IN THE LAND OF PURGORITES

Sebastian Grubb

Table of Contents

Chapter 1

A Year of Peace

"Keep your damn shield up, Simon. It's no good holding it about your waist. Do you want to take a sword blow to the skull?" I asked somewhat angrily of Simon.

"No, Commander Kane. I'm sorry. I let myself slip for a second." Came the guilty response from Simon.

"You can't afford to slip, Simon. You know this. That slip will be your undoing. Now, let's go again, and remember….SHIELD UP!" I ordered.

I once again hammered Simon with a combination of blows from the right and left, high and low, to see how he responded and to test his instincts. I used my training sword to avoid drawing any real blood, but I had no intention of making it comfortable on Simon. Praise be, he did manage to adhere to my advice and keep his shield where it was needed to deflect my strikes. We had been practising in the west yard area of Gutvast Palace almost solidly for over an hour, and honestly, both Simon and I needed to rest, and so we did. It was still only mid-morning, so the sun had not reached its zenith, but we could tell it would be a scorching day.

I did not realise that Lord Vincent Harbrandt and his lady Vivian had been watching our training session. Both began applauding and cheering as soon as Simon and I began making our way to the water trough to slake our thirst. Vincent was my long-standing friend and battle brother, not to mention the current Keeper of the Lafroide Valley and head of the Harbrandt dynasty. He was a high-ranking and respected noble who employed hundreds of people in his enormous estate in the east of Halia.

"Excellent Simon, your shield work is quite incredible. I know Marcus agrees, but will not tell you so." Complimented Vincent, a broad smile on his face.

★ ★ ★

This part of my tale begins roughly one year after the intense battle atop Mirgot's Pass in which we had triumphed and managed to throw back the Purgorite forces. Our capital city of Farchester had been saved, thanks not just to Halian forces, whether dead or alive, but even South Utreshian warriors who had travelled far to bravely offer their assistance.

Simon was by this stage a muscular and athletic eighteen-year-old. He had proven his worth in bloody battle against tough opponents and his combat skills were well advanced for his age and experience. So, I had decided to take him to the next level. I knew that Simon had the potential to become not just a great soldier, but a LEGENDARY swordsman and warrior. He was tall, only an inch shorter than my height of six foot three inches, and possessed quick reflexes, great coordination and an eye for openings and weak spots. For proof of these attributes, one only needs to look at how he manoeuvred behind the beast Brutuck and slashed into his slightly exposed ankle during the intense battle atop the walls of Mirgot's Pass.

Since repelling the invaders and celebrating our victory, we had slowly rebuilt Halia piece by piece. We had planted new fields, rebuilt destroyed buildings, forged new riverways, and recruited new soldiers from Halia's willing and able youth to replace those lost during the brutal struggle against Va'heash and his brutes. It had been an arduous process, but we had been together, each man and woman picking up a spade, a sickle, a hammer, a brick, a plank of freshly cut wood or even a sword to do what they could.

If ever I needed inspiration to keep building, to keep endeavouring, to keep hoping, I thought back to what my departed friend Kurt had said atop those high walls just before the battle began. I recalled his stirring words of encouragement and his sword shining in the gloom as a beacon to lead us to victory. I thought of what Kurt died for and what he lived for. I must confess, even now in times of dark despair when I feel weak, I travel back to that moment on the battlements when Halian warriors stood strong together and prevailed against fearful odds. I find that even the darkest gloom can be banished, and the longest nights always end with a rising sun and a new day.

I had been promoted by the military hierarchy from the post of Captain to Commander in response to my efforts during the Purgorite invasion. This made me one of the more senior officers in the realm of Halia. I no longer slept in simple quarters within Carnagon Castle with the rest of the soldiers, but instead was gifted with a stout mansion house around six miles South of the castle itself. I lived there alone, beside one servant and one cook. The servant was a helpful young lad in his twenties called Tarmon, and the cook was a lovely old dame called Betsy. In truth, I did not really live alone, as I had adopted a three-year-old Bullhound dog named 'Morse' shortly after taking residence within the mansion house. Morse had lived around soldiers since birth, and whilst he had never been bloodied in battle or taken another life, I could just tell that he had a warrior spirit, and his physicality alone made him built for combat. Fully grown, he weighed around 150 pounds with most of it being muscle. Morse was possessed of a strong, wide jaw and a set of fierce-looking teeth. He seemed to eat as much as a fully-grown man. Luckily, I had the means to feed his healthy appetite.

As for Vivian, she was Vincent's lady. In fact, he had offered her a proposal of marriage only three months before watching Simon expertly fend off my sword strikes in his yard. Vivian had gratefully accepted. Vivian was a lovely woman, and beautiful to boot. She was tall, with flowing fair hair and sparkling blue eyes. Vivian was the daughter of a very wealthy Farchester merchant named Stephan De'Witzer. The two had first met whilst the battle survivors were resting and recuperating a little within the confines of a cosy Farchester tavern. Vincent had actually mistaken Vivian for a barmaid, a mistake which Vivian corrected in good humour. This led to further conversation, and things seemed to go from there. The couple seemed very happy, and I was happy for them. Vincent had taken a step into my comfort zone by asking me if I was looking for any female companionship. I was somewhat caught off guard, as we had never really discussed romance; however, I responded by telling Vincent that I had really always been a soldier and fought for Halia. I focused on my duty and my tasks. I had never felt the 'need' for a woman, odd as that sounds. Vincent accepted this explanation, and the issue was never raised again.

In the year since Mirgot's Pass, we had not heard a whisper from Va'heash or the Purgorites. We had almost forgotten about him, and many had even thought to write the invasion off as history, or as some nightmare that was over once we could see the blue skies and bright sun once again. As new concerns arose, Va'heash kept getting pushed further back into the realms of "old news". But we were fooling ourselves, and we had been fools to think that Va'heash had simply disappeared. For the subject of Va'heash was put firmly back on the table during an officers' meeting one sunny Veronot★ day.

Chapter 2

The Meeting at Farchester Castle

The meeting in question was to take place within the confines of Farchester Castle, a solid stone structure which boasted formidable walls, imposing-looking towers and a heavily defended entryway. The castle itself was surrounded by a moat roughly eight metres wide. Access was afforded by a staunch drawbridge which tended to be lowered during the day to allow access to visitors, officials and castle staff. Prior to the meeting, I had never actually been within Farchester Castle, so this was something of an experience for me. I raised my head to see the proud Halian flag fly from the battlements, the slight wind causing it to ripple and dance. As I gazed upon the emblem of the black castle upon a sky-blue background, I was momentarily taken back to my frantic ordeal on the Mirgot battlements, where the mere vision of the flag was enough to induce me to claw my way back from death.

I was roughly one hundred feet from the entryway into Farchester Castle when I heard my name being called from behind me. I turned to see my comrade Major De'Beresford, who had stood boldly with us at Mirgot's Pass. The Major had ultimately held it all together and directed the Halian response during that unforgettable battle. As Halians, we would always be in his debt.

"Ah, a pleasure as always Major. How is life treating you currently?" I asked the old warrior.

"To be honest, it is all a little boring, Commander Kane. I am still stationed at Mirgot's Pass, and whilst I do not particularly welcome another thousand-strong horde of barbaric invaders trying to take the place over, I would welcome some action." Replied the Major, somewhat downbeat.

I could fully understand where the Major was coming from. We were soldiers, we were trained to fight, and if necessary, to kill. Sometimes, we needed to feel a sword grip in our palm, a good, solid shield on our arm. Sometimes, we needed an enemy to slash a deadly weapon in our direction to give us some purpose. Once you got a taste for battle, a dark part of you wanted to keep eating.

"I have a feeling, Major De'Beresford, that action will be coming our way. This looks to be a fairly important meeting that has been called. My invite arrived on the finest quality paper and was very fancy looking, with signatures from all five of the Higher Cadre." I reassured the Major.

The 'Higher Cadre' were a five-man team of elected officials (almost always from the Farchester aristocracy) who oversaw the ruling of Halia. Generally, the 'Cadre' would reign for five-year stretches, whereby nationwide elections would determine any changes to the five. Halia had operated under a structure of monarchy for centuries; however, this system of ruling had been abolished following a series of bloody civil wars some 150 years prior to this tale. But that is another story altogether.

I had a query I wished to make of the Major, concerning his title.

"Major, would it be imprudent of me to ask why you were never promoted for your efforts following the battle? You were basically leading our war effort and had tremendous responsibility. I must admit to feeling uneasy that whilst I am now a Commander, you still answer to the rank of Major. Don't misunderstand me, 'Major' is still a worthy rank, but should you not have risen the ranks?" I asked of De'Beresford, knowing that I was probably overstepping some mark of manners.

Luckily, De'Beresford took the question well and was perfectly open about the situation.

"Oh, it's not like I walked away from that battle empty-handed. The battle essentially ended the Purgorite invasion and saved the realm. I am sure that the Cadre recognised this and saw fit to reward me. I was promoted from third-Major to first-Major, granted new lands, 200 units of gold and a large Manor House near Gloombest Lake with five acres of land. The Manor House will pass to my son Nathaniel when I am gone. So, you could say I was rewarded in other ways. In all honesty, I think that the Cadre want to keep me monitoring and overseeing Mirgot's Pass. I have been in charge there for ten years now and seem to be good at my job, if I may be so immodest! I know the troops well and have their respect. Overseeing that final barrier into Farchester is a huge responsibility, and I have a strong feeling that the Cadre do not trust anyone else with it. Were I to be promoted to a higher rank, I may be sectioned off to another area, leaving Mirgot's in 'lesser hands'." De'Beresford explained.

I realised that the Major and I would be late for this meeting unless we got a move on, so I suggested that we speed up our pace. The Major agreed, and so he and I made our way over the sturdy drawbridge, through the powerful-looking gatehouse, and across the main courtyard towards the towering structure of the Keep, where most of the administrative tasks took place.

The meeting was held on the top floor of the Keep, as if to give extra weight to its importance. This also meant that all attendees had no choice but to climb the several staircases to reach the large chamber in which a long, polished Oak table had been set ready for nine places. The chamber had a large gable window at one end of the room, with a high vaulted ceiling and a fine woven rug gracing the wooden boards. Nine of us were to attend this confidential meeting, with each of us being greeted and our identity confirmed by two armed guards at the door.

Once inside, I approached the table calmly and made my greetings to the two members of the nine who were already seated and remained seated as I spoke. These are two of the five-man Higher Cadre. They were Lords Gerard Huscliffe and Wolfgang Schnieder. Both were serious-looking men in their early sixties dressed in embroidered ankle-length robes, belted at the waist. Besides their robes, they wore no real finery. They greeted both the Major and me with minimal fuss and without changing facial expression. The looks on their faces remained serious. It was clear that we were not here for chatter or to exchange pleasantries. In view of this, the Major and I seated ourselves and simply sat in silence, waiting for the meeting to begin.

Luckily, we did not have long to wait in this state of awkward tension. Within the next ten minutes or so, the other five attendees had arrived and presented themselves. Some of the attendees were already known to me, as we had met during Halia's invasion, if not before. Captain David Stire, once second in command to the gallant Kurt Winters, sat down next to me after offering a brief smile and nod of the head, which I returned. Captain Stire had been placed in charge of overseeing the safety of Barford Castle, which was still in the process of being rebuilt, although by the time this meeting took place, it was almost back to its former glory. Captain Stire was not a large man in stature, but very competent and strong in battle, with excellent sword ability. Although I may have failed to mention it, Captain Stire, then 'first ensign' Stire, fought alongside the men on the battlements of Mirgot's Pass. He and I had spilt blood together.

The other attendee I already knew was Joseph Fullcowen, who had become Captain Fullcowen following a promotion. Fullcowen had worked alongside me very ably, guarding the rear of the company as we traversed the daunting miles from Valmere Valley to Mirgot's Pass, both above and below surface level, both in relative darkness and almost utter darkness. Captain Fullcowen was a man I knew that I could trust if it came to further battle. Further battle was something that I saw on the horizon somehow, and I knew I was not alone. The other three military officers were unknown to me by person, but I had heard mention of their names. They were Major Johann Heven, Major Francis Biller and another Commander, by the name of Lucius Vorgo.

Once all nine members had taken a seat and looked ready to begin, Lord Huscliffe stood up from his expensive high-backed chair at the head of the Oak table. Instinctively, the other seven military attendees also stood as a sign of due respect. However, Lord Schnieder calmly remained seated, his face still a mask showing no emotion. Lord

Huscliffe indicated that we should sit, with a gentle movement of his right hand. There was no preamble, as Lord Huscliffe launched straight into why we had been summoned from our important duties from all over Halia. He opened the meeting with these harrowing, but not totally unexpected words;

"Officers of Halia, I thank you for coming here at short notice when there is still so much to do in our land. However, it is clear this is a matter that cannot wait. We have received solid intelligence from agents overseas, in North Utresh, that Lord Va'heash has not given up on his plans of conquest in Halia. In fact, he is, as we speak, planning another invasion. This invasion, our sources tell us, looks to be many times larger than that which was experienced only one year ago. This time, Va'heash is looking to summon allies to his banner. We are now convinced that Va'heash is looking for Purgorite expansion and domination of all lands south of the Palmoria Ocean. He is not greedy or foolish enough to believe that he can conquer the whole of Valamantus, but it seems he still wishes to stretch his grasp as far as he can. If this is not concerning enough, some of these sinister "allies" are known across the globe for their cruelty, to the degree that even the Purgorites seem fairly tame by comparison. Gentleman, need I say that Halia cannot even begin to contemplate a further invasion, let alone a combined effort from multiple enemies? I say again, this planned invasion CANNOT happen."

There was a pause around the table as each soldier drank in this information in his own way. If any one of us had believed the Purgorite invasion to be over, they were fools, not just to themselves but to Halia as well. Maybe I was a fool alongside them, as what had I done to prepare for a further invasion other than entertain my ego with some half-boiled plans which had never amounted to much more than late-night notes and sketches in my study? What had any of us really done?

As if to indicate his ability to read minds, it was Major Biller who responded to the question I was turning over in my mind.

"My Lord Huscliffe, I would thoroughly agree that we should take every action to prevent any further invasion, rather than deal with it when it arrives…"

I knew that a "but" or "however" was coming sometime soon from Major Biller. Luckily, we were not left waiting long.

"…but, if the inevitable invasion did happen, our defences are in a better state than a year ago. The only way for the invasion to reach our land is across the sea to the North. North Utresh lies some 400 miles away, and it would take weeks for their ships to traverse the Palmoria Ocean. Whilst we would struggle to defend all seventy-five miles of our North coastline, it is clear that the transport ships would only be able to land safely at certain stretches of the coast. Over the past year, I have been working alongside local administrators and construction teams to erect sturdy barricades, lookout towers, catapults and even proper fitted guard barracks. It's not like I have been sitting with my thumb up my backside."

There was a pause as the table looked toward the two members of the Cadre, to see how they would respond to this colourful explanation from Major Biller, which came close to sounding like a rebuttal. Both men remained calm and as stern-faced as ever, once again betraying no sign of emotion.

"No one here is accusing you or indeed anyone else of sitting… 'with their thumb up their backside'…as you word it. I am grateful for your efforts, Major Biller, as is the rest of Halia. Those Northern defences were much needed, and it is a shame that it took such an event to wake people up. I admit that it should have been the Cadre who ordered those defences built, long before the Lord Va'heash paid us his visit. The well-being of Halia is under our overall responsibility. I can make no excuses for our inability to take better control during the Purgorite invasion. Truthfully, only two of the Cadre were active within Halia, and even before the invasion, we were faced with numerous problems, as many of you are now aware. The invasion came at the worst possible time, and quite simply, we found ourselves overwhelmed," explained Huscliffe, his face and tonal expression not quite reflecting the apologetic theme of his words.

"Luckily, strong soldiers of Halia were able to take the stand and save Halia from damnation. I refer more specifically to any and all soldiers who fought tooth and nail at Mirgot's Pass. Commander Kane, Captain Fullcowen, Captain Stire, Major De'Beresford, Halia owes you all a tremendous debt of gratitude. You held that wall long enough for the Halian army to arrive and help crush the invading forces," came the congratulatory remark from Lord Schnieder.

I felt that as a Commander, it was time for me to make my presence felt, to contribute. I spoke up, asking the question which must have been hovering just above the table, but needed to be voiced out loud.

"My Lords, if we are to halt this invasion before it has even begun, I assume you plan on directing an assault across the Palmoria Ocean, into the lands of North Utresh?" I enquired.

"You have assumed correctly, Commander Kane. This is the matter I was about to delve into," came the quick response from Lord Huscliffe.

"Yes, it is the will of the Cadre to send troops into the very heart of the enemy. I realise how daunting this sounds, but it is a necessary action. We think it best that we send a smaller troop unit as opposed to a full steel invasion. We do not know North Utresh well enough for such a bold and expensive move. A full invasion with the Halian Navy and ground army would mean taking our ships across 400 miles of Ocean, where anything could happen. Even if the ships managed to get near North Utresh, their coastal navy and defences could be such that the Halian ships were destroyed before even touching solid ground. This would be an unmitigated disaster and leave Halia totally open to attack.

No. It is the decision of the Higher Cadre that a smaller unit move in covertly, under the guise of foreign Mercenaries from the neighbouring land of Kazbare. This smaller unit will perform reconnaissance, survey the land, enemy movements and locations and perform any necessary actions to disrupt the Purgorite effort. Be it burning supplies, disabling outposts, destroying roads as to make them impassable," continued Lord Huscliffe.

"Lord Huscliffe, may I ask what are your instructions regarding Lord Va'heash himself? Should this covert unit look to cut the head off the snake and lead the Purgorite invasion leaderless?" asked Commander Vorgo.

I took this opportunity to study Commander Vorgo more closely, the only officer around the meeting table to match me in rank. He was a tall, powerfully built soldier with a strong, leaderlike face and deep commanding voice. He looked at Lord Huscliffe with piercing blue eyes as Huscliffe responded to his question.

"Commander Vorgo, I would not suggest that this unit, professional as they may be, tackle Va'heash directly. We have received further intelligence on this Lord Va'heash over the past year, from Halian paid spies and scouts hidden within the Purgorite circles. Unfortunately, none of this intelligence works in our favour. Firstly, Lord Va'heash is primarily stationed within a nigh on impregnable fortress called "Balostroma", which roughly translates into Halian as "Playground of Pain", which tells you what manner of abode Va'heash oversees. This "Balostroma" fortress makes even our toughest and most formidable fortresses look like a wooden peasant's shack. The stone walls are too thick to break through, too high to climb and tunnelling under would be impossible given that this cursed place is built into the side of a mountain range. Brutal guards patrol the walls and surrounding areas relentlessly. It is even rumoured that Va'heash has winged creatures flying the foul skies above the fortress, constantly scouring the ground for signs of unwanted visitors.

Secondly, trying to kill Lord Va'heash himself would be no mean feat. In fact, it would be extremely foolish to even try to assassinate Va'heash. Commander Kane, you are the only officer at this table to actually see Lord Va'heash in person, at Carnagon Castle. You have seen something of him, but even you did not see his true self. Va'heash modified his appearance somehow to appear more…man-like…so that he would be more easily accepted by your nobility as a potential ally and even friend. The scouts who have been lucky, or should I say UNLUCKY enough to see Va'heash in person, with any disguises removed, report on his horrific and unnatural appearance. Had Va'heash approached the Halian nobility in his truer form, the nobility would likely have run screaming in terror instead of welcoming into their home.

Va'heash's powers of mind control and what we would call "dark magic" also go further than we thought, and our blood curdles merely contemplating his reported abilities. Although this cannot be totally confirmed, we have had reports that Va'heash can cause a person's blood to boil in their veins, causing a most painful death. Va'heash can enable this horrific fate by merely channelling his mental focus in a certain direction, although, of course, how he does this is beyond our understanding. Va'heash can also burden a person with unspeakable nightmares night after night, which eventually drive the person to insanity. Allegedly, Va'heash only need speak particular incantations in a certain voice, and direction, to cause this constant psychological torture. I know that this sounds far-fetched to us as Halians, but we need to understand that these Purgorites are not even remotely like us and follow different laws of existence. Truthfully, we do not know where Va'heash's abilities end. He is not a man like us, but a demon from somewhere we do not even want to dwell on.

If these two reasons to avoid Va'heash are not enough, there is also the matter of Lord Va'heash's personal guard: a close-knit unit of eight carefully selected and elite warriors who guard their Lord with hound-like loyalty. Va'heash has even got himself a new 'Champion' to replace Brutuck. We cannot confirm this creature's name or its origins, only that the creature seems to be even more deadly and capable than Brutuck, as well as being thoroughly dedicated to its master's safety."

The table was once again quiet, as the officers digested this harrowing information that they likely wished they could just pour back out of their minds like a man might pour spoiled milk down the drain, before walking back to their castles and getting on with their peaceful Halian existence. Forgive me, but I wanted that myself. It was one thing to plant your feet on familiar Halian soil, surrounded by your battle brothers, and fight against a foreign enemy who had no right to be there. But to travel across a vast ocean into the heart of the enemy in unfamiliar and most likely frightening territory, with no real army at your back? That was something else altogether.

The silence was broken all too soon as Lord Huscliffe continued with his presentation.

"The Cadre believed it prudent to inform you of our planned expedition into North Utresh as soon as possible, as to give each of you adequate time to make appropriate preparations." Advised Huscliffe.

This sentence caused no little stir around the table. Concerned glances and even murmurs were exchanged between the attendees around the table. It was actually Major De'Beresford who stood up and voiced the question we all had in our minds.

"Excuse me, Lord Huscliffe, 'appropriate preparations' for what, exactly?" queried the Major, making no effort to hide the concern from his face.

"It is the decision of the Higher Cadre, that you, Commander Kane, will be in overall charge of this expedition."

These were the next words from Lord Huscliffe. He may have said some other words directly afterward; only I did not digest them fully due to the shock caused by that particular twenty-word string of varying syllables. I had just been told that I was not only travelling into the dark and dangerous land of the enemy, but that the lives of countless people were being entrusted to me. I managed to regain focus and pick up on Huscliffe's hopefully very good reasons for throwing my life into turmoil.

"…you proved yourself a true leader in escorting and guarding a large body of Halian citizens, both civilian and military, to a place of relative safety, and once there you continued to fight valiantly and without pause until the battle had been won and Mirgot's Pass secured. You have a decorated history of leading and directing troops in battle and it is clear that you inspire loyalty and bravery amongst those soldiers following your command."

I was about to speak out in protest and had even opened my mouth a little to vocalise my first syllable, when I was cut off by Huscliffe as he specified the next member of this already unpopular journey. Maybe it was best that I had held my tongue, as thinking back to that moment, my reason for not wishing to be sent to North Utresh did not extend much past "I don't want to go", which would not have been an excuse likely to recuse myself as a leader.

"Major De'Beresford, you also proved yourself at the battle of Mirgot's Pass, if proving yourself further was even needed. You did your job ably and thoroughly in overseeing the security of that final vital stronghold before the enemy could descend on Halia. You are also a proven leader with many years' experience in the field under a variety of harsh conditions. Like Commander Kane, you have travelled far and wide over your years of service and taken vital roles in numerous military campaigns. The Cadre therefore dictates that you accompany this expedition and serve as Commander Kane's second-in-command." Lord Huscliffe instructed firmly to an equally perturbed Major De'Beresford.

The Major and I both remained silent, which was wise, as Lord Huscliffe identified who would be following us on this dangerous errand.

"Captain David Stire, our late comrade Captain Winters spoke very highly of you and always valued your presence as his second in command, even when the Cadre had other suggestions for that post. Before your posting at Barford Castle alongside Captain Winters, you spent years specialising in clandestine operations, work which could be categorised as 'behind enemy lines'. It is our belief that your skills, experience and overall expertise in reconnaissance and scouting will make you an invaluable addition to this group." Complimented Husliffe, if such a term can be used, given when the recipient of the compliment had basically just been ordered to jump in on a suicide mission.

"Major Johann Heven, it has come to our attention that you have travelled through parts of North Utresh during your military service and have even been helpful enough to create maps detailing distances, geographical features, main roads and built-up areas. Whilst these maps are very useful for reference, and have already been consulted, it would be even more useful to have you there again in person. Your knowledge of the landscape, even of the peoples, the language and the potential dangers of the place indicates to the Cadre that you should make up the fourth Officer partaking in this exercise," explained Huscliffe.

At this stage, Lord Schnieder, who had remained silent for a while, took over and explained why the remaining three officers had been invited to the meeting.

"Commander Vorgo, Major Biller and Captain Fullcowen, you three will not be taking part in this expedition directly."

As I looked at the faces of the three Officers in question, they remained attentive and emotionless in terms of facial expression. I could not tell if they were relieved to be out of harm's way or devastated that they were to miss out on an adventure full of danger and mystery.

"Instead, you will remain in Halia and undertake the duties of the Officers whilst they are away on this exercise. Commander Vorgo, you will take temporary charge of Carnagon Castle and the surrounding regions. You will oversee military matters in the area and respond to any issues or disputes that arise. Please confer with Commander Kane about a handover, so that you know all you need to know before he leaves. I leave the both of you to organise the specifics."

At these words, I looked over at this Commander Vorgo and found his piercing blue eyes meeting my gaze. I failed to really read his expression. This man, whom I did not even know, but who would be looking after not only my castle but my people. It was no good to ask if I could trust him. I had no choice in any of this, it seemed. None of us did.

"Major Biller, you already have experience of managing Mirgot's Pass as you were Major De'Beresford's predecessor. It is the Cadre's ruling that you temporarily take up your former post again and command the Pass in Major De'Beresford's absence. We can think of no-one more suited to this vital role in Farchester's safety. I will leave Major De'Beresford to update you in depth about any and all changes to structure since his leadership began." Lord Schnieder explained to Biller, who nodded graciously at this decision.

"Captain Fullcowen, the Cadre would be delighted if you would oversee the command of Barford Castle during Captain Stire's absence. You were stationed there as an Ensign for several years and know the Castle well. You also have adequate experience and ability in the command of soldiers and local management. Again, please liaise with Captain Stire about a full handover in good time," entreated Lord Schnieder.

I need not relay the rest of the meeting word for word; however, I will surmise the rest of the Cadre's instructions. Lord Huscliffe advised that any further meetings regarding this expedition need not involve the three lords who would be staying in Halia and would be carried out in secrecy, with only the necessary attendees invited. There would be more meetings to follow in time, where the many specifics would be ironed out. Lord Huscliffe offered some words of reassurance in that the expedition would not actually be going ahead for some weeks, and the Cadre deemed it prudent to update the expedition leaders as soon as possible, rather than shock them with some manner of last-minute emergency order.

Upon the Cadre's offer to answer any questions the table might have regarding this daunting expedition, Major De'Beresford spoke up.

"My Lords, forgive my boldness, but I am slightly curious as to why Commander Vorgo, Captain Fullcowen and Major Biller were invited to this particular meeting in which specifics of the operation are being discussed, if they are not actually part of the operation itself. Do they really need to know what we will be doing out there?" Enquired De'Beresford.

The Major's question was one that I had already alighted on in my mind, but perhaps was not forthcoming enough to actually voice it, in the moment.

"The cadre had entertained the idea of keeping the three named officers in the dark about this expedition and simply tell them that the officer who had been occupying the post they were being asked to fill had taken a leave of absence or even been dismissed from the Halian forces. However, we ultimately decided to invest our trust in Officers Vorgo, Fullcowen and Biller and involve them more closely in these proceedings. This way, they can offer you more support in the coming weeks. I have followed the track record of these three esteemed officers, alongside speaking to their senior officers, and have full confidence that they will maintain secrecy regarding the information they have entrusted with so far." Lord Huscliffe explained to the Major.

The Major simply cast his eyes towards the table as if in further thought and nodded in response.

Once the meeting had been drawn to a close and the attendees all thanked profusely for their help and cooperation, as if any of us had a choice, we were all dismissed from the chamber.

Chapter 3

A More Private Meeting

Once outside the castle walls, officers Vorgo, Fullcowen and Biller all travelled off on their own separate ways after a brief farewell. I spoke briefly with Major Heven, who also had to leave Farchester immediately to attend to fairly urgent matters. That left Major De'Beresford, Captain Stire and me, who retired to a certain watering hole we had become familiar with. "The Wyvern's Way" was a pleasant, three-story tavern not far from the main city entrance. It was still relatively quiet when we three entered, so whilst Major De'Beresford made his way to the bar to order three jugs of much-needed brown ale, I selected a nice table in a remote corner of the tavern where I did not believe that eager ears would reach.

Soon enough, the Major brought over the three jugs, before sitting himself down with a sigh. De'Beresford rubbed his tired-looking face with his strong-looking hands before opening what was essentially a more relaxed follow-up meeting to the one just experienced.

"Ughh, I don't know about this Commander Kane, I am almost fifty-four years old now. I thought my days of high adventure were behind me, but it seems not. I feel like I belong here, in Halia, defending Farchester, not running off to some dangerous land of savagery to carry out some behind-the-lines bollocks." The Major expressed, looking at both of us with eyes full of expression.

I was glad that the Major could now unburden his true thoughts and feelings, away from the frosty glare of the Higher Cadre.

"My feelings mirror your own, Major De'Beresford. I would rather we stay here in Halia if we are to be invaded. I would rather commit myself to training more soldiers, building more defences, purchasing new and better weaponry, even fitting out new warships and sea defences. What if we are stuck over in North Utresh when the actual invasion comes? What good will blocking some road 500 miles away do then?" I responded to the Major in an empathetic manner.

"Commander Kane, I would have you address me as 'Ralph' whilst we are alone and not in the presence of troops. Whilst 'Simon' is officially my first name, I have always preferred to be known by my middle name, which is Ralph. We have fought side-by-side and spilt blood together. I know it may be against protocol, but in all honesty, this 'expedition' feels like it's against protocol." Ralph continued.

"Very well then, I will acquiesce to your request, Ralph," I responded.

I did not ask Major De'Beresford to address me by my first name, as I was a senior Officer to himself, so the power dynamic was different. The time may come when I did offer this privilege, but it was not there in The Wyvern's Way.

"I would also rather remain at Barford Castle. There is still so much to do there, and I feel like it is my calling. I was directly involved in the rebuilding of Barford Castle and worked day and night in my pursuits. I have nothing against Captain Fullcowen, but do not feel like I should just be handing over the reins to him out of nowhere. Ultimately, the Cadre orders, and we must obey. We can sit here griping about our misfortune all day...."

Captain Stire suddenly paused in his heartfelt monologue and corrected himself, realising that he may have just accused two senior Halian Officers of the shameful act of "griping".

"Forgive me, Commander Kane and Major De'Beresford. It is I who is doing the griping. I would not seek to criticise your thoughts, actions or dare to suggest what we should or should not do. I spoke to you in a way most unsuitable." Captain Stire confessed, his face reddening and his eyes fixed on the table.

"There is no need to ask forgiveness, good Captain. You fought with us on the walls of Mirgot's Pass and have worked hard to both defend and rebuild Halia. You have as much right to voice your concerns as Major De'Beresford and I." I reassured the Captain, whilst looking him in the eye.

Ralph did not bring attention to the fact that I had continued to refer to him by his full and proper title.

After some more discussion about what dangers we were likely to be facing over there, about Lord Va'heash and his sinister capabilities, about this murky new champion of his to replace Brutuck, about the weather, about what we would eat, we bade farewell to each other and made to go on our separate journeys. The questions that had been raised during the discussion will be answered later in this tale, believe me.

Upon leaving the Tavern, I made my way smartly to the nearby stables where I had left my trusty horse 'Palladin'. Palladin was a sturdy Stallion of a lovely dark brown shade, with bright eyes and a luxurious, flowing mane of night black hair. He nodded his large head and danced around a little when he saw me approaching. I stroked his

long, noble nose before untying his rope from the post and climbing into the fine leather riding saddle. I threw a silver unit through the air to the dirty-looking stable boy before nudging Palladin into action. The young lad caught the coin and nodded to me in appreciation.

As I cantered along with Palladin northward, back toward my mansion house, I soon enough found myself passing through the gateway of Mirgot's Pass. Before passing under the formidable walls, I raised my head to scope the battlements high up. I would always see the shining sword of my friend Captain Kurt Winters up there, whether it was actually there or not. For me, it was more than a piece of steel behind held aloft. It was and still is a symbol of Halian strength, courage, spirit and fortitude. It is a light in the darkness. A glimmer of hope when lost in a sea of despair.

I found myself smiling a little as Palladin and I came out of the other side of the Pass and continued northward on the main dusty road.

It was a pleasant enough day with a bright sun, and a fair wind blew from the East. Despite the harrowing information I had been exposed to in our earlier meeting, I for some reason felt…free. The pure Halian sun was in my face, the air smelt fresh, and the wind felt refreshing upon my cheeks. I could feel the powerful bulk of my good friend Palladin between the rough ground and me as he dutifully bore me from one place to the next, never complaining.

"How would you like to go for a little run, my friend?" I asked Palladin.

Palladin, as horses tend to go, had no powers of speech, but did seem to whinny in some manner of agreement. So, taking his noise as an affirmation, I found myself putting my spurs to him and increasing the pace. The ground began to roll by faster and faster, and faster. Soon enough, we had broken into a full gallop and were likely going faster than I had ever gone on ANY horse. I use the term "we" as I felt like I was running just as much as Palladin, even though my legs were barely moving. My spirit was running, though it was in fact flying.

"Let's go Palladin, let us fly!" I roared into the sky.

By now, local workers and farmers were pausing in their duties to gawp and marvel at the finely dressed officer charging along on a powerful Stallion whilst laughing and roaring like a maniac. I can admit that it must have made a sight indeed! I paid them no heed, however, as Palladin carried on driving north like some equine God of speed itself. I honestly felt that no living being could be faster than Palladin was right then.

I slightly regained my composure to see that we were already nearing the wide River Sovern, that blessed path of water which had stalled the Purgorite invasion and bought us invaluable time. Several bridges had already been rebuilt across the river and were perfectly safe to use; however, I directed Palladin towards the unfinished bridge, which still had a gap of ten metres between the opposing sides. Ten metres of thin air over a fast-moving river. Looking back, it was beyond reckless to do what I did and to subject both Palladin and me to such potential danger. We could both have been severely injured or outright killed, but I just knew that we would make the jump, even if I could never explain it to anyone logically. It was feeling deep in my gut, deep in my heart, even.

As Palladin barreled toward the unfinished bridge, the various craftsmen involved in its construction looked on in shock as they saw what we meant to do. I recall seeing numerous sets of hands held up as a means of warning and dissuasion. I recall the pale, startled faces mouthing words that we should halt immediately. But I was deaf to the warnings, for there was no going back. Palladin knew what he had to do, so he tore off the dusty ground and onto the bridge itself, by now an embodiment of thunder and lightning itself. Palladin was a living storm, and I the rider.

I saw the ten-metre gap rushing up to meet us at an insane speed. From my position, the gap looked impossible, and the sane, reasonable part of my brain tried to surface to tell Marcus Kane to stop before it was too late. But that voice of reason was lost in the storm of wild energy that seemed to surround Palladin and me. God damn it, this jump was OURS! I found myself taking a deep breath just before I knew Palladin's strong hooves would leave the earth for better or worse. Then, I found myself flying. For Palladin, my brave boy, soared clear over those ten metres. That was another moment of my life that will never leave me. The exhilaration of Palladin and me jumping as one was beyond words. My trust in him and his trust in me. Our time in the air cannot have been more than a few mere seconds, but we seemed to fly for much longer. Then, all too soon, Palladin's strong hooves hit the other side of the sturdy bridge, and he drove forward.

Now that our epic run and gravity-defying leap had taken place, I came back to my senses a little more and slowed my good horse back to a sustainable trot. He had performed an incredible feat, and I knew that he needed to regain his wind. I still had to remind myself that Palladin was no God, or supreme being, although it seemed that he had a speed beyond any living being without wings. As we continued

North, I patted Palladin's strong neck several times and whispered words of thanks.

Later in the afternoon, after several hours of riding and a few breaks, I pulled Palladin into another stable and again tied his rope to a wooden post. This was my own stable, which made up one of the outbuildings of my small complex. I gave Palladin a nosebag full of good apples before leaving him to rest and heading toward the mansion that I will begin to call 'Castle Kane,' as I had never been told of any real name for the place other than a basic address for administration purposes.

As I entered the large entrance hall of Castle Kane, my trusty servant Tarmon greeted me kindly, as was his usual manner.

"Good evening, Commander Kane. You look like you've had a hard ride. Do you wish for me to see to Palladin?" enquired the young man.

"Oh no, Tarmon. I have left him with a nose bag and a trough of water. He will be fine." I responded.

"No problem. Brother Abel came around only around thirty minutes ago. I hope this is okay, but I asked him to wait in the parlour as I knew that you were due back before nightfall." Tarmon continued, hoping that he had not offended his master.

"That's fine, Tarmon, you did right. I will go and see Abel as soon as I have taken a moment to reset myself a little." I reassured Tarmon.

Tarmon had been assigned to me shortly after I was handed the keys to Castle Kane. During our discussion early into Tarmon's posting with me, he told me that his father worked as a tradesman and that his mother sadly died during childbirth. Tarmon never mentioned any siblings or cousins. I did ask him why he did not take up a trade like his father's, as the income would have been better than that of a house servant. Tarmon confessed to me that he wasn't very good with his hands and felt that being a servant was more his calling. I doubted this very much, but did not tell Tarmon at the time of the conversation. It was my belief quite early on that Tarmon was capable, able-bodied, bright and could even be inventive and think on his feet. It was his lack of self-esteem which delayed him and a little and dampened his prospects. He did not believe in himself. It was only later on in his posting that I tried to increase Tarmon's confidence and get him to see that he could do greater things if he applied himself. It was ultimately up to him to make that leap though.

Chapter 4

About my Father

I found Brother Abel standing in my parlour and perusing a series of regional maps mounted on the stone walls. The maps had been left hanging by one of the previous military officers who resided within what was now Castle Kane. Brother Abel turned when he heard my approaching footsteps, his weathered old face breaking into a warm smile.

"Greetings, Commander Kane. I trust you have had a pleasant ride back from Farchester?" Abel enquired in an interested tone.

"Please, my brother, call me 'Marcus'. You are one of my oldest friends and we are alone in my home. No need to be so formal," I offered to Brother Abel.

"Okay, 'Marcus' it is then. I would not refuse the order of a decorated Commander." Abel replied, somewhat jokily.

After sharing a brief laugh at this jest, I asked Abel to please take a seat in one of the armchairs which were situated around the small table I tended to use for drinks and small plates of food whilst entertaining guests. I returned to the parlour shortly with two mugs of hot spiced punch and a plateful of bread-based snacks.

Abel gladly helped himself to one of the small snacks and thanked me as I passed him one of the steel mugs. I did not mention anything about today's meeting to Brother Abel, or even my death-defying charge and leap over the River Sovern. Truthfully, Abel would know about the expedition in time. Instead, after a few minutes of small talk, Abel began on what specifically had prompted his visit.

"Marcus, I have a serious concern to raise, and I thought best to raise it as soon as possible, rather than wait for your next visit to

Carnagon Castle, as understandably you cannot be based at the stronghold all the time," Abel advised me, the concern of his voice and expression ensuring my full attention.

"I was this morning treating a young private in my infirmary. The soldier had suffered a nasty bite from what looked to be a rodent. There was a small set of teeth marks on his ankles, which were red around the edges. The soldier complained of ongoing pain in his lower leg, almost certainly brought on by the bite. I wrapped his ankle carefully in a clean bandage after treating it with the relevant ointment. I advised the soldier to come back to see me in a few days if the pain did not abate. When I asked the man if he had actually seen the creature that had bitten him, he told me that he had; however, his description of what had bitten him was disturbing. He described looking immediately down after feeling the pain in his ankle and seeing what looked to be a grossly deformed rat scuttling away into the darkness. This rat was apparently larger than normal, as well as possessing an extra clawed foot and a thick tail which seemed to whip around of its own accord, as if the rat could 'wag' its tail like a dog.

This report would have been of some concern taken alone, however, I have seen with my own eyes larger than normal droppings around the lower areas of the castle, like the cellars, and also in some of the wooden sheds in the gardens. I have been thinking about this information today, and find my thoughts going in a certain direction, a direction which I shudder to progress down in all honesty," Brother Abel continued in a most grim fashion.

I felt like I knew where Brother Abel's deductions were going, but I remained quiet and let the learned man finish his concerns without trying to beat him to the mark, as if we were playing some manner of game.

"Marcus, is it possible that something of the Purgorite invasion survived and is now surfacing? We saw the devastation caused amongst the livestock, and all those piles of burning carcasses. We remember all too well the disease. What if that disease was only lying dormant, and is now rearing its ugly head to spite us some more? Maybe the soldier was only seeing a standard rat and his mind played some tricks on him. Maybe whatever vermin left those larger droppings has just been at the castle's food refuse. I would like to think that, but my instinct tells me that something more sinister is in progress." Abel finished, looking at me directly as if to invite my response.

"Thank you for bringing this to my attention, Brother Abel. I will not sit on this information. I will instruct a team of specialists to scour all areas of the lower castle and the gardens to search for signs of infestation and do whatever it is they need to do. Please let me know of any further concerns, and also could you let me know if the private's health gets any worse? You may be right about something of the plague surviving, but I don't want to jump at shadows yet and invite hysteria. We need to find out the facts first. I'm sure you understand." I responded to Abel.

"Of course, Comman… I mean 'Marcus'. Any action you can take would be most helpful. I do hope that my fears are not getting the best of me and halting my powers of logic and reason. I am content for the specialists to do their work and take appropriate measures. That is fine." Abel assured me.

There was a slight pause before Abel ventured somewhat tentatively into another realm of discussion, one that caught me quite off guard. For Abel wanted to speak of my father, a man named Harald Kane, who was long dead and who had not come up in our discussions for several years.

"Marcus, I knew your father quite well, as you know. He was very much an adventurer and explorer, always tackling some wild mountain or some deep and dark uncharted cavern. I believe there was NOWHERE he did not fear to tread. I actually accompanied him on some of these slightly less hazardous and gruelling trips in the capacity of gathering fresh herbs and plants for medicinal use in my general work. I have told you that he was good with animals, but I felt that it went beyond that." Abel told me, whilst fidgeting with his hands a little.

I must admit that at the time, I was interested as to where all this was going. What did my father being an animal lover and naturalist have to do with anything?

"What I mean is that your father seemed to be able to communicate with animals on a primal level. He could almost talk to them, in a way. I don't mean the way a dog owner will speak lovingly to his pet canine, only for said canine to look dumbly at their master with big eyes, not understanding a word of what is being said. It was more like your father could COMMAND animals and summon them to this presence. He could not say, issue a set of complex directions and get the animal to perform tasks at a human level. He could, however, bend nearby animals to his will, up to a certain point. I would not say your father was any manner of sorcerer or magician; that would be folly. However, he had a skill and ability that could never be taught. It was in him all the time. I only mention it now, as I see how well your horse Palladin and your faithful hound Morse respond to you and obey you. It is my belief that something of your father's strange ability has been passed down to you, even if you do not know it." Abel finished, turning toward me to see how I was taking this explanation.

As for my reaction to what Abel had been telling me, I was dumbstruck and knew not what to say next. If I did indeed have this hereditary ability, how had I never actually come across it in my forty-six years of life? I was not my father. I loved Palladin and Morse as companions, but I had never felt that I could speak to them beyond basic orders. I had never felt that I had some type of mind connection with them, beyond that of any other animal owner with their pets.

I voiced these thoughts to Abel, who did not press the issue any further, but just told me to keep what he had said in mind and not write it off altogether, strange as it may sound. I thanked Brother Abel for his visit and waved him off as he departed on his own sturdy palfrey into the setting Veronot sun. That evening, I thought over all that Abel had told me whilst tucking into the delicious fish stew which old Betsy had prepared. The possible vermin issue had to be dealt with quickly and effectively. I knew that I needed to focus primarily on the upcoming expedition and handing over duties to Commander Vorgo, and something like an outbreak of pestilence was the absolute last thing any of us needed.

Chapter 5

The Next Meeting

The next meeting concerning the upcoming expedition actually took place not in Farchester Castle, but in the command room of Barford Castle. The meeting had been scheduled to take place one week after that first induction meeting, where the scene had been set. This location had been chosen as it was a more central location for the parties involved, as opposed to all of us having to travel South to Farchester. I did appreciate not having to travel so far, and even thanked Lord Huscliffe for this before the meeting began.

"Oh, do not mention it, Commander Kane. In all truth, the decision was not entirely altruistic, for both Lord Schnieder and I had business to conduct in the more Northern lands of Halia earlier today. Plus, I wanted to see with my own eyes how Barford Castle was faring. I am impressed with what I see. The outer wall is looking strong and the awful damage to the East tower has been patched up so expertly that one may never have thought the castle had ever been attacked at all." Explained Lord Huscliffe, his face perfectly composed.

"If only our internal scars could be patched up so easily," came the hard voice of Captain Stire, from behind us.

I knew that Captain Stire had never forgiven the Cadre for their lack of action during the Purgorite invasion. He had never forgotten how they preferred to sit behind their nice high walls whilst Halian men, women and children died in the towns, in the streets, in the tunnels and of course at Mirgot's Pass. I could not disagree with Stire and did not really like the Cadre much more than he did. But I was older, slightly more diplomatic, and better at guarding my tongue.

Huscliffe did not answer Captain Stire with words, only inclined his head slightly to show that he had heard and processed the Captain's remark.

The meeting attendees once again sat around a long rectangular wooden table, although not quite as long and fancy as the one which graced the chamber in Farchester Castle. The Command room was stone-floored, with the only floor covering being an inexpensive woollen rug, which was spread under the table. Several tapestries and paintings adorned the stone walls, as well as various wooden cabinets and sets of drawers. I did notice that one of the paintings seemed to illustrate Halian men fighting gruesome monsters atop soaring battlements. Whilst it was clear the artist had not actually been present, I assumed that the painting depicted our struggle atop Mirgot's Pass. The painting had clearly toned down the horror and desperation of the scene, as no corpses or blood could be seen anywhere in the picture. Only strong-looking Halian soldiers fighting valiantly against Purgorite invaders, who had been scaled down both in terms of size and how fearsome they actually were. Whilst I appreciated what the painting represented, it was sensationalising what was a horrific struggle for survival. I was about to speak to Captain Stire about the painting when Lord Huscliffe formally opened the meeting in his usual stern and attention-commanding voice.

"Officers, once again, thank you for attending this meeting. Whilst the meeting one week ago was to set the scene and let you know our intentions, as well as of course giving you due notice before your journey, this meeting will be a case of setting down specifics. I am convinced of the safety and security of this meeting room and that no prying eyes or ears will intrude upon us. Now, we, the Cadre, have arranged for this expedition to set forth in three weeks' time. The fully laden and equipped transport ships will set sail from the Northern port of Hawk's Hope on the fourteenth day of Aogasti*. The entire team travelling from Halia to the East coast of North Utresh will number twenty men. I would ask that each of you four officers, Commander Kane, Major De'Beresford, Captain Stire and Major Heven, each recruit two trusted soldiers to accompany you on this mission. I leave the actual selection to your reliable jurisdiction. The other eight soldiers will be made up of specialist reconnaissance troops of the cadre's choosing. I can assure all present that these are elite troops who have proven their ability beyond doubt. They have already received instructions about the expedition and have been ordered to report to Commander Kane at the port before you are set to depart.

Now, as I mentioned one week ago during our meeting, you clearly cannot stroll into North Utresh bearing Halian colours and Halian appearance. Prior to departing, you will assume the appearance of Kazbarian mercenaries. This entails shaving your head totally and keeping it shaved throughout the duration of the expedition. You will also be marked with the relevant tattoos, which tend to grace the neck, forearms and chest. I would prefer that, for the sake of authenticity, tattoos be inscribed in all of these bodily areas. I would rather they were there and not needed, than needed but not there. Do not worry, these tattoos are not permanent and will be removed upon your return to Halia. Other than the hair and tattoo situation, Kazbarian men do not look unlike those of Halia. Kazbarian mercenaries tend to be heavily built and muscular in appearance, with darker skin and a weathered look. I need not worry about that aspect, as you four Officers are already in good military shape and thanks to your days of hard working and fighting in all types of weather, possess that certain look not attained by those more clerical types who spend their days sitting behind a desk writing with a quill.

Now, I am sure that you will be wondering about the language barrier. Fear not, as the land of Kazbare is diverse and most residents speak several languages, one of which is Halian, although they call the language 'Halaze' over there. But it is still the same language, and you will be understood by almost all other Kazbarians. If you are experiencing doubts or concerns that Kazbarian mercenaries who do not speak the regional dialect will stand out and draw attention, do not worry, for there are different tribes in that diverse land, many of which only speak one particular language, like Halaze, Kazbat, which is the official language of the land, Utreek, which is the primary language in neighbouring Utresh, both south and north. Halaze is still a fairly common tongue in North Utresh as well.

To make things smoother, however, the Cadre has arranged for a Kazbarian interpreter and Halian friend named 'Ule-Romesh' to meet your ships at the North Utreshian coastal port of Tol'mral. I apologise for your having to learn these various bizarre names on top of everything else, but I'm sure that Ule-Romesh will be very helpful in aiding your understanding of this foreign land. Major Heven, I am not sure of how far your grasp of Utreek extends, but please offer whatever assistance you can.

The ships themselves will depart from the port at eleven of the clock in the morning, so please all be assembled by the ships with all your gear ready for departure. There will be plenty of food already purchased and on board to last for the journey, which we estimate will be five to six days, depending on the manner of weather you may encounter. I appreciate that very few of you have direct sailing experience. Do not fret about this matter, as a team of experienced sailors will see to the running of the ship. You will be travelling on two ships as opposed to one, just in case all is not lost in the unlikely event that one ship is sunk. The two shipmasters in question are named Sea Captain Barlow and Sea Captain Bostone.

Your actual dress and weaponry will be supplied before the date of departure and delivered to you by a dispatch rider. It is essential that you arrive at the port looking like true Kazbarian mercenaries, suited and booted. The dress will be a padded leather gambeson about the torso with a vest of light chainmail over the top, with thick trousers and knee-high fighting boots with knee guards to complement your lower body. Luckily, the Kazbare mercenaries tend to fight with longswords similar to us Halians, although slightly longer and heavier and made of a different quality of metal."

Once again, I will not recount every word that was uttered. Lord Huscliffe gradually drew the meeting to a close, after advising that other meetings may occur with certain attendees prior to the departure in three weeks; however, this would be the last official full meeting.

I rode part of the journey back to Castle Kane, accompanied by Captain Stire, as he had to pay an overnight visit to another castle. We rode side by side, I mostly listening, as Captain Stire vented openly about his thoughts concerning our upcoming task. He was giving voice to that which he could not express in the presence of the Cadre.

"…and the temerity of that old fool to say shite like "to fight with longswords similar to US Halians" as if he has even held a sword or risked his life in desperate battle. No, the Cadre are happy to sit behind their comfy desks in nice safe castles and send BETTER men off to fight and die in foreign mud. The kings of old fought from the front and led men gallantly into battle. They risked all for those from whom they asked loyalty. No, I speak wrongly, they didn't ask for loyalty. They EARNED loyalty."

I continued to listen as Captain Stire unloaded. I knew that Stire was breaking code by slandering the Higher Cadre in the presence of a senior Halian Officer, and that I could easily have had him reprimanded for such behaviour. As long as Captain Stire did not go overboard and suggest something criminal or outright treasonous, I was content to merely listen quietly to his passionate monologue. Truthfully, Stire had been raising some good points, many of which I agreed on.

Around eight miles from Castle Kane, Captain Stire and I parted ways as he took a more Easterly route to his destination. I rode on alone, deep in thought about whom I should recruit as my two agents for the upcoming expedition into the dangerous realms of North Utresh. I would have to give some more thought to the second agent, for after some careful consideration and mental weighing, I had decided whom I would first approach with the offer of high adventure.

Chapter 6

Commander Vorgo

The next morning, long before the bright sun had reached its fiery zenith, I managed to find young Simon Fester polishing his steel breastplate and using a whetstone to put a keen edge on the cutting edge of his longsword.

"Ah, First Lieutenant Fester, always one to make a good impression. I am sure that I would be able to see your armour in the dark, it shines so much. Your sword looks sharp enough to cut the air itself!" I complimented my young comrade.

Simon stood smartly to receive my greeting, dropping the cloth with which he had been using to buff the steel.

"Please sit, Simon. I have something I would like to discuss with you. How would you like to come with me on an adventure?" I offered to the young soldier, his eyes already glowing with interest.

Simon and I sat alone in the Carnagon armoury, quite undisturbed and in confidence, as I ran through the particulars of the expedition and what I would be asking for as the leader. I told Simon, reminded him really, that whilst he was young and still lacked experience, he was sharp-minded, quick-witted, had a keen eye for weak spots and seemed always ready to embrace a new challenge. I was about to tell Simon that I was not forcing him to attend me on this mission, and he could, if he chose to, remain at Carnagon Castle. This turned out to be unnecessary, as young Simon keenly agreed to take part in this exciting-sounding expedition. He was young, full of fire and was looking for just this type of hazardous but hopefully thrilling adventure to satiate the soldier in him.

Looking back, recruiting Simon for this purpose was a foolish decision to make and, given what happened, one I deeply regret, but what's done is done. The past is the past, for better or worse.

The next few weeks were a very busy time for those of us involved in the expedition. Alongside managing our usual duties as ranking Officers, we also had to prepare for our journey as well as liaise with and gradually hand over responsibility to our temporary replacements. I use the word 'temporary' as no-one wanted to break the comfortable illusion that everyone would be returning from the trip to North Utresh all safe and well with the job completed. We had to keep up high spirits publicly for the good of Halia, despite our internal thoughts and feelings.

I found myself getting on well with my replacement, Commander Vorgo. Vorgo was slightly older than I and more experienced to match. He had been fulfilling the rank of Commander elsewhere in Halia for the past ten years. From further research and asking around the right circles, I had, since that first meeting in Farchester, found out a little more about Lucius Vorgo. He was clearly a capable Commander and wasn't afraid to fight in the deepest and bloodiest part of a battle. I was told that Vorgo was a highly skilled and relentless warrior who had felled countless enemies on the battlefield, and even some OFF the field. I had also been warned that he was dangerous and not someone you want to make an enemy of. Making him an enemy was the last tactic I wished to employ, for he would be managing my region whilst I was away. So, I made sure to give him no motive to dislike me. I was always polite, respectful, understanding, generous and even complimentary in my dealings with Commander Vorgo. Fortunately, at the time, at least, Vorgo returned my good graces, and we enjoyed pleasant conversations and a healthy working relationship.

As part of the handover process, I gave Vorgo a full tour of Carnagon Castle, which would be his primary responsibility and office of work. I went to the length of inviting him into the treasury room and briefly going over the various financial ledgers and rent records. I introduced Vorgo to the castle treasurer, Stegan Lemore, from whom

I obtained permission prior to allowing Vorgo to see the confidential records contained in the somewhat dusty wooden cabinets. As Commander, I did not actually need to ask Lemore's permission to share any such records, but I felt that extra level of respect conducive to my style of management and leadership.

I also introduced Vorgo to the head cook, Chef Ramon Dalfrey, a portly, red-faced and jolly looking man who ably oversaw the sustenance of the castle's occupants. For I recall being told that an army marches on its stomach! Nearby, we came across the captain of the guard, one Captain Gustav Hamst. Gustav and I had fought side by side against the Purgorite threat and I had promoted Gustav to this important role, knowing that he was more than up for the task.

Next, I took Vorgo to meet my trusted old friend Brother Abel. We found Abel alone in his infirmary, taking advantage of a quiet moment to sort out his medicines. He appeared to be rearranging the varying sizes of glass bottles in some certain order when I spoke to him.

"Brother Abel, I'd like you to meet Commander Lucius Vorgo. Commander Vorgo, as you know, will be taking control of the region whilst I am away on business matters."

Brother Abel turned smartly at my words, his eyebrows raised and his face pleasantly surprised. He skipped over to where Commander Vorgo stood and offered a large hand in greeting.

"Oh, a real honour to meet you, Commander Vorgo. I truly look forward to working under your command. I have heard great things about you." Abel began, beaming up at the taller man with a broad grin.

Lord Vorgo promptly took the offered hand before giving it a few firm soldier-like pumps.

"My reputation does precede me; I hope I am not immodest in saying so. I have also heard great things about you, too, good Brother. I heard that you were one of the few medical practitioners assisting the large party that travelled South to Mirgot's Pass. I have no doubt that your skills were invaluable during that most difficult time." Offered Vorgo in a congratulatory tone, as a smile also alighted upon his usually stern face.

"I have also been informed about the potential rodent issue by our good Commander Kane, so rest assured, I will follow this issue up without hesitation. I believe that the specialist team in question have already been hired. The last thing we need is mutated rats scurrying about, spreading disease," continued Vorgo in a more serious tone.

"Thank you for saying so, Commander Vorgo. I did what I could given the terrible circumstances and lack of supplies and equipment. But honestly, it was really Marcu…I mean, Commander Kane, I'm sorry, and the late Captain Winters, who led us so bravely through the most harrowing ordeals." Brother Abel replied, nodding toward me in recognition and respect.

"Commander Kane is indeed most brave. Halia forever owes him a debt of gratitude. I clearly have a big spot to fill going forward." Vorgo complimented.

Although Vorgo's words were respectful and he gave the outward appearance of sincerity and gratitude, I could not help but detect a glimmer of something in his eyes. I could not tell if it was deceit, or mockery perhaps? It just struck me that he spoke of the 'big spot to fill' as if he didn't plan on me returning to Halia.

It was that same evening when I was visited by the artist who had been instructed to inscribe the necessary markings onto my skin for the upcoming expedition. The actual work was done in my downstairs study, with me sitting in a wooden chair, clad only in underclothes and trying not to wince as the artist used a sharp pen to sketch out the patterns in a dark ink. The pain was surprisingly intense, even for a hardened warrior like myself who was no stranger to the rough and tumble of bloody battle! At least the markings were only temporary; I only hoped at the time that removing them would not be quite as painful as adding them.

Chapter 7

Setting Sail

Finally, we found ourselves rising bright and early on that fourteenth day of Aogasti. I got up from my familiar and cherished four-poster bed in my large chamber, which lay at the East end of Castle Kane. I drew back the heavy velvet drapes and looked out at the beautiful rising sun and lush green fields of Halia. I knew that I may be seeing the last Halian sunrise I would ever see. The sight was therefore both beautiful and painful. I dressed myself in the Kazbare mercenary garb which had been delivered to my home a few days previously, knowing that my appearance would be altered even more drastically when I arrived at the port. I would be turning from a noble Halian Commander into a rough, hard-living Kazbarian mercenary. From a man who fought for his country, to a man who fought for gold and even for dark thrills.

I had already spoken to both Betsy, my cook and young Tarmon, my servant, about my upcoming trip out of the land. I had broken the news to them that as of the fourteenth of Aogasti, they would cease to be under my direct employ, but would be referred to Commander Vorgo, my replacement, for alternative work. Betsy took the news well, bless her, as she had changed from master to master so many times over the years that it was business as usual. She kindly wished me the best of luck in wherever I had to go and told me that it had been a real pleasure working for me. Tarmon, however, was slightly more unravelled by the news and he even went to the extent of asking to come with me and continue to serve me.

"No, Tarmon, you can't follow me, I'm afraid. I cannot go into detail about where I am going, but it is no place for you. I am certain that other work will be found for you very soon, maybe even as an apprentice to a skilled craftsman. You need to believe in yourself more, my lad." I had said to the gloomy youth.

North Utresh was no place for Simon either, so it turned out, but at the time I naively thought that his skilled swordplay and firsthand account of battle with the Purgorites had "prepared him for anything", as the saying goes.

The day before my departure, I had arranged for my beautiful horse Palladin and my trusty hound Morse to be looked after at the nearby stables and kennels, respectively. I did not have the option to take my two four-legged brethren with me and could not really ask attendants to visit my castle daily to feed and exercise the animals. I knew the owners of both establishments and trusted them to take good care of my two companions. Castle Kane would be securely locked and bolted during my absence. With all the servants and animals going elsewhere, there was no reason for anyone to go in or out whilst I was away.

It was also the day before departure, the night before, to be precise, when I opened my chamber closet door to retrieve a certain item which I had not held in a long time. The Cadre had advised us clearly that weapons specific to the region and peoples we were meant to be mimicking would be provided to us as part of our guise. There was one weapon which I was not leaving behind, though, as this weapon was to me more than just a weapon.

In Halia, it is and has always been customary for a soldier to be buried with his longsword. As to the origin of that custom, it has always been a point of contention. Some folk say that the sword helps define the soldier's purpose in life. Some disagree and argue that the custom allows soldiers to fight on in the afterlife, whatever that is supposed to mean. Some Halians even believe that the swords are left in the soldier's wooden casket as offerings to the Gods. I never knew which of these rumours to believe. Our brave and fearless comrade Mordak had been buried with a standard Halian longsword, alongside all other Halian bodies found in the aftermath of the battle of Mirgot's Pass. But I did not bury Mordak's true weapon, the one he wielded in the *Lenfer of battle.

As I stood in my chamber closet on that red evening of the thirteenth day of Aogasti, I looked up at what I fondly referred to as

"Mordak's Might". For his trusty, modified and brutal looking hammer had been residing in my closet ever since I took ownership of the mansion house. The treasured item had not been cast in the closet like some lost pair of socks to be buried under piles of junk, actually quite the opposite. The solid hammer had been resting on a bed produced by two long sturdy nails which had been driven deep into the wood at the back of the closet. I wanted Mordak's Might kept somewhere safe and secret, somewhere a thief, should they somehow manage to break into my castle, would not immediately think to look. As I gently lifted the mighty weapon down and held it in both hands, it struck me once more and more strongly than ever, that what I held was more than a weapon, it was a symbol. It was not just a lump of hard steel to be swung around, it was a physical statement of Halian strength, fortitude, pride, endeavour, and wrath. I felt that by wielding that hammer, something of Mordak's huge strength would be passed to me. That I might be imbued with his bottomless battle rage and fighting spirit when the time came. So, I lovingly wrapped Mordak's Might up with the rest of my luggage as I murmured a quiet prayer to Mordak's soul, wherever he might be now.

Riding on a rented horse, a sturdy Chestnut mare whose name I did not know, I trotted into the district of Hawk's Hope at around half past the hour of ten. I had left Castle Kane very early, as it was a good fifteen-mile trip to the port. I observed a large gathering of dismounted soldiers waiting outside one of the port's large administration buildings. Even from a fair distance, my trained eagle eyes could spot several familiar faces and several unfamiliar ones. I continued my mare down the wide dirt path toward the port, my luggage case securely fixed over the mare's ample rump.

The first familiar face I encountered was that of Lord Vincent Harbrandt, who was engaged in conversation with Major De'Beresford as I guided my mare towards them. He was embracing his beloved fiancée, Lady Vivian, with one arm whilst he gesticulated passionately to the Major with the other. Vincent paused as he saw me approach and raised a hand to his eyes to shield his eyes from the worst of the dazzling Halian sun.

"Ah, Commander Kane. I was just telling Major De'Beresford about my efforts to re-grow the Diromale Forest. It is slow work planting new trees and watching them grow, but patience is a virtue of course. In truth, I came here this morning not to talk about new forests, but to wish you good men luck and see you all off. My lady Vivian has never even seen the Palmoria Ocean, so I thought this would be a golden opportunity to broaden her horizons!" Vincent declared.

"I am very grateful for your concern, my Lord. I feel that we will need all the luck we can get. It would be good to have you again at my side, Lord Harbrandt, but I appreciate that you have so many matters to attend to here, not to mention a beautiful young fiancée to look after and a wedding to plan. You look radiant this morning, Lady Vivian. I hope that the beauty of the Palmoria Ocean is all that you hoped it would be." Came my address to both Lord and the future Lady Harbrandt.

"Absolutely, Marcus, it is most stunning. I hope one day to go sailing across it, as you will be, although maybe not so far." Lady Vivan answered energetically, her golden hair glowing in the sunlight.

Looking back, little did Lady Vivian know at the time that she WOULD be sailing across that Ocean before too long. Just not at all in the way she envisioned.

Lord Harbrandt excused himself and his lady from our party, as he had to attend to business elsewhere in the port. I shook hands with Major De'Beresford once we were alone and could communicate more freely now that we were no longer in the presence of high nobility. Do not misunderstand me, Vincent was very much our battle brother and had shed blood with us, however, local customs still needed to be observed, and rank respected.

"Commander Kane, how are you this morning? May I ask which two soldiers you chose to accompany you on our expedition?" asked the Major.

"Good morning, Ralph. As to your first question, I am understandably nervous and a little excited. I have not partaken in an expedition of this nature for….well, never...to be totally honest. As far as companions are concerned, I have recruited First Lieutenant Fester and Second Lieutenant Palos. I believe that you know both of them, to some degree at least." I responded to the Major, ensuring that no-one was in earshot to hear me addressing him by his first name.

"Oh yes, I do know both of those fine Officers. An excellent choice if I may say so. This will be a valuable experience for young Lieutenant Fester. He is still young and there is so much of the world to see. People say that Valamantus is a small world, but when I go to the Farchester Observatory and gaze at all the maps pieced together by different explorers, it seems that the world is endless. There is much that we haven't seen." The Major reminded me.

The Major was right on that last line. That was indeed much of the world that explorers had never ventured into and remained a mysterious blank on the Valamantus global map. Even then, I had an uncomfortable feeling that some parts of the globe were better off being unexplored, and that some dark lands were better off left well alone by nosy intruders looking to stake their name to a "new" patch of land.

"Commander Kane, please come with me, I would like to introduce you to two of my younger Officers who will be accompanying us on this expedition." The Major said, already moving off in his desired direction. By this stage, I had already dismounted my rented horse and left her at the port's large stable block.

The Major approached two young Officers engaged in conversation, who stood up smartly as he approached. Both Officers were smartly presented and well–built. Although both men were strangers to me, one did look familiar. I had seen a little of that face in someone else, but where, and whom?

"Commander Kane, I would like to introduce you to First Lieutenant Harold Parcher…" Major De'Beresford spoke in an official tone, indicating the Officer nearest to him, who bowed to me respectfully whilst acknowledging me simply as "Commander".

"…and this is Captain Laurent D'Arten." Finished the Major, indicating the other Officer whose face had seemed so familiar.

"Good morning, Commander Kane. I believe that you knew my father, Henry D'Arten, late Constable of the Eastern District?" Enquired the young Captain, a certain knowledge alive behind those gazing blue eyes.

I must admit that I was for a moment at a loss for words. For an instant, I found myself back on the battlements of Mirgot's Pass, surrounded by enemies and desperate, yelling at Captain Winters to murder the father of the young Captain standing right before me. I once again saw Henry D'Arten's lifeblood spill shockingly to the brickwork and the light leave his eyes. Laurent most likely resembled the soldier his father Henry had been earlier in his life, before rich living and lack of exercise reduced his once strong body to that of a paunchy quill pusher. Laurent knew, he knew what I had been a part of.

"I did know your father a little. He fought with us at Mirgot's Pass…and fought bravely. I look forward to having you with us on this expedition, the both of you." I offered, after that slight hesitation.

I feared that the workings of my mind had carried over to my facial expression, and that young D'Arten recognised my lip service for what it was. However, after the brief introduction, I excused myself and carried on to catch up with Captain Stire and to meet his two selected companions for the mission.

Whilst the tattoo artist had visited the expedition's participants on a castle-by-castle basis over the past week to scribe the replica Kazbarian markings (which were a pattern of jet black spikes and swirls slightly resembling creeping thorns), the head shaving was to be done communally, at the port. It was around half past eleven when all of the assembled troops were asked to line up smartly outside of an unremarkable medium-sized building. I, as the leader, set an early example by being first in line for this unpleasant but mandatory requirement of the trip. I, for one, treasured my shoulder-length locks, which were still primarily a nice dark brown, with only a few telltale strands of silver. It would not be easy to see the whole lot sheared away, leaving me as bald as either a newborn babe or an elderly man sitting out his last years of life.

We were invited into the room four at a time and politely asked to sit in a chair by one of four well-kept and finely dressed barbers. A sheet was draped over our seated upper bodies, specifically around the neck, before being tied comfortably. Each barber then proceeded to use razor-sharp shears to expertly and rapidly remove the main bulk of the man's hair, before applying a rich lather of soap to the scalp and using a much smaller blade to take the hair right down to the scalp. Fortunately, or unfortunately, I was not blind to this ongoing transformation, as I was enabled to watch this change via a finely polished mirror which had been fixed to the wall around four feet in front of me. The low pain of seeing my locks removed was almost negated by the thrill of seeing how expertly and deftly my barber worked with his blades. In a sense, he was almost as good with a blade as I was, only on a much smaller scale of work!

After a space of only ten minutes, the first four men had been de-haired, cleaned off and the sheet untied. I even fumbled in my trouser pocket for some silver units with which to pay the kind gentlemen; however, this offer was politely refused with a slight smile and a shake of the head. As I left the barber's floor, I could not help but run my hand over my now totally bare head. All I felt was the tiniest inkling of stubble. From a large stack of shaving kits, I had been handed one by the barber and reminded to shave my face (which I had always done anyway as a matter of principle) and head on a daily basis, in the morning if possible. I certainly felt the wind much more acutely on my scalp the moment I left the building, which I knew was just another thing I would need to endure. A soldier's life was not meant to be sunshine and Begonias, so honestly, a colder scalp was hardly an ordeal.

Soon enough, the twelve Halian Officers stood outside with their clean faces and hairless domes. Any men with beards had also had those taken off. One particular officer, a Captain Lane McAdams, looked barely recognisable after his long hair and heavy hedge of beard had been stolen from him. It was like actually being able to see his face fully for the first time. I recall thinking how exposed he must have felt and not envying him. There was no strict code for hair growth in the Halian military. It tended to be up to the regional Senior Officer to dictate such rules of appearance. Long hair was never really an issue in battle, as the hair tended to be secured under a helmet or tied back so as not to impede the vision of the combatant.

The eight Cadre picked "specialist reconnaissance troops" were the last to arrive, not long after the point of midday, or high sun. They had clearly been given a more leisurely arrival time than the rest of us. The eight troops rode in a fairly tight formation, each sitting atop matching black Stallions. They were already shaven-headed and displayed similar markings to the rest of us who had by then been waiting for well over and a quart. It seemed that the ship departure time of eleven of the clock dictated by the Cadre was merely a number to ensure that the Halian Officers were there in good time. In fact, the two ships, named Oceanwolf and Farseer, did not set sail until half past the hour of midday.

I got to meet the Sea Captain of the ship Oceanwolf, which would serve as my home for the best part of the next week as she made her way across 400 long miles of open ocean. Christoph Barlow was a powerfully built, stocky man of average height with a ponytail and a medium scruff of beard. His red and weathered face told of years on the sea with a salty wind constantly rushing to meet him. He shook my hand with one of his own meaty paws and told me most genuinely that it was a pleasure to be escorting me on this trip, and that I should not hesitate to ask him for any assistance should it be required. He addressed me as "Me Lord", despite my rank of Commander. Given that Sea Captain Barlow was not under my command and actually doing us all an invaluable service, I did not have the heart to correct him. Let him address me in his own way, as long as he got us across all that ocean in one piece.

Sea Captain Barlow was in charge of a group of six other experienced sailors, who would be tending to the operation of the ship and fulfilling the various duties that needed undertaking. Whilst I had travelled on different waterborne vessels of various sizes across the seas many times, it had only ever been in the capacity of a soldier who needed to get from one place to the next. I had never troubled myself too much with how the different sails worked and how the sailors had to respond accordingly to wind changes and sea conditions. During my years of campaigning, I had bunked on ships ranging from the smaller and lighter Schooner, to hulking town-sized Frigates bristling with mean cannons and carrying hundreds of men. Both Oceanwolf and Farseer were of the Schooner class and could easily accommodate both sailors and soldiers, with room to spare. The ships were nearly identical in appearance and dimensions, it seemed. They ran for a length of 140 feet and were around twenty-four feet at the widest point, which allowed for sufficient free movement. These were sleek ships designed more for transport and to navigate inland waterways. They were most certainly not built to withstand the pounding of multiple enemy cannons or take much direct assault from the mean-looking ram of enemy ships. So, if we happened to encounter some hulking behemoth looking to make a tasty snack out of our pathetic little Schooner, then we were in deep trouble. Or, if a boatload of angry sea bandits wanted to climb, jump or leap aboard to take our supplies, and most probably our freedom, if not our lives, then all we would have to fend them off would be melee weapons and projectile arrows. Fortunately, Sea Captain Barlow was no stranger to these seas and knew how to avoid trouble and outsail and outmanoeuvre larger, more cumbersome ships.

As Commander, I had separated my nineteen men into two separate travelling groups before leaving the port, as was my privilege. Ten men on each ship, of course. I had split the group so that six Halian Officers and four of the Cadre selected scouts would travel together on each ship. That way, we could become more familiar with each other in terms of establishing a working relationship. I knew next to nothing about any of the eight scouts that I would be commanding, so felt that our days on the vast ocean together with little else to do would be something of an opportunity. Of course, I expected each and every man to follow my order to the letter, but I would prefer not to be seen be a faceless official barking orders from on high. It was my personal stance that fighting men operated better if they at least knew and respected the Officer passing the orders and leading by example. At the same time, I did not want to be seen as a "friend" more than a commanding Officer, as that made insubordination that bit more likely to rear its ugly head. I did not want to find myself in a position where my order of "guard that supply cache" was met with a surly response of "I'll do it tomorrow when I feel better" from a nonchalant and slouching soldier who had become so comfortable as to mistake a direct order for a polite request.

Accompanying me on Oceanwolf were my two selected Officers, Lts. Fester and Palos. Jerome Palos was a tall and well-built soldier whom I had known for around five years by the time of the expedition. He had already travelled to and fought competently in "darker lands" and proved himself in various elements of war, so I felt him a natural choice to recruit. Also aboard Oceanwolf were Major De'Beresford and his two recruits, 1Lt. Parcher and Captain D'Arten, whom I introduced earlier. The Major had informed me that both of the Officers had served in scouting-type roles before being stationed at Mirgot's Pass. They both struck me as fairly quiet and brooding men, but a certain glint in their steely eyes told of a danger that lay within. I had the early impression that when it came to battle, those two would be the kind of fighting men you wanted at your back. The Major had known them both for several years and told me that he barely had to spend a thought on which two men to recruit, as they both stood out immediately as perfect choices. D'Arten still seemed to regard me with a certain detachment, but seemed content to at least follow my instructions.

The four Cadre selected scouts accompanying us, six Halian Officers on Oceanwolf were named Darkwolf, Smoke, Midnight and Shadowprowler. As one can imagine, these were not their birth names.

It was not like a set of proud young parents decided to name their ruddy-faced bundle of joy "Darkwolf" upon seeing him open his innocent little eyes for the first time. These were instead names chosen by each soldier as he was inducted into the clandestine brotherhood of what tended to be called the 'Halian Scouts'. These eight men had no rank amongst themselves; the closest they came to rank or title was inserting the word "Scout" before their chosen name. I had met all four individually before leaving the port. The interestingly named scouts were polite and engaged in whatever conversation I opened, although they were also taciturn and guarded with regard to actually sharing information. That did make sense, given the shady nature of their work. I respected their need for distance and did not impose on them any more than I had to. I did not really care how little or much that any of them said, as long as they followed my orders without question and carried out their tasks ably. I had little doubt that they would, given that these eight troops had been selected specially by the Higher Cadre from a huge pool of possible candidates. I knew that the Cadre did not make their selections on a whim or without serious thought and discussion.

The first two of the six Halian Officers who would be experiencing the joys of the Palmorian Ocean whilst riding the Farseer were Captain David Stire and Major Johann Heven, Heven being the only Officer with direct experience of Utreshian life. Major Heven was a towering man of over six and a half foot, taller even than I by several inches. He possessed a tough, angular face and the eyes of a warrior. I can imagine his intimidating appearance would have fitted in well in the clearly harsh lands of North Utresh, where it was live strong or die weak. Not only was he tall, but broad of the body with strong arms and a deep chest.

The four less senior Officers accompanying Stire and Heven were two First Lieutenants, Bartolo Demetri and Justain Smith, alongside Captain Lane McAdams and First Lieutenant Siegfried Schmidt. I didn't know much about these four lower Officers as the expedition began; I could only trust in the good judgment of Stire and Heven and look forward to getting to know the young Officers once we reached North Utresh.

Military rankings, of course, differ from nation to nation, and even tribe to tribe. But as far as Halia is concerned, the rankings work as follows from lowest to highest: we have Private, Second Ensign, First Ensign, 3Lt., 2Lt., 1Lt., then to Captain, Major, Commander, Warmaster and finally Battle Commodore.

Chapter 8

Pillards Attack

Once the sea voyage got underway, the men quickly fell into a routine. Anyone who has spent not just hours but DAYS on a smallish ship with nowhere to go will know all too well how slow time seems to move. You have little to do but sit somewhere out of the way of the busy sailors and wait, and talk, and maybe eat some dry, unexciting food, then wait, and talk, and use the ship's basic privy, and then sleep away some more boring hours. Even the discomfort of seasickness can alleviate some of the boredom, macabre as that may sound. Whilst I did entreat my troops to keep themselves active with fairly stationary bodyweight exercises like push-ups, squats and jumping jacks, there was simply not the room on deck or anywhere else on the vessel to engage in sword practice, whereby large men would be stepping to and fro often without really looking where they were going. The combatants would be knocking into things, tripping over ropes, maybe even causing damage to Navy property, which never goes down well.

It was on day three of the otherwise unremarkable sea trip, however, where we were FORCED to use our swords, specifically the Kazbarian blades that had been issued to us as part of our clever guise. As explained to us earlier by Huscliffe, the blades were slightly longer and heavier than our standard Halian longswords, but fortunately, the difference was minimal. The Kazbarian blades in question were maybe one and a half inches longer and one kilogram heavier. This is a difference easily worked around by powerfully built warriors very used to wielding a longsword in all manner of situations. Whilst I am no metallurgist or even competent blacksmith, the Kazbarian long blades did seem somehow tougher than our Halian Steel, as if made of a denser metal. This was a difference that worked in our favour, as by basic rationale, the stronger the metal, the stronger the armour that it could penetrate.

It was actually Sea Captain Barlow who first spotted the approaching vessel using his board-mounted spyglass, at around two hours after sunrise. From that distance, he could not quite make out the ship's nature, insofar as was it a trading, military, exploratory or transport vessel. He could therefore not easily discern her intention. His disquiet was such that he summoned me to his position and even bid me take a look through the spyglass at the mysterious vessel. Barlow did not want to promote unnecessary concern, though, so he merely instructed his crew to proceed onward and told me that he would, of course, react accordingly should this mysterious vessel prove to have sinister intentions.

To our shared dismay, the mysterious vessel only drew closer to the Oceanwolf. It was not our imagination or paranoia; the vessel was clearly making for us and at quite a rate. By this stage, the occupants on the deck of the ship had spotted this incoming vessel and many appeared to be straining their eyes to make out details. As I observed Barlow's face, which was fixed behind the spyglass, I saw that it grew alarmingly pale and concerned. This concern naturally spread to me, and I feared his next words, which were nothing less alarming or shock-inducing than…

"It's a large Pillard ship, Commander Kane. They are just dropping their flag. I can already see a load of armed men on board who seem to be looking right back at me. They are not here to trade, believe me. I cannot outrun them even in this ship. What do you wish to do?" asked a harrowed-looking Sea Captain Barlow.

I had come across Pillards before on previous sails to foreign soils. They were vicious looters and murderous sea scum who would violently storm ships, taking whatever they wanted from the vessel and killing anyone foolish enough to stand in their way. They were sometimes so cruel and savage as to go from bow to stern, crook and cranny, looking for any hiding bodies to murder. They would then take anything valuable from the still warm corpse, even going to the extent of prying out gold teeth or cutting off a finger to the root, simply to obtain an inexpensive ring which might fetch a few units of silver. During my previous encounters though, strength had been on our side, as I had been sailing on a much larger and stronger ship which carried many times the fighting men that Oceanwolf presently did.

"We cannot fight them off from a distance or even stop them from boarding the ship. We can only be ready for them when they do arrive. Now, listen Captain Barlow, I understand that you usually command this vessel, but right now I need you to listen to me, and trust me. I want you and the rest of your sailors to lower one of your wooden tender boats into the sea and sail off, making sure that the Pillards see you." I basically ordered, to an increasingly astonished and disbelieving Sea Captain Barlow.

"B..but..my ship…I will not lose my beloved Oceanwolf without a fight, or simply hand it over to sea scum freeloaders." Protested an understandably belligerent Barlow.

"You will not lose the ship, trust me. The Pillards are brutal, but they are not ready for us. The only thing they will get from this ship is a painful and bloody death. Get in those boats and row out and leave the rest to us." I almost snarled at Barlow through gritted teeth.

Barlow must have seen the rage in my eyes, for he stepped back, nodding in an almost puppy-like fashion, before rushing off to gather the rest of his sailors from wherever they were on the ship. Luckily, he had not gone far before three of his sailors converged on his position, clearly eager for orders.

My plan to deal with the Pillards had been formulated almost off the hoof, but I had to believe that it would work. I prayed that the Pillards would see the sailors rowing frantically away from the ship and assume that the vessel had been abandoned by underpaid workers not wanting to face death at the blade of a Pillard's much-used blade. As soon as I had been told of the ship's identity by Barlow, I had whistled to my troops on board before giving a hand signal which indicated that they should hit the deck and hide themselves immediately. I therefore hoped that the Pillard lookout hadn't spotted too many bodies on board and that there was a general assumption that any other ship occupants would be close behind the first boatful of sailors in other Tender boats.

With the sailors appearing to obey my highly unusual orders and rushing towards the single, smaller row boat, which was large enough to carry all seven of them, I lay down before crawling low behind the cover of the wooden railing. The railing ended around four feet above the wooden deck, allowing plenty of room for even a very large crawling soldier to remain unseen. As soon as I got within earshot of most of the troops, I spoke forth so that all could hear, before the Pillards could possibly get within earshot and hear me over the sound of the waves and wind.

"Listen, those are Pillards approaching, they plan on boarding this ship and fleecing it dry. Obviously, that cannot happen. Negotiation is already off the table, so we will resolve this situation with a brutal and vicious attack applied without remorse. Each man hide out of sight as best as possible, then, on my command, rise and attack. Pick an enemy body as early as you can, then move onto the next. They outnumber us, although by how many I do not know. Just keep killing until they are no more." I ordered sternly, already feeling my pulse race and the adrenaline build.

I took pride in seeing nine sets of hard eyes gazing right back at me, all hungry for some much-needed exercise.

I quickly chose my own hiding spot behind two large barrels of ship equipment. Despite Oceanwolf being only a Schooner, it was surprising how many hiding places could be found on the craft. I saw nimble young Simon crouch low behind a pile of dirty sails, his sword firm in hand. I looked to my left and noted that tough old De'Beresford was standing upright, as still as a statue behind a large wooden post. Further down the ship, the four scouts impressed me as becoming almost invisible, as if they could blend into any background. Even I could not spot them exactly with my trained eyes, but I knew that they were there, and ready.

I was just taking deep breaths and steeling myself for the upcoming fight when I noticed something large and solid sliding across the deck toward me. I looked down and immediately spotted my beloved Mordak's Might almost at my feet. My first fanciful instinct was that the spirit of Mordak was somehow watching over us and had sent his hammer forth from the afterlife. However, that romantic image was dispelled all too soon when I saw the grinning face of 2Lt. Palos peering out from under a pile of rope like some demon from a nightmare. I had told Palos earlier about the weapon, after he had seen it wrapped up in my luggage. He had clearly had the good sense to quickly procure it once he understood the incoming threat. I nodded at him, grinning wickedly myself. I closed my right hand around the leather wraps and once again, gazed the length of the brutal swinging death giver. Mordak's Might had begun as a humble Blacksmith's hammer used by an Otter's Wall tradesman, before Mordak discovered it and proudly made it his own. He had adapted the hammer over time, strengthening it, increasing its size and weight, making it more deadly in battle and able to work against tougher armour. Mordak's Might final form was a three-and-a-half-foot-long, thirty-five-pound behemoth of a weapon. The most dangerous part was, of course, the head, a brutal lump of solid steel which had been finely shaped into a wicked, armour-piercing spike on one side and left a dull bludgeon on the other side. A further three-inch spike also graced the top of the hammer head, making enemies even less likely to want to get close. The once purely wooden handle had been expertly strengthened by carefully placed and welded rods of steel. If this purely physical aspect was not enough, Mordak had managed to bore a two-inch long, narrow hole into the hammer head, before inserting a few grams of a potent, powered chemical named 'Dyoxytrite'. Whenever the hammer head connected with another object at force, the powder would effectively explode, giving the hammer swing a further concussive effect, as if the weapon was somehow not deadly enough!

By this stage, I was almost going totally off sound and vibration, as I dared not risk peeping out from behind the barrels and revealing myself. The element of surprise would be beyond vital for this ruse to work. I heard the enemy ship draw nearer. I heard the bark of many angry voices. Then, I heard the sound of what I could tell were long and heavy wooden planks dropping loudly against the side of our ship, the Oceanwolf. I did, however, look further down the ship and made eye contact with 1Lt. Parcher, who was hiding silently behind the accommodation deck and had a clearer view of the invading party. He held up both his hands with fingers splayed three times, as if to indicate that we were about to deal with at least thirty intruders. He was struggling to keep his nerves in check, judging by his facial expression. I nodded in recognition and indicated for him to stay hidden and stay back. Young Simon locked eyes with me as we heard the first heavy footsteps on the deck, on OUR deck. I for a moment found myself back atop Mirgot's Pass and reliving that terrible moment when the first Purgorite brute had jumped off the ladders. Then, I recalled that we had WON that battle, and we would win this one too.

The sound of more footsteps joined that first pair, and within seconds, the deck of the Oceanwolf shook with their combined weight and movement. The Pillard voices were loud and merry-sounding. They thought that they had stumbled upon easy pickings. *'Fine'* I thought to myself, *'let them keep talking. It just lets us know when they are close enough.'* I knew that none of us had been spotted by the Pillards despite the proximity, as I had heard no sound of struggle or outcry, or clash of duelling blades. When I heard the nearest loud voice only two feet away, just above the barrels, I knew that it was time for combat.

I gripped Mordak's Might with both hands, took a deep breath of the rich Palmorian air, before rising boldly to my feet. Whilst I rose, I also stepped and pivoted with my brutal length of killing steel. I also roared one word at the top of my lungs and again prayed that my men would react and join me in bloodshed.

"NNNNOOOOOOOWWWWWWW!!" I screamed, whilst unleashing Mordak's Might.

That unfortunate nearest Pillard, standing with sword in hand, but with said sword dangling loosely at his side, ate the full blast of my hammer strike. I just had time to witness a shocked face, before it was violently transformed into a huge spray of bone, brain and head innards. It was like my hammer barely stopped, and I barely felt any actual contact. As I dashed forward to handle the next Pillard, already a corpse who was still standing, I took the deepest pride that from all around the ship, my troops rallied to the call.

The old Major stepped out from behind his wooden post and keenly set to with his Kazbarian blade. I knew that he was no fool with any sword and quickly decapitated a hapless Pillard after the briefest series of exchanges and parries. I looked to my right and saw young Simon slice low at Pillards' poorly armour legs, causing a shocked scream and a jet of crimson gore to shoot over the deck. Simon promptly followed up this blow with a wicked neck slash, which almost beheaded the foolish intruder. I took care of the next Pillard, a large man holding a sword and a puny-looking wooden shield, with a strong overhead vertical strike. The man tried to guard himself against my blow with his shield, but the wood would have needed to be four times the thickness to save him. My blow drove right through his flimsy shield and mangled his arm whilst dragging him messily to his knees. Mercifully, I silenced his awful screams with a follow–up blow to his skull. I was not looking for a lengthy battle here.

I quickly snapped to my right to fend off a sword strike from a snarling Pillard, who, alongside his fellow pillagers, had recovered from their shock and started to fight back. I knew that these men were experienced and brutal killers and not to be taken lightly. I also knew that my comrades and I were highly trained, experienced and deadly soldiers of Halia. I found myself laughing at this, for some unexplainable reason. I was laughing madly as I drove the reinforced handle of Mordak's Might up into the Pillard's nose, crushing it into his face and knocking him flat. I laughed aloud as I saw one of the Scouts, I cannot recall which, seem to materialise twenty feet in the air before dropping down to plunge a blade through a Pillard's neck. All around me, I saw still and bloodied Pillard corpses. I spotted young Captain D'Arten skewer a Pillard through the torso, before deftly sliding out the gory blade and dismembering another enemy like a ravenous diner carving up fresh steak with a sharp blade. It was clear that the battle was going our way and my ruse had worked. The battle was going our way, but it was not quite over. I turned to my left and saw that on a fairly open space of deck, a body of maybe ten remaining Pillards had wisely formed something of a phalanx. They stood shoulder to shoulder, terrified and trembling, maybe for the first time in their wretched lives, but certainly for the LAST time. We were not taking prisoners. I once reestablished my firm grip on Mordak's Might, and holding it aloft, I could almost feel its power coursing down my arms and through my body, through my veins, through my very being. I barreled towards this last phalanx of Pillards, already sensing my troops at my back and sides.

"Stay to the sides and pick off any remainers," I ordered as I charged fearlessly into this last pathetic emblem of hopeless resistance.

Mordak's Might began swinging, and it was like the weapon was controlling me, such was it's power. We carved wicked figure 8s through the air again and again as we drove forward, each swing and strike felling another enemy to the music of death screams and crushing bones. The enemy could do little to fight back. They made cursory efforts to lash out with their puny blades, but our force was such that it must have been like trying to fight off a Tornado of steel and rage. I knew that if any Gods of War existed and were watching from on high, they would have been proud of the gore-slicked fiend driving his hammer through enemy after enemy. My troops duly waded in from the sides, slashing, hacking and slicing into the fearful mass. As my bloodlust and rage slowly dulled and cold reason returned, I saw that there was nothing around me but a small sea of broken bodies, blood and innards. No enemy was left standing. I looked around at the Halian men and they duly returned my gaze from wild-eyed and blood-soaked faces. I was panting heavily and shaking with the comedown as my adrenaline levels returned to normal. I noticed that all nine other warriors were whole and standing, although some sported nasty cuts and were limping a little. All in all, a good result. I raised Mordak's Might high in the air, enemy blood still running off it, and gave forth another almighty roar, this time of joy and triumph. My cry was taken up by each and every Halian soldier standing there with me. Our voices seemed to spread so far and wide that everything from deep swimming Whales to soaring seabirds must have heard our calls.

With regard to what our brother ship Farseer was doing whilst Oceanwolf was being assaulted, they had not been loitering and callously leaving us to our fate. It had been pre-agreed and discussed before departure how each ship would operate during such an assault at sea. If it were one enemy ship attacking, they could only really focus on and board one of our ships. The other ship was then to manoeuvre itself in such a way as to circle around and ram the stationary enemy ship, causing serious structural damage as well as giving the ramming ship's fighting occupants the chance to swarm the enemy vessel whilst hopefully most of her fighting occupants had already departed on their mission of appropriation by force.

In this instance, Farseer had most duly and ably carried out her duties and driven herself right into the side of the Pillard's slightly larger Brig. As soon as contact was made, the gigantic Major Heven had led his armed and eager troops in a tight formation aboard the Brig, which we noted was named "Bloodshark" to wreak havoc, whilst my group was busily wreaking havoc against our Pillard intruders aboard Oceanwolf. There had only been a small handful of armed resisters aboard Bloodshark, who were deftly dispatched before the ship was secured. My troops were not savages and would not have harmed any unarmed sailors or staff, even if I had not given strict orders that any such brutality would be treated as murder and dealt with accordingly. As I said, we were not taking prisoners, and we didn't. After relieving Bloodshark of whatever food, supplies, equipment and general war material that our two combined ships could safely carry, we left the non-combatants on board Bloodshark unmolested and advised them not to set sail for at least two hours and keep their distance should they ever see us again, which I did not doubt that they would. The ship was not damaged beyond sailing, but she was in condition to go on rampaging anytime soon.

Chapter 9

Talking with Friends

The next day, day four, settled into much the same tedious routine as before, to such a degree that it was like the previous day's intense burst of bloodshed and rage had barely happened. We had unceremoniously dumped what was left of the Pillard bodies directly into the sea to be eaten by whatever beasts lurked in those dark depths. We did not have the energy, patience or desire to show any funreal rites to sea scum who would have butchered us like cattle before leaving our corpses to reek and rot in the heat and sun. We also all got down on our hands and knees, regardless of rank and did our best to scrub out the gore from the deck. Sea Captain Barlow almost had a fit when he and his sailors returned once the battle was over to see the state of his beloved Oceanwolf. Although he was thankful that no damage had been done to the ship itself and everything was still in working order. The goods we had procured from their vessel, most likely goods they have procured from someone else, would be put to good use.

It was on the evening of day four when I sat down to talk with 1Lt. Fester on a slightly quieter part of the ship. It was not long after we had feasted on an evening meal of dried salt beef and biscuits washed down with watered ale. I found young Simon leaning against one of the masts, quietly writing on parchment. I waited until he had finished his last sentence and rested his writing hand before enquiring as to what he was writing.

"I'm….I'm keeping a journal, a record of this trip. Just so that if and when I get back to Halia, I will have a written log of all that happened. Don't worry, if we come across sensitive information and secrets, I will not go sharing them. I will guard this log with my life, Commander!" Simon replied with a smile, as if jesting, but I could tell that he was sincere in his desire to maintain confidentiality.

"I did not mean to interrupt you, Simon." I apologised.

"No worries, Commander. I had just finished today's record in all honesty. Not a great deal to write. Yesterday's log was slightly more exciting." Explained Simon.

I lowered myself and took a seat next to Simon, our backs against the strong wooden mast and our eyes gazing out toward the calm sea, towards the sun disappearing in preparation to rise in another part of Valamantus.

"Mordak would have been proud of how you put his hammer to use yesterday, Commander, even if it was against measly sea-scum and not armoured Utreshian brutes. I feared to get too close lest you cleave me in half with that thing!" Simon complimented, and admitted, to me.

"It is a truly awesome weapon, and too good to sit on a shelf gathering dust. I think that Mordak would be proud that it was being wielded after his death against ANY enemies of Halia, or anyone trying to harm his friends. You know Mordak better than I, I think?" I asked Simon.

"Very likely, I think. I knew him before the whole Purgorite invasion, we had done some weapons training together and even travelled in the same unit. He had the heart of a lion and was the strongest man I had ever seen. I recall him carrying two wounded men up a mountain without a word of complaint. I also remember him ripping a door clean off its hinges whilst we were resting in the town of Leven's Mill, because he thought he heard the sound of a woman being indecently assaulted within. It turned out that the… erm…indecent assault was actually just overly noisy consensual coupling. Mordak profusely apologised for his error, before wishing the couple all the best and leaving several gold units to replace the damage he had done to the door." Simon fondly recounted, before tentatively encroaching on a more current subject.

"D'Arten the younger seems a very skilled fighter. I saw him slice through at least four of those Pillards like they were barely moving. I have spoken to him a little about various aspects of the soldier's life and the interesting places we've travelled to. I haven't yet mentioned his father, Henry, and neither has he. May I ask a bold question which may be above my rank, Commander?" Simon posed, his voice mirroring the uneasy caution marked across his face.

I nodded briefly, allowing Simon to progress.

"Do you think he knows exactly what happened to his father. I mean, about what Captain Winters did at Mirgot's Pass?" Simon asked, lowering his voice to little more than a whisper.

"I think he knows; however, we have not discussed anything on the subject. When we do reach North Utresh and get ourselves settled a little in our temporary accommodation, I will speak privately with Captain D'Arten and set the record straight. Henry D'Arten was not a good man and even went to the extent of sealing a pact with a Demon. But he was still a father. His son deserves the truth." I answered, sincerely, for I had every intention of doing just what I had proposed.

It was at this moment that Major De'Beresford asked if he could sit and join us. After I offered no resistance to this plea, the Major somewhat stiffly lowered himself down next to me and assumed a position similar to that of Simon and I.

"Ugghh…my body is protesting much after yesterday's excursions. I haven't had a fight like that in quite some time. Although I am in some discomfort today, it did me good and I needed the exercise. Almost took me back to my youth, hehe!" The Major finished with a chuckle.

"I had little doubt that you would finish that battle on your feet with a well-blooded blade, Major. You are a tough old warrior, far too tough for some nameless sea scum to put down. You have fought much tougher than those Pillards, so have I." I offered in congratulatory tones to the Major, even though he did not need such.

"Luckily for us, they were lightly armoured, undisciplined and not ready for any real resistance. You could tell that they were used to just hacking down the odd rent-a-guard, or poorly armed sailor wilding swinging some old cutlas. Poor mistake to take on the cream of the Halian warrior class, I would say. Haha." The Major stated, his bald head gleaming in the last of the sunlight.

"See, you are still not too old to fight, Major. There is plenty of adventure left. None of us are getting any younger, but we are hopefully not ready for the grave yet." I told the Major.

"I know, Commander. In truth, a large part of me WANTS to die before I grow old. I want to die sword in hand, preferably covered in my enemy's blood. I do not want to rot away to nothing, maybe not even able to see, move, hear or think properly. I saw my dear Father die slowly over many months. It was not good for any of us, and frankly, I was glad when it was over. I want to die….whole, whilst I am still strong, if that makes sense." Declared the Major.

"I absolutely understand. I also want death to just…happen, to be quick, and for me to die like I have lived. Standing, and proud. There is nothing wrong or selfish in that, Major." I responded emphatically.

After a while, the conversation died down, and each man went his own way to take his bunk. Luckily, I slept well, for the next day brought further adventure, threat, danger and not least the sight of North Utresh itself.

Chapter 10

Sea Beasts

Day five progressed fairly uneventfully for the morning. Men arose, ate a basic breakfast of heated oats, dried fruits and heated Halian tea, before engaging in a quick wash in the ship's basic onboard privy. Then some Officers exercised, or read, or gazed out to sea, or waved and yelled to the men aboard the ship Farseer or even played some of the string instruments which had been installed on the ship for our entertainment and time passing. It was not long past high noon when Captain Barlow spotted yet another ship, which caused him disquiet. Once again, he was fixed behind his spyglass for some minutes in a state of anxiety. Even from my unassisted point of view, I could tell that this ship dwarfed the Bloodshark and looked like a warship built to not only defeat but EAT smaller ships like our meagre Schooner. If it meant us bad intentions, I doubted that even Mordak's Might would be able to save us. I figured that there could be score upon score of armoured warriors on that ship, not to mention possible cannons, catapults, crossbows and other large machines that flung unpleasant things at high speed toward anyone unlucky enough to have incurred the ship's wrath.

I noticed that Farseer was drawing much closer to us than normal, almost like two brothers stepping closer to protect themselves and each other against a larger aggressor. I had little doubt that Sea Captain Bostone had spotted this large ship and was making his own assessments and going through his own possible options.

"Mariner Jessop, go grab that book of national flags from my cabin. You'll find it on my desk, right there. Go now, Jessop!" Order Barlow in an urgent tone.

"What do you see, Captain Barlow?" I asked, stepping closer to the man.

"Something I don't like one bit, Commander, that's what." Replied Barlow, most brusquely, still glued to the spyglass.

"I have the book here Captain Barlow, how can I help?" Offered Mariner Jessop upon his prompt return to the Bow.

"Now listen carefully. Look for a flag which displays what looks to be a barking dog surrounded by a spiked circle which is dripping blood. The colours are black on white with dark crimson blood." Directed Sea Captain Barlow.

Jessop quickly scanned the possible flags with his trembling finger before apparently alighting on the relevant flag. His answer only deepened our anxiety and justified our growing sense of fear.

"I've found that flag, Captain Barlow. It is called "Ul'Modek" and is the flag of North Utresh, specifically the Purgorite Clan." Announced Jessop.

So, here we were again. Time to meet our old friends. Instinctively, I felt my hand lower to grasp the handle of my Kazbarian blade. Mordak's Might was once again safely wrapped up in a lower part of the ship.

By this stage, we were nearing the waters of North Utresh, although still many miles from the coastline itself. We should have expected warships to be prowling the territory, looking to intercept any threat before it reached Utreshian soil. As the Purgorite ship drew closer, for it was most certainly centring in on us, its full strength became more apparent. For this vessel was nothing less than a floating fortress. At least forty cannons poked menacingly out of the ship's side I could see and were almost certainly mirrored on the other side. The ram of the ship was so large and solidly shaped that I knew it would literally cut Oceanwolf clean in half like a keen woodsman's axe through flimsy wood. There would be no hiding from this beast, as I knew that once she was up close, any eyes on deck would only need to look straight down to see the entire deck of Oceanwolf. I could already see armoured troops lining the ship's sides, appearing to stare straight at us with cold eyes.

It became clear that the Purgorite vessel meant to sail between our two ships, Oceanwolf and Farseer, and there was nothing we could do to stop this. I knew that we could not deal with this situation with violence or force. This situation would call for my utmost skills of diplomacy, tact and brains. I steadied myself and tried to focus and think about what I would say if I were even given the chance to speak. *'Focus, Marcus, focus, think deep'* I told myself quietly.

The hulking Purgorite vessel did indeed come to a pause between our two ships, as both Sea Captains had wisely brought their vessels to a total stop. There was no running or hiding; the Shark had caught the Salmon, it seemed. By now, all of my troops were standing on board, weapons sheathed, but never far from their open hands. We were all looking up at the mean, brutish faces regarding us from on high. There was maybe twenty feet of open water between Oceanwolf and the side of the enemy vessel, the name of which I could not translate, as it seemed to be a series of runic emblems, as opposed to familiar lettering.

It was not long before a stern-looking, robed official presented himself at the side of the Purgorite boat and looked down on us. For a terrifying moment, with the sun at the wrong angle and my mind already unsettled, I thought that I saw Va'heash himself and was possessed of an insane fear that this demon would simply boil us all alive or cause us to hurl ourselves into the deep and dark sea whether we wanted it or not. Then, after a moment, I saw that the official was not Va'heash, only another of his underlings and servants.

"Greetings, do you speak the tongue of Halia?" asked the robed official in a loud and clear voice.

Damn me, I was so close to simply answering "yes" and basically giving us away. Luckily, I actually used my mind before my mouth and gave the answer.

"We speak Halaze. We are men from Kazbare. I am sorry, we do not speak Kazbat or Utreek." I spoke aloud whilst affecting a foreign guttural accent, for many Utreshians knew what Halian's sounded like by this stage.

The Purgorite official was quiet for a moment, clearly still cautious and not satisfied by my response.

"You are mercenaries, is this correct?" Enquired the official.

"Yes, we are fighting men looking for work in North Utresh. We are looking to sail to the port of Tol'mral, then to offer our services." I responded, trying desperately to believe what I was saying in order to avoid displaying the telltale signs of lying.

In a sense, I WAS indeed telling the truth. We were fighting men. We were looking for work in North Utresh. We would be sailing to the port of Tol'mral. As far as our physical appearance went, we were from Kazbare. I found myself gaining confidence in what I was saying and felt increasingly that we would be allowed to proceed onward.

My confidence level was checked when there came a cry from up high on the deck of the Purgorite ship. The official looked quickly to his right in response to the sound of the alarm, before an Utreshian soldier moved to his side and spoke quietly to him. After a few sentences appeared to have been exchanged between the two Purgorites, I saw the face of the Utreshian soldier who had almost certainly issued the cry. Even at that fair distance, I recognised the face. I had last seen it whilst in the dank cell at Carnagon Castle. It was that same jailor who had been frantically banging on the cell door after I had jammed the keyhole and was in the process of escaping.

"This soldier declares that you are not who you claim to be, but a Halian soldier named Marcus Kane." Challenged the official.

It was at this moment that I experienced a most bizarre sensation. I felt like I could somehow sense living beings below me in the deep waters. My mind flitted back to that conversation with Abel about my father's odd connection with wildlife, which I had basically written off as absurd at the time. Only now, something was happening. I knew that I needed help, I needed to focus, I needed….to call.

"He is mistaken, I have never even been to Halia. I do not know anything of this 'Martus Karn,'" I declared, deliberately mispronouncing my own name in a bid to sound confused.

"Stay put, I am sending some agents on board to investigate both of your ships and those apparently genuine Kazbarian markings. Something is not right here." Answered the official, now more serious than ever.

The conversation was over. If armoured troops came aboard the ship, looking everywhere and asking all manner of questions, it was all over; they would somehow find us out. I knew it. That sense of living things below me was getting stronger and stronger, though.

Focus, Marcus, focus.

I did just that, I closed my eyes and seemed to reach out through the deep waters. It took a lot of effort, but at that moment, I had dozens of lives to save. I had Halia herself to save.

Finally, I made a connection, although my head felt like it was going to explode from the level of mental exertion demanded. This deep mind belonged to something truly gargantuan. Some primal sea beast from deep waters uncharted, who could offer us aid in this vital moment. So I called to it, I asked it for help, I pleaded. I continued to focus as I heard shouting around and above me and heard the sounds of metal hooks digging into wood near me. I was dimly aware that Purgorites would soon be sliding down onto the ship in numbers, so I continued to call. The beast was moving now, I could feel it rising through the waters at terrifying speed towards the large dark object between the two much smaller objects.

"Yes, the large shadow in the middle. DESTROY!" I felt myself say, or communicate, to the beast.

For the connection was beyond words. We did not share any language, only an intent.

I opened my eyes and found myself gasping for breath and my vision blurry. At first, I thought that I was dreaming or hallucinating. Immediately in front of me, I saw several hugely thick dark green tentacles rising up out of the water to a dazzling height and slamming against the enemy vessel. The beast that the tentacles belonged to must have been something straight from a nightmare, only it was a nightmare for our enemies. For us, the beast was a friend, at least temporarily.

The Purgorite ship was shaking under the beast's assault, despite its formidable size. Already, large cracks and holes had appeared in the ship's wooden sides, and seawater was pouring in. Large chunks of wood, bodies, shreds of sail and all sorts of other material were being flung far through the air in every direction. I saw Purgorite soldiers rain down from the ship deck, preferring to risk drowning than being violently crushed by some monstrous, raging tentacle. Within sparse minutes, as my men watched on in wide-eyed awe with mouths agape, the once mighty floating fortress was half submerged as the mighty tentacles continued to pull it down into the murky depths. Our two ships were being rocked on the waves caused by all this commotion, but were too far away to be swept down with the rest of the Purgorite ship. Some debris did land on our deck, but thankfully, it neither caused any structural damage nor injured anyone. The Sea Captain Barlow had wisely kept his resolve and got Oceanwolf slowly moving as soon as he had recovered from the initial shock of seeing a huge sea monster rise from the depths. The Farseer Captain, Bostone, had done likewise, so that both vessels had escaped the worst of the range of damage.

Soon enough, the tentacles retreated back to the deep waters where they belonged, leaving only a miniature sea of floating refuse and floating Purgorite bodies, some already dead and mangled, many still alive and desperately clinging to planks of wood for support. We had no choice but to leave them to their fate, although oddly enough, I did not find myself exactly in moral turmoil as we sailed onward. I did try and thank our deep-sea friend, but the connection was long broken.

The best I could do was never forget the service it provided. The fact that it helped pathetic surface dwellers to whom it owed nothing.

I knew that word of the ship's loss would feed back to Va'heash, and that he would somehow know that I was involved. He would not be happy about such a loss of an expensive ship and so many useful warriors, not to mention the personal offence he would no doubt take. I felt a strong sense that I would have to answer for this act eventually, but would cross that bridge when I came to it. For now, the immediate threat was over, and we could proceed onwards, hopefully unmolested, to Tol'mral.

Once the men had regained themselves after witnessing the rather unusual event of a giant sea creature destroying a full-sized warship, it was Major De'Beresford who first broached the subject of what I seemed to have done. The Major asked what that creature was, and how on Valamantus I had managed to summon it and direct it, and also how it left our two ships alone despite us being an even easier snack than the Purgorite vessel. I answered the old soldier honestly and openly.

"Truly, I have no idea, Major. I just found myself making a connection with something huge below the waters and sending out a mental distress call. I managed to direct the monster to the enemy ship with the intent of destroying it. Then the connection was broken. Funnily enough, Brother Abel told me about an ability that my father had during a recent visit to my home. An ability to communicate with animal life in a way that other people cannot. I thought he was speaking nonsense at the time, but now, I do not know. I have serious doubts that I would be able to do the same thing right now. For one, it took a huge toll and left me light-headed and in pain." I divulged.

"Yes, I can see. Your…erm…your nose is bleeding a little, Commander." Advised the Major, pointing delicately to my nose, which was indeed spilling out a little crimson.

I quickly wiped the embarrassing leakage away with a handy face cloth I always carried in my pockets. The nosebleed made sense, given the amount of pressure I felt building inside my head during my brief "conversation" with the sea beast. Even then, it had occurred to me that the larger the creature I was trying to summon, the more of a strain it placed on my mental faculties. Connecting with a Rabbit or a Cat must be so much easier than connecting with a deep-dwelling, tentacled behemoth. I would not have been able to keep up that connection for much longer without simply passing out, or worse.

"Land ahoy, North-West direction." Came the loud cry from one of the sailors presently on lookout duty.

A flock of eager men, both soldier and sailor, rushed toward the front of the boat to see if their eyes could detect this land. I myself failed to spot anything despite some hard scouring; however, without the aid of a spyglass, I was at something of a disadvantage. After only a few brief minutes, Sea Captain Barlow approached me and provided an update.

"I have checked several sets of maps and am certain that we are looking at the East coast of North Utresh itself. We are now a matter of hours, not days away." The Captain reported in a confident manner.

It was easier for Sea Captain Barlow to be confident. He and his crew would be offloading his cargo, both sentient and non-sentient, before restocking on food and supplies and departing back to the relative safety of Halia. He would not be enduring life in the dark and foreboding lands of North Utresh. Part of me wanted that sea trip to continue, dull as it was, as at least then our mission in North Utresh could remain something abstract, like a nightmare which had not yet happened and which I could put off. I knew that as soon as those ships docked at Tol'mral and we stepped off the gangplank and onto the walkways of the port, that it was real, and the nightmare would truly begin. Of course, these were thoughts and doubts I kept to myself and only noted down here. I did not voice my fears to the soldiers under my command. As far as they were concerned, I was a qualified expert who was fearless and led by example.

I made the decision that we would dock the ship early the next morning, rather than rush in and make a nighttime entrance. I felt that sailing in quietly under the cover of darkness would arouse more suspicion, as I had been informed by the Cadre that business at North Utreshian ports was conducted from dawn until dusk.

That final night on the sea was unnerving for all of us. The men were quiet and many brooded alone, dealing with the reality of the situation in their own manner. None of us knew exactly where we would be spending the next night, only that accommodation had been arranged and that our contact Ule-Romesh would act as our guide for at least the first few days. But what would that accommodation be like? What would be the risks and difficulties? Only Major Heven had direct experience of life in North Utresh, and I didn't know if that knowledge was a blessing or a curse for him as we sat waiting. Well, the mystery was about to be over, for better or worse. For tomorrow morning, we would be sailing into the land of the enemy. We would be in the land of Purgorites.

Chapter 11

The Horrific Port of Tol'mral and Meeting Romesh

Both Oceanwolf and Farseer sailed into the busy port of Tol'Mral early the next morning, side by side, at least until uniformed officials holding writing boards guided us into separate docks, luckily neighbouring docks. Once the two vessels had come to full rest, both Sea Captains wasted no time in throwing their long, tough ropes to waiting port workers so that the vessels could be secured. Then, the gangplanks were lowered from the ship's deck to the port platform before being secured by the same port workers. The Sea Captains were the first to disembark from their ships and make their way down the gangplank to greet the uniformed officials and declare the nature of the ship and the cargo they were carrying. Both Sea Captains Barlow and Bostone had been briefed carefully on what story they would give and what details they would provide when prompted. Fortunately, from my position still upon Oceanwolf's deck, I could see that the official seemed satisfied with what he had heard and the two Sea Captains were shortly issuing hand gestures to those still on board the vessels. The process of transferring ourselves and our equipment to the port itself then began.

There is a famous and highly regarded Halian painter named Rudvick Boder, who paints vivid and unforgettable depictions of "Lenfer", the word we Halians use to refer to the fiery punishment that awaits evildoers upon their mortal death. The paintings are usually awash with torment, hideousness, deformity, demonic entities, depictions of pain, and much worse.

Walking away from the Oceanwolf and into the port proper was almost like walking directly INTO one of Boder's frightening paintings. I will try to put into words what we saw with our own eyes whilst at the port, although I shudder now to do so. Prepare yourselves.

Firstly, the sky was that same sickly yellow colour which had been blighted upon Halia just over a year ago. If anything, the sky was worse, more oppressive and malignant. Just looking up at it almost prompted a feeling of nausea. The sky seemed to be alive and moving, but I in the worst possible way. It was like the sky itself was a constantly shaking sea of hate which wanted to take its venom out on the groundlings. The groundlings, however, much not much better. It was clear that slavery was big business in Halia, for we saw long lines of emaciated chattel being driven together like animals, chained and shackled, by huge, brutish masters who carried barbaric-looking whips. I could not tell if these bags of skin and bones were even male or female, as any muscle, body fat or telltale curves had rotted away, leaving only a shell. To the person, these creatures were hollow-eyed and nearer death than life. The heavy metal chains and shackles that secured them likely weighed more than they did.

One of these poor skeletal figures actually made eye contact with me. During our brief but wordless exchange across a space of maybe 200 feet, it was as if this person, broken beyond repair, was desperately trying to reach out and tell someone, anyone, that they were still a person. I could still detect some emotion in their eyes and face. The exchange ended all too soon, however, when the brute master roared a command at my loitering watcher. I could not understand the nature of the command from where I stood, but figured that it was a command issued to get the poor husk moving again. When the figure continued staring at me, not wanting to break contact during that moment of even minor comfort, the brute master became enraged at his property disobeying orders. With one hard and powerful wrench, he pulled the chain attached to the husk's neck manacle with such force that the husk's light body flew through the air toward him. The husk landed messily and grotesquely at the master's feet, their feeble neck clearly broken at a terrible angle and their face now totally lifeless, instead of semi-lifeless. At least now their pain had ended.

"Commander, I...I...I...look at that. Look at...at...at th...those d...d...dogs!" young 1Lt. Fester was stammering in my ear.

I looked to my left and saw more emaciated slaves. More hulking brute masters wielding evil-looking tools used to establish their dominance. I also saw the dogs to which young Simon had been referring. I use the word "dogs" but these Purgorite-led beasts were a far cry from the bright-eyed, loyal friends that a Halian countryman might stroke by their hearth on a cold night. No, these four-legged forms were more like the size of a smaller Halian Cow. They were incredibly powerfully built and looked to weigh upwards of thirty stone in weight. A huge meaty block of a head bared not one but two sets of sharp yellow teeth, which looked like they could chew through a solid wooden door. The mutt's eyes were a ferocious and unnatural green, as if Lenfer itself looked out through them. Foul-looking drool splattered against the port ground non-stop, from the jaws of these abominations of a "dog".

It seemed that another unfortunate piece of walking property had drawn their master's wrath and was about to pay a gruesome price for their supposed felony. We could not help but watch on as a feeble figure was cast to its knees and unshackled. Only the poor wretch was not being freed, at least not in any sense they could benefit from or enjoy. We all knew that they were only to be freed from the shackles of whatever life they had experienced up until that moment. At the master's calling, one of the four-legged lumps of meat ran up to the wretch, before hungrily enclosing its vast jaws around the wretch's upper arm, or what was left of it. With a sickening and powerful shake of its head, the mutt ripped the wretch's arm clean out of his or her shoulder socket. The beast continued to crunch and chew on the slave's arm as the slave faded out of this world due to the immediate shock and blood loss. The rest of the chattel only looked on with their sunken eyes and blank faces. They had been beaten beyond any ability to display emotion, even shock.

Moving on from those two gory displays of what happened to "disobedient" slaves, we pressed on, trying to remove ourselves from that darkly picturesque and vivid nightmare of a place. But there was still more to see. Piles of rotting carcasses seemed to be almost everywhere, giving off reeking fumes which I could almost see in the fetid air. The carcasses seemed to be indiscriminate and belonged to everything from rats to large horse-like beings. The stench was overwhelming, but it seemed that the port operatives and even patrons were not bothered by any of it.

I also spotted several beings bearing horrific physical deformities. One such being was entertaining a group of bored sailors by dancing around on their six uneven and different-length legs in a way which was shocking to me, but oddly enough hilarious to the sailors. It was clear that the six-legged "person", if I can use such a term, was in pain and not enjoying any of this, but this was of no concern to the bored sailors who just wanted some fun before their next long and boring voyage. The next deformity belonged to that of a tall woman who most unnervingly had three heads, cramped grotesquely onto her disfigured neck and shoulders. A finely dressed merchant, accompanied by two sturdy-looking guards, appeared to be closely inspecting this woman, as if wishing to hire her services for some manner of cheap court performance. The merchant, totally without shame and without even checking to see who was watching, ordered the poor three-headed woman to perform a very intimate act upon him, which I will not detail but only leave to the imagination. I could only imagine that such unfortunate souls had to demean themselves in such a way simply to make a living.

"Is that a cat, or a rat, or a bug…what the lenfer is that thing?!" Asked Captain David Stire in a state of disgust.

I believe that we all saw this bizarre creature around twenty feet away. We had to walk past it to leave the port, and as I passed it, I could not help but observe it up close due to morbid curiosity. It was close to being a huge spider, maybe one foot wide, including leg span. It had around ten long and thick legs, which seemed to be constantly twitching and spasming as I looked down for those horrible few moments. Its main body was like that of a cat in shape, only covered in nasty-looking and uneven spiky fur, which looked like it could cut you just by touching it. Its head was more like that of a rat, with beady black eyes and a wretched mouth containing long fangs. As we walked by, this hideous creature hissed at us in some manner of warning or threat. The sound was so loud and terrible sounding that even some of my troops, hardened warriors who had slaughtered countless men in bloody combat and seen terrible things, took a step sideways as if to be away from this awful and accursed specimen. I knew that several of the troops were not good with certain insects, so seeing some hideous amalgamation of all that was creepy about insects and hearing it hiss at them could not have been very pleasant at all.

It was as I was nearing the top of the final set of steps out of the port, carrying my luggage and very eager to just get away from that pit of despair and disease, when I was confronted by a darker-skinned man with piercing, almost yellow eyes and long, tied-back hair. The man wore a tough, knee-length leather coat and sturdy fighting boots. He carried two short swords about his waist.

"Commander Kane, I presume? Please, call me Romesh. I will act as your guide. I would ask you to follow me. I have transport waiting."

Chapter 12

The Journey to Our New Home

Romesh curtly escorted us across an expanse of dirt road to a large waiting transport vehicle. The vehicle was essentially a large and basic-looking rectangular wooden box with three window holes per side. The transport was mounted on six broad wheels and had four large horse-type creatures patiently tied up and waiting to be spurred into action. The North Utreshian "horses", which would be providing our momentum, were maybe one and a half times the size of a good Halian Stallion, but with a shorter and thicker neck and head. Their legs were also thicker and more muscular. I was just glad in the moment that the horse beings were only pulling our transport and not charging towards us in battle. A whole cavalry of those galloping beasts was not something I would ever wish to face in battle.

Romesh caught my eye and felt the need to give some explanation as to our freakishly large equine companions.

"These beasts are called 'Drutzers', they are prized as both combat animals and to pull heavy burdens at good speed, like they will be doing very shortly. Their combination of strength, speed, energy and resilience is legendary around much of the Northern zones of Valamantus. They do not come cheap, though. Please, let us board and be underway." Came Romesh's explanation.

Once my nineteen other troops and all of our luggage had been loaded aboard the spacious transport, the whips cracked and the four Drutzers immediately lurched into action and picked up a respectable speed in seconds. The ride was slightly bumpy as we traversed basic dirt roads at some rate, but it was no real discomfort compared to sailing across the Palmoria Ocean for over five days. I sat between Major De'Beresford and Major Heven during the ride, speaking little.

We all knew that the expedition was truly in tow now that we were on enemy soil, and during that ride in particular, no one seemed to feel like socialising. I saw several men gaze out of the window holes at the passing landscape, as one is wont to do, especially when in new territory. The landscape was not picturesque or beautiful at all, but was nonetheless interesting and very different to Halia.

I saw no rural villages or even small towns with unprotected homes, gardens and buildings. It seemed that in North Utresh every such settlement was contained within some manner of formidable-looking walled compound, often with guards seen patrolling the walls or manning the tops of towers. I saw several lakes, rivers and other waterways, although they did not look like the kind of places you wanted to wash in, let alone use to slake your thirst. Occasionally, I saw large, towering rock statues of warrior-like figures rising proudly into the sky. The Purgorites were very much of a warrior culture, and whilst North Utresh was home to other tribes and clans, the Purgorites were by far the most powerful, influential and deeply entrenched. It seemed natural they would choose to honour warriors and warlords as opposed to Philosophers, Chemists, Writers, Bishops or Explorers.

After a few hours' travel, the transport was brought to a rest at Romesh's bidding. The troops were allowed a chance to relieve themselves within the relative privacy of a large, wooded area by which we had stopped. The four hard-working Drutzers also had a chance to briefly rest their bodies and take in some water. Full leather flasks of water were also kindly provided for the troops. Romesh confirmed that this water did come from a more purified source than the rank-looking water of the lakes and rivers we had passed and was plenty safe to drink. As we drank together, I raised the matter of the hideousness we had witnessed at the port of Tol'mral, specifically the emaciated slaves.

"Oh, those slaves are no good for manual labour anymore, or even basic household duties. For whatever reason, they were allowed to become feeble and wasted. They were in the process of being...erm... 'dissolved'. I mean this quite literally, I'm afraid. Such slaves as are seen to be of no use are forced into a process whereby their bodies are dissolved in a large tank of chemical solution before being excreted into the coastal waters. They are seen as so low that Lord Va'heash does not want even their corpses polluting his soil." Reported Romesh.

Romesh must have seen not only the look of disgust in my face, but also my recognition at the name of Va'heash. He continued.

"Make no mistake, Lord Va'heash basically IS North Utresh. He is not registered as any official ruler in any kind of stately document, as would be the case in Halia. But his name is known throughout these lands as a ruthless tyrant to be feared and avoided. In all honesty, I am surprised that you survived him. The Cadre told me a rough history of the Purgorite invasion of Halia." Romesh informed me.

"We were instructed to avoid Lord Va'heash and his stronghold, this…Balostroma? This is not an assassination mission by any means." I declared to Romesh, being careful not to divulge many details about what manner of mission we were actually on.

"Good. Balostroma is not somewhere I would go with an entire army at my back, personally. Over the years, several invading armies have tried to capture the fortress by force and failed miserably every time, with horrific losses. Not only is there the fortress's imposing physical aspect and geographical location, but the place's many guards, both winged and land-based, and we are not even speaking of Va'heashes' unworldly powers. Powers that no man should be able to possess. Only Va'heash is absolutely no man. No one even knows how old he is or from whence he came. He has no family to speak of. I do not even think he was born of a woman as you or I were." Romesh answered in somewhat hushed tones, as if he believed that even the trees had ears and would report back to Va'heash.

As it was time to be underway again and hopefully reach our destination before early afternoon, we all climbed aboard before the transport got rolling.

After another few hours of travel through the same kind of landscape, we approached our destination, or should I say our accommodation. We were to be housed in a remote and carefully chosen former military compound, one with easy access to several roads and paths.

Chapter 13

Welcome to Tol'Trevel

Once our transport stopped outside the large wooden gates of the compound, the gates were slowly rolled open on command from a hand signal issued by Romesh through the window space. Once the gates were fully open, the horses once again moved forward at a gentle speed to take us into the compound's gravel courtyard. So, this was to be our new home for however long our mission took. Already, my troops were peering out of the window spaces to point at and comment on aspects of the compound layout. I spotted several large single-story stone buildings dotted about, but couldn't immediately work out their purpose due to their likeness. I saw one building which included a tower, which I assumed was a lookout post. I kept quiet, however, and trusted that Romesh or one of his agents would grant us a brief tour.

Once we had been invited to disembark and transfer our luggage into smart piles in the courtyard, Romesh provided such an introduction to my troops and I as we stood in a rough line formation, with me at the front.

"Gentlemen, please be welcome at Tol'Trevel. The building to your right is the barracks, where you will find comfortable accommodation and wash facilities ready for you. To your left is the kitchen block and dining hall. In the larder, you will find a trapdoor hidden beneath a movable section of flooring. It leads to an underground tunnel out of here, should you find yourselves compromised. Behind me, and ahead of you, is the command block, where you will find meeting tables, work desks, good writing and messaging equipment. You should find everything you need there, although I see that you have brought your own materials as well. There is also a stable block on the compound with eight horses currently accommodated. I would ask that you tend to their feeding and care yourselves. There is also a small infirmary building with basic medical supplies, which lies right next to the barracks. You will also tend to your own cooking and cleaning duties, I'm afraid. The Cadre explicitly informed me that no unauthorised parties should access Tol'Trevel during your station here, this of course includes cooks, stableboys and cleaners. I can still be reached, though, should you need anything. You will find a messaging torch in the tower of the command block with the appropriate codes. I have agents monitoring that tower who will report to me at once should you require assistance. Thank you, Gentleman."

With a brief smile and a quick bow, Romesh finished his introduction, most likely impressing all of us with his keen and modern grasp of the Halian language. Romesh then moved toward me and quietly bid me farewell whilst dropping a set of large iron keys into my hand, signifying that Tol'Trevel was now mine to command. Romesh then gathered his agents and remounted the now almost empty transport, before circling around in the wide courtyard and disappearing down the round in a moving cloud of pounding hooves and choking dust.

'Right, time to be a Commander again' I thought to myself, before turning around and addressing my troops, who were clearly waiting for orders and looking for a little guidance in this alien land.

"Okay, men, let's first of all check out the accommodation, see what the beds are like and where we can store our gear. Just relax a little if you wish, we've all had a rough journey both on sea and land. I'm going to check the water pumps and the stove and see if I can't get a good brew of tea going. I would like us to convene for an afternoon meal in about two hours or so, though. If you want to leave the compound and walk around a little to get the lay of the land, that's fine; we'll have to do that anyway soon enough. Just be very careful and of course don't give any info to nosy locals, if you do come across any. Major Heven is the best man to speak to in terms of everyday hazards you might face in North Utresh, so speak to him if in doubt. Carry on gents." I finished with a wave of my hand.

I did not want to immediately start barking direct orders within the first few minutes of arriving at a strange place in a strange land. These were still my comrades, my countrymen, my brothers in battle. If I were to rule by absolute force and brutality, would I be much better than those rotten slave drivers I had seen at that sewer of a port? I knew that at some stage I would have to give orders though, which would not go down well and might be very difficult to follow.

The barracks turned out to be decent enough and actually better than places most of us had bunked during our military careers. I had before slept in a self-dug trench in an unbearably humid and damp jungle, with insects crawling all over me uncontrollably whilst lying in an inch of foul water. At least the dorm room was clean, with a solid level floor, four walls and what appeared to be a solid roof. I had no idea what the weather was like in this part of the world, at this time of the year. The land did look more arid compared to Halia and I doubted that we would be experiencing the same heavy downfalls that we did back home. A leaky roof over our heads was just another issue I could have done without. The beds were of very basic build with thin mattresses and one feather pillow each. Each bed had a small table next to it and a leather trunk at the foot of the bed. I noticed that there were no privacy separations between the beds or a separate room for the "leader", so once again I would be bunking with the troops, like in the old days.

"Alright, just pick a bed, guys. You don't need me to allocate you one. I'll take the one nearest the door, just in case we're attacked in the night." I told the troops as they walked slowly down the corridor between the rows of cots, studying the beds, as if they were not all exactly the same.

After I had deposited my gear in my leather trunk, I walked through the courtyard to check out the rest of the compound and what it had to offer. It seemed that Romesh did not feel a personal guided tour necessary, as if he were a property agent trying to sell a nice country estate.

My first stop was the kitchen block and dining hall, which were enclosed in one long, high-roofed building. A solid square chimney provided an exit for the cooking fire's smoke. Within, I found a series of long, plain trestle tables with basic wooden benches on each side. The kitchen itself was spacious, well laid out and in good order. After scouring through the various cupboards and shelves, I ascertained that the place provided sufficient pots, pans, plates, mugs, utensils and whatever else might be needed for some serious cooking and eating. I knew that I would have to work out some duty rotas for the cooking and cleaning, whereby everyone, regardless of rank, pulled the same weight and got their hands dirty. I just hoped that there would be no moaning or griping from the men. Even a minor mutiny was not something I needed on my hands at that time.

I found Major Heven already in the Command block, studying the local maps, which had helpfully been fixed to a north-facing wall. There was a large rectangular meeting table in the centre of the main room, with various desks, cabinets, shelving units and other furniture lining the edges of the room. Major Heven turned as I walked in.

"Commander Kane, I hope you don't mind me being in here, taking a look at the place. I must say that these maps are very detailed. We brought our own maps, I know, but these no doubt show things that our maps missed." Heven reported.

"No problem at all, Major Heven. We are all on the same team and this block is as much yours as it is mine. Please don't think that you cannot be here without a superior officer present. What do you think of the place so far, may I ask?" I enquired of Heven.

"Oh, by North Utreshian standards, this place is like a top-rated Inn. Much of this land is poverty, hard living and discomfort. I know that the towns might look grand behind their high and strong walls, but believe me, the streets themselves can be pretty dire. Piles of rubbish crawling with vermin, families of five crammed into a single room, life expectancy of barely forty, disease rife with little in the way of medication." Heven told me, his face serious.

"Well, count us lucky then. I have been in places far worse than this. Major Heven, please join me in climbing to the tower. Let's see this place from the best viewpoint we can." I part offered; part ordered the Major.

The sight was something, and whilst not exactly Mirgot's Pass, we could see clear over the compound walls for miles around. The compound was situated at the top of the west slope of a sizable valley, with the land gently rolling away to the west. The tower was maybe fifty feet high from the ground to the peak of its tiled roof. Looking about, I saw no other buildings or signs of dwellings nearby. The nearest other building was around two miles to the Northwest and looked to be some manner of Storehouse with a high fence surrounding it. I had been advised, whilst still in Halia, that to purchase food we would need to travel ten miles south to the trading station of Beltreke. We had been provided with enough food for twenty men for three weeks; however, any longer and we would need to provide ourselves.

"Does this bring back any memories, Major Heven?" I asked the Officer.

"Not really. I was working more in the West of the country, and the landscape was very different to this. Much more crowded and none of these open barren spaces. There was constant noise day and night and people bustling around wall to wall. This is so much more peaceful." Major Heven answered, almost seeming to enjoy his current predicament.

The afternoon meal was a joint effort, with myself and four other officers toiling away in the kitchen. Whilst we were preparing the hearty spread of boiled ham, mashed potatoes and diced carrots, other Officers were setting out the table places and making sure that everything we would eat off and with was nice and clean. There was plenty of larder space for our food supply, whether it was stored in sacks, boxes, crates or nets. There was also a decent-sized cold room for foodstuffs best kept at lower temperatures.

The conversation at the table was jovial enough, with each Officer conversing with his neighbouring fellows. During something of a lull in the conversation, I asked the assembled soldiers if any of them had left the compound and done a take of the surrounding lands. It was one of the Officers I was not so familiar with, 1Lt. Demetri, who responded to my question.

"I have, Commander. I walked West for a few miles to see the place from the ground, so to speak. I did not see any living people, just animals." Demetri reported.

"Animals? What were they exactly?" I asked the young soldier.

"They looked to be like some manner of wolf. Jet black hair and about the size of a Halian Mastiff. They had those telltale yellow eyes which seemed to glow in the dark. They were staring at me from the cover of one of the few wooded expanses around here." Demetri detailed.

"Major Heven, does this description sound familiar to you?" I asked, hoping for further clarification of our nearby fanged neighbours.

"Sounds like a Bletzvelt to me. They are quite cautious alone or in twos during the day, but at night and grouped in larger hunting packs, they are vicious bastards. Keep an eye out for them." Heven advised the room, in general.

"I think I can handle a wolf half my size, Major Heven. I have already taken dozens of lives of tougher creatures, whether they were on two legs or four." Demetri responded in cocky tone I did not care for.

"Major Heven speaks wisely. We need to be alert to ALL dangers in this area. We do not need to expose ourselves to undue risks or underestimate threats." I said sternly, not just for the benefit of Demetri but to all the soldiers under my command.

Demetri nodded a little at my warning, before returning to what was left of his meal. I had a gut feeling that he was too headstrong and proud to heed my words of caution. Once the meal was concluded, the dishes and cooking material washed and set to dry, I stood up and briefed the room whilst we were still gathered in one place.

"Everyone, I would like to hold a meeting at six of the clock in the Command block to draft out a plan for tomorrow. I already have several areas of interest that I, or we, need to pursue and devise a plan of action for. I will not go into any further detail right now. Please all be in the block at six prompt." I commanded.

Chapter 14

A Plan of Action

I spend much of the hours between the meal and the six of the clock meeting in the Command block going over the information and working out some strategy. Working with me were Majors De'Beresford and Heven, and the scout Darkwolf. By the time of the meeting, I felt confident that we had made some progress. I had my papers and written notes in order, and I was ready to update the company.

I was quietly impressed to see nineteen other bodies present in the Command block, all sitting quietly around the main table, at six sharp. I wasted no time in opening the meeting.

"Gentlemen, thank you for being prompt. We have a full schedule ahead of us, so let's get straight into it. Some preliminary study of the surrounding area, as well as information from our very helpful sources, have alerted us to three points of interest in this part of North Utresh which require further investigation. The first is a major supply route for Purgorite war materials, which runs on a North-South line several miles east of the valley next to us. The second is a medium-sized Purgorite military outpost and training ground, which we could do with disabling. This outpost lies eight miles West of us, where the ground is slightly less open. The third operation concerns a communication office which enables the exchange of messages, letters and other information vital for Purgorite functioning. By disabling all three of these locations, we will be delivering a heavy strike in terms of disrupting any plans for a foreign invasion of Halia. This is why we are here, men. For the safety and security of our homeland.

Now, whilst these tasks may sound insurmountable right now from this room. We will work together and take these tasks step by step, not acting until we are ready and have our information correct.

Darkwolf, as the temporary acting leader of the scouts, you will take your seven-man unit out tomorrow morning and travel to the military outpost. Passing yourselves off as Kazbarian mercenaries looking for employment, you will hopefully be able to gain access to survey the camp from inside and outside. Please make note of any features you deem useful, in as stealthy a manner as possible. I know that you are experts in this line of work and so I do not need to go into further details. If you feel that the ruse is not working and you are suspected of infiltration, please do not hesitate to leave as quickly as you can. Do not engage in combat unless you are attacked first. You do not want to bring down an entire armed base on top of you. There is a stable block around three miles south of here, you will trek there and hire eight horses for the journey using the Utreshian coins you will shortly be provided with.

Major Heven, you will take your two Officers, Captain McAdams and First Lieutenant Siegfried Schmidt, as well as First Lieutenant Demetri, to survey the supply route. See where the weak points may lie, such as bridges, stretches of road underneath outcrops of soil or rock, stretches near bodies of water, which could be flooded with some excess of redirected water. Study the surface and structure of the route. I would ideally suggest carrying out this type of work under the cover of darkness; however, the lack of light would make the job difficult. Plus, if you were to work by torchlight at night, such light may draw unwanted attention.

I will take Major De'Beresford, Captain D'Arten, 1Lt. Fester, 1Lt. Parcher and 2Lt. Palos and travel toward the Communication Office, which lies some five miles in a South-East direction. We will need to cross the valley; however, I have a fairly easy route carved out. We will enter under the premise of being Kazbarian mercenaries wishing to send and receive reports from our employers. We cannot enter the premises armed, and I have been advised that all patrons are searched at the doors, so please, take no weapons. Once within, stay calm and do not draw any aggression. I have a paper document for each soldier to carry, which can pass as a communication, should they be questioned. Like with the military base, once inside it is our job to scope the place out and look for weak spots and see what the overall security is like.

Captain Stire. It is my desire to keep this compound manned and staffed at all times around the clock. You will keep station here, alongside 1Lt. Smith, to maintain a presence and keep an eye on the surrounding area.

Of course, each day will be different, and the unenviable task of remaining at the base will fall to different Officers depending on what exactly needs to be done that day. Okay, a lot to take in, but I am ready to field questions. There must be some." I said to the assembled team.

There were indeed questions from different Officers around the table. Questions about leaving time, what they needed to take, were they travelling on horseback or on foot, what food to take, how long should they spend out there gathering information. I will not clog up my tale with the minutiae or give a word-by-word account of question and answer. Let's just say that I tried to remedy the doubt of each inquisitor as best I could.

Chapter 15

Speaking with D'Arten

It was that first evening when I saw an opportunity to clear the air with Captain D'Arten. I saw that he had opened the gate of the compound to step outside, closing the gate again behind him. I followed and found him just outside the gate, lighting up a pipe, the glow of the powdered leaves lighting up his face a little in the slowly darkening day. We were alone.

"Captain D'Arten, how are you feeling about tomorrow's mission?" Was my opening question. The words I chose to break the ice.

"How am I feeling? I am not really feeling anything, Commander. I have been assigned to a task and I will carry it out. I am not nervous, if that is what this is really about. It is not a combat mission, just looking around some kind of Post Hall." D'Arten responded, staring out across the expanse of open land in front of him.

"I know, it is just a mission to gather information and intelligence. I know it may sound boring, but we were not sent here to get involved in large, pitched battles. That may well come later at another place and time but is not our purpose right now." I said to the Captain.

The Captain said nothing, just continued puffing on his long carved pipe and staring out into the wastelands.

"I know that there will be Purgorite guards about the place. I am not looking forward to being so close to them again, especially without a sword near hand." I said, primarily to keep the conversation going.

"It wasn't Purgorites who murdered by father, from what I have heard. I have one of my own to thank for that it seems. One Captain Kurt Winters." D'Arten said, his tone grave.

"Captain D'Arten, what have you actually heard about your father's death?" I asked D'Arten the younger, feeling a little relief that I was finally broaching the subject.

"I heard several rumours from people who were apparently there. One was that Winters stabbed my father during a drunken argument in the Mirgot's Pass dining hall before the battle had even begun. Another was that Winters was some manner of sorcerer who summoned a demon to slaughter my father over some perceived slight. Yet another tale tells me that Winters hurled my father from the top of Mirgot's Pass, hoping his tumbling body would knock some of the climbing Purgorites from their ladders. I was on campaign elsewhere at the time, so regardless of what happened, I was not there when my father needed me. I also heard that Winters was my father's half-brother, which could perversely link that murderer to me in some way," D'Arten said, the anguish in his voice clear.

"Listen, I was there. I saw your father die. Yes, it was Captain Winters who issued the killing blow. I would not deny something so serious. But you need to know why. You need to know the hard truth, not silly rumours by people who were clearly nowhere near to see the incident occur." I admitted to D'Arten.

Then, starting from the beginning, I took Laurent through the whole story. Starting with Kurt's discussion with the Mooden-thing in the endless abyss and ending with the summoning of the shadow demon whilst Henry D'Arten's blood was still hot. It was not at all easy for either of us, as I had to try and tell Laurent that his father had made a selfish deal with a demon and allowed one of his own soldiers to suffer terribly.

There was an uncomfortable silence that followed after I had finished my recounting, as both of us stood quietly. At least I had done all I could and given the whole truth, hiding nothing. I had even mentioned that I was there and had urged Winters to make the killing blow. I had told Laurent that I was not hoping for his forgiveness. It was his to give or keep.

Captain D'Arten finally broke the silence.

"Well, that is certainly a lot to take in. Thanks for speaking the truth though. Please excuse me, Commander Kane." D'Arten said, before turning and walking back through the main gate.

Chapter 16

The Communications Office

The first breakfast in North Utresh was a fairly simple meal of oatmeal, dried fish and fruit. Those of us going abroad on missions had a potentially long and hard day ahead of us, so needed to fuel well. No-one had to be forced out of bed, as we were all military men used to daily routine and discipline. We were all breaking our fast by half past eight of the clock in the Dining Hall. For a midday meal and hydration, we would be taking packed supplies and filled water flasks. There was a limited supply of clean washing water at our compound fed by a primitive pipe system, but only a very desperate man would drink it straight from the pump. The water was not even particularly safe after being boiled. Instead, we took our drinking water from large heavy barrels kept in the larder.

The scouts were the first team to set out, to make their way toward the stable block. Darkwolf led his squad out of the gates not long after the breakfast refuse had been cleared. As well as Smoke, Midnight and Shadowprowler, who had accompanied me aboard Oceanwolf, there was also Eclipse, Unseen, Wraithven and Creeper. I knew that they must have felt exposed with their bare shaven heads and so much exposed skin. I knew that they likely felt most at home in cloaks, masks and hoods. The Cadre had selected them for a reason though, as I have alluded to previously. I had spoken to most of the scouts individually at some point. They were polite and cooperative in our discussions, but still took care to guard their tongues and were far from being the most chatty soldiers I had come across.

I took my team out of the gates next, and duly headed east at first to find the route that would take us across the valley and towards the Communication Office. We were, of course, clad in our Kazbarian mercenary garb, just without any weaponry. There was no point even taking weapons as far as the outpost doors, as if found, they would likely be simply 'taken' as if in punishment.

I took the lead, consulting the map regularly, whilst my five comrades followed behind in relative silence. It was slightly tricky ground to traverse, so attention needed to be paid to foot placement. I was grateful for the tough build of the fighting boots, which we had been issued. I recall barely feeling the ground beneath my feet, like I would do in thinner soled shoes.

Whilst the distance to the Outpost was not that far, it was the effort of descending and ascending which elongated the trip, especially in the heat. Despite the arid look of the landscape, the air was surprisingly muggy and could be hard to even walk through. There was not even a mild wind to provide refreshment, and I, for one, could feel myself sweating under my armour. I had reminded the men to stay hydrated and look after themselves especially carefully. The more exhausted the men, the more likely the risk of illness, which would only make our work out there harder. In addition, exhausted bodies often lead to unalert minds and eyes, which was another setback we could do without.

Finally, I found myself nearing our destination. The Communication Office was an austere and depressing-looking two-story stone building surrounded by a seven-foot wall, which was decorated with mean-looking metal spikes, should anyone be foolish enough to try and climb over uninvited. The entryway was flanked by large and armed Purgorite guards, who stood ready to interrogate all patrons as to their purpose. I held my head high, tried to look confident, and walked toward the entryway, fully expecting to be challenged by one of the guards. My expectation was met as the guard to my right stepped slightly in my way and held out a huge spade-like hand, before uttering something in a language I did not understand. I had anticipated this and responded accordingly.

"I am sorry. I from Kazbare. I only speak Halaze and not Utreek. Do you speak Halaze?" I asked the large, imposing guard.

The large and intimidating guard only stared back at me blankly, seemingly understanding about as much as I had said as I had understood of his guttural barking. In that instant, I cursed myself for not bringing Major Heven with us as he was the linguist, but back at the compound, I had my reasons for assigning each higher Officer to his specific task.

I was about to repeat myself slowly, as if the guard was a dullard, when a familiar voice spoke up from behind the guard. Romesh stepped toward the guard and spoke a few verses in a language clearly familiar to his ears, as he nodded a little and stepped out of my path whilst lowering his slab of a hand. Two other nearby guards then went through their all-too-familiar routine of checking all six persons for anything that could be classed as a weapon.

Once passed the guards after a satisfactory safety check, I promptly led my troops through the gateway, glad for that minor hold-up to be dealt with and over. I shook hands with Romesh and thanked him for his very timely intervention. Romesh was unarmed like the other patrons, but otherwise was dressed much as he had been the day prior.

"No worries, Commander Kane, I have been assigned to act as your guide and translator, up to a certain point of course. I cannot be party to your specific intentions and plans. I saw your group traversing the valley and figured that you were coming here. I was coming here anyway and felt that my linguistic skills may be of use." Romesh explained, before lowering his voice and moving away from the large meatsacks guarding the gate.

"In truth, many higher administrators and more educated North Utreshians do speak Halaze, as well as the local Utreek, but guards like the ones just encountered tend to be army rejects who can only find employment in terms of intimidation or dishing out street-level violence. Many can barely spell their own names." Romesh revealed.

Romesh smiled, bidding us farewell, before carrying on to another part of the large block building. I wasted no further time in entering the Office building itself, my soldiers following closely behind, already taking information in with their trained eyes. I saw more armed thugs inside the building, mostly loitering around, establishing something of a presence. I did not make eye contact as I continued down the main corridor. I kept my eyes straight ahead, only deviating to quickly check signs indicating various rooms and sections of the building. Fortunately, the signs were listed in various languages, given how many different tribes and peoples moved through the building and conducted business there. I spotted a sign clearly marked 'Main Communication Office' with an arrow indicating a left direction. I duly followed these directions, which took my soldiers and I into a large, high-ceilinged room with a balustrade. There were many wooden desks set both around the walls and centred as a block in the middle of the room. There were also large sacks of what looked to be unsorted communications dotted around. Uniformed workers moved to and fro around the room, paying no heed to the six tattooed and bareheaded Kazbarian mercenaries who had just entered. The room was fairly loud with the din of conversation taking place, trolleys being pushed around and documents being stamped every few seconds.

I knew that even with all the other activity going on in the room, we could not just stand there looking around, as we would only begin to draw unwanted attention. I moved forward and occupied a vacant desk, holding one of my 'dispatches', which was really nothing more than random, fabricated code. I only hoped that an overly studious administrator would not walk by and demand to interrogate what I was sending. My soldiers followed suit and took up positions at vacant desks, before pretending to engross themselves in writing, reading and checking. Of course, each man was sneakily glancing around to observe specific aspects of the room and look for weaknesses. Anything from a feeble-looking windowpane, to a potentially loose wall sconce, to the best place to start a fire, to potential escape routes and choke points for combat. It was all being digested as my soldiers furtively glanced around and made mental notes.

After around fifteen minutes of such behaviour, I bade most of my troops to remain in the main room whilst Major De'Beresford and I made our way upstairs under the premise of wishing to speak to one of the senior staff about a missing communication I was expecting from a particular North Utreshian Lord. It will come as little surprise to know that no such piece existed, but it was a good excuse to scope out the lesser-walked corridors and gain a measure of whether an incursion via the first floor would be possible.

It was as I turned into a long corridor that I received an almost destabilising shock, to the extent that the good Major had to grab my arm and steady me before I totally lost my feet. For I had seen the beast Brutuck standing at the end of the corridor, quiet still and glaring at me. He was clad as he had been atop Mirgot's Pass in his heavy armour and Rhino head helmet, which was almost grazing the high ceiling. I looked again once I had come to my senses a little, only to see nothing but an empty corridor with the odd chair, desk and set of drawers as furniture. I relayed to the Major what I had seen, he being none the wiser and claiming to see nothing. He reminded me that Brutuck was dead, his huge skull kept as a morbid keepsake within Farchester Castle whilst the rest of his body was long rotted away in an unmarked pit. It occurred to me that the Major had never directly faced Brutuck, for he had been fighting elsewhere at the Pass when our small group had defeated the beast. He had never experienced Brutuck and did not have those wicked eyes and savage face imprinted on his memory like I did at the time, and honestly still do to this day. Even then, I had a good idea that an outside force was somehow playing on my fears and showing me terrible things to unnerve me. I also had something of an idea of who or WHAT was behind the vision. I just knew that the demon Va'heash was behind this somehow.

Once I was able to focus on my task again, I walked along the unattended corridor to check the first of four identical-looking windows. They were fairly thick plate glass held in place by some manner of fine cement. Window glass was a fairly recent introduction to North Utresh, I had been told, and only wealthier establishments could afford the cost. As I studied the window closely, I believed it possible that access could be gained via blunt force effort. It was just a question of whether the breaking window would be heard by guards in the locality. We could not exactly carry a long ladder all the way from our Outpost to the Office, but we did possess climbing ropes with attachable metal hooks, which were used for the very purpose of ascending walls and other vertical or very steep surfaces. I had also been looking out for internal lockable gates or doors whilst walking the corridors and thankfully had not seen any. Many of the doors to private rooms or offices featured keyholes; however, we were not looking to gain access to those rooms. Our primary aim was to take the Office out of operation totally.

Once I felt that a sufficient diagnosis of the building's inner security and layout had been made, I returned to the main post office to find the rest of my soldiers still engaged in their acting work. I quietly gathered up the troops before leading them toward the building's main double doors. The doors themselves were made of thick wood reinforced with metal strips, which looked to weigh hundreds of kilograms each. I had also noticed two sets of heavy locks fixed to the doors as I passed. Breaking through those doors with brute force would not be easy. The locks also looked fairly advanced in terms of design and enough to cause even a seasoned lockpicker some bafflement.

I admit that I felt a wave of relief wash over me as we all passed safely out of the Communications Office, not just unharmed and undetected but with our task accomplished. *'A good start to the mission,'* I thought privately to myself at the time, not realising just how quickly the mission would turn bad.

I gave instructions that we should find somewhere out of the way and take some sustenance and water, given that it was by then early afternoon. Whilst I chewed away at a dry loaf with some meat and washed it down with clean drinking water, I re-checked the maps of the immediate area, seeing how best to spend the rest of the afternoon. I knew that there must be areas we could check out during the day without arousing suspicion from passers-by.

I decided on scoping out a Storehouse which lay three miles to the north of the Communications Office, according to my map. I was interested in seeing what manner of goods it stored. My plan was to approach and see if I could speak to a security officer about a possible purchase of goods, obviously at a rate favourable to the officer themselves. I would even offer to throw an extra commission in if such a practice were common in North Utresh. Sometimes, a daytime approach with smiles and empty hands worked better than a night approach with cloaks and daggers.

After briefing the troops on our next motion, we set off in our northern direction toward the Storehouse. The heat continued to be oppressive and relentless, but it was just another aspect of life in that place we had to endure and tough out as fighting men with duties to perform. We passed various small groups on the track north, mainly traders, merchants, and some hefty physical labourers with big, rough hands and even rougher faces. We did not see any groups likely to pose a threat or give us a challenge. I was very mindful that we were still unarmed and not prepared for any physical conflict should it be forced upon us.

As I neared the building, I noticed a similar high wall surrounding the structure itself, similar to the Communication Office. It seemed that any semi-important building outside of a fortified settlement was basically a castle in its own right. I even saw the same fearsome metal spikes adorning the top of the thick walls. Again, a wide gateway gave access to the Storehouse itself, which was a very tall block of a building which looked to be made of stone for around twenty feet from the base, then a mixture of strong wood and metal frame for the upper structure. The gateway was apparently guarded by the same manner of 'rent-a-grunts' who had been gracing the entryway to our earlier destination. I approached, fearing that my words of explanation would be falling on incomprehensive ears. If that was the case, I would just nod and turn around, counting our losses. We could not exactly try to force our way past them. Both grunts were larger than us, better armoured and carried six-foot weapons which looked like an even more gruesome perversion of the Halberd. Plus, there would be more guards inside, no doubt. I presented myself anyway and asked if either guard spoke Halaze. After a brief moment of silence, both guards mutely shook their heads. Their faces still set in stone. Their hands never leaving their long killing sticks. I was about to turn about, content to have at least tried, when I heard a voice respond to my question.

"Yes, I speak Halaze, how can I help?"

I looked toward the speaker, and took in a uniformed attendant of medium build with long hair flowing out from underneath his cap. His hands were clasped in front of him, and he was smiling warmly, seemingly pleased to be able to offer service.

"Ah, we are from Kazbare and here on business, you could say. We are wondering if it be possible to purchase some supplies directly from your Storehouse. We can pay good coin." I said, in my best "Kazbarian" accent.

"Well, that is possible. What is it exactly you are needing?" asked the man, who had not yet given a name.

"We are looking to obtain travel clothing, boots, camping tents, cooking equiptment maybe even some weaponry. You see, we may be here for some time and will be moving around a lot. I have tried to go to Beltreke, but they no have what we look for." I told the Storehouse agent, trying to sound convincing.

"That sounds true enough. Beltreke is lacking in the kind of supplies you are looking for. Well, you have come to the right place. Please, come inside and I can show you what we have and maybe we can come to an arrangement." The agent offered.

I heard Major De'Beresford whisper quietly from behind me that he did not believe this to be a good idea, but in the moment, I merely raised a hand to quiet him as I walked forward through the gateway. My troops began following my lead, until the uniformed agent instructed otherwise.

"Please, just yourself, sir. I would prefer your men to remain outside the gates, if this is okay." The agent directed.

After a pause, in which I seriously considered insisting that I enter the Storehouse accompanied, I begrudgingly agreed to go alone. I had the feeling that I had little choice, despite the agent's polite way of phrasing his demand as a question. So, after turning around and ordering my men to stay put with a hand gesture and a nod, I followed the agent across the yard area and towards the structure itself. In that moment of brief eye contact with my soldiers, I had seen the alarm and dismay on their faces. Their commander was going into an enemy location unarmed and alone. I could understand their concern, I only hoped that I could play my part right and get out of there alive and with knowledge of the building's contents and layout printed in my memory.

The agent and I accessed the large Storehouse via an entry door large enough to admit carriages and other larger wheeled transporters. As soon as we entered, I noticed more armed thugs patrolling the various aisles of the Storehouse, which seemed to be one enormous high-ceilinged space. I spotted numerous buyers and traders perusing the goods on show. The shelves themselves extended several stories high in some areas, and had to be accessed via iron walkways, ladders or moveable sets of steps.

The agent finally introduced himself, as we neared the particular shelf he seemed to be taking me to.

"I am named Petrok. I am the Officer who oversees the operation of this Storehouse. It is unusual for armoured men like yourselves to just turn up at my gates unannounced and try and negotiate the purchase of goods. However, I am not so foolish as to turn away good coin, so I will not make an issue out of your somewhat unorthodox way of trading." Petrok told me.

"I am Suvest Kra'mang. I am the leader of my team of fighting men and responsible for their provisions. I apologise for coming here unannounced to trouble you. It is just that we are in desperate need of these goods." I explained, sincerely and humbly.

Petrok paused, a look of puzzlement spreading across his face.

"Kra'mang, you say. Wasn't that clan name outlawed over a hundred years ago? What part of Kazbare do you come from, Suvest?" asked Petrok, now looking at me carefully.

I felt my whole body tighten and my pulse quicken as I had to think on the spot and try and keep up the charade.

"To be honest, my family are outlaws. That is why I left the land to do what I do. That is why I have not been back to Kazbare in so long. I was born in North Kazbare, in a small settlement called Tel'Masok." I responded in a steady voice, trying my utmost to remain calm and confident.

"Interesting story, Suvest. Your men outside, how long have they been under your command? How long have they been, how do you call yourselves...'mercenaries?'" asked Petrok, his face getting closer and closer, as if looking for any signs of telltale lying tics.

Instead of continuing to play whatever game Petrok was playing and digging myself only deeper, I looked him straight in the eye and pushed back a little.

"Petrok, my business and that of my men be of no concern to you. Either you exchange your goods for my coin, or I take my business elsewhere." I answered sternly.

Petrok stepped back a little and seemed to concede, for he simply showed me the shelf he had been guiding me to.

"You will find some good equipment here and on the neighbouring shelves, Suvest. Once you have gathered what you need, take it over to the desk at the north end of the House where the purchase will be transacted." Petrok directed, before bowing slightly and making his exit.

I did not feel like dallying long, given that I was alone and the Stockhouse supervisor was already suspicious. So, I took some basic items from the shelf that we didn't really need merely to justify my presence at the place. Once I had taken the items to the purchasing desk at the north end of the building (walking somewhat slowly and appearing to gaze around in awe at how large the place was!) I carried my bag of goods back out through the large Stockhouse doors, back through the premises gateway and the surly guards, and into the somewhat relative safety of my waiting circle of troops.

"We were very concerned, Commander. That was a rather painful twenty-five minutes. Well, it's a relief to see you whole and with some supplies in tow." The Major reported.

"I admit it was a risk, Major. But here I am again. Let's go back to base. Later, we can see how the other teams fared," I suggested.

It was on our journey back West, towards the valley, when we first spotted what looked to be a sizeable Purgorite armed force. They were gathered not far from the Communication Office, and some were pointing towards the large building. More alarmingly, I spotted a few pointing roughly in our direction. Heads looked to be turning in all directions, as if checking for something…or someone. They were still a fair distance off, too far for my group to look like anything other than standard Kazbarian mercenaries. I had no intention to get much closer, and did not want to find myself in a situation where I was challenged and had to answer questions.

The Major stepped to my side, clearly sharing my thoughts.

"I would be quite surprised if they are not looking for us. Most likely, some agent at the Office became suspicious of us and called in the boys. How shall we pass them?" The Major enquired.

"Let's skirt around in a North-West direction so that we do not get too close. As long as they stay put, we should be okay." I told the Major, the word "should" given a certain uncomfortable emphasis.

As I led my soldiers in said North-Westerly direction, trying to become as invisible as possible, but totally unable to simply hide any of us from sight, I became increasingly confident that we would be okay and make base. So it can be understood why my heart sank when I saw around ten of the armed unit break off from the pack and come towards us at a trot. I was in no doubt that they were coming straight towards us, as there was not really anything else in our vicinity, we were walking through an open desert expanse. Unarmed, outnumbered, no Captain Winters to ride to our rescue, no shadow demon to appear from a portal, I felt fear once again. It was then that I felt sand brushing against my exposed skin. I paid it no mind at first, as I was so focused on trying to somehow outwalk, or if it came to it outrun the approaching Purgorites. Only if we did break into a run, it would only make it obvious that we had something to hide and were most likely the people that the searching Purgorites were seeking. The wind seemed to be picking up pace, blowing more sand at a greater speed against our bodies. I could feel that the strong wind was blowing almost directly from the North, so would be hurling stinging sand straight into the faces of anyone travelling directly North. I figured that if I took my unit directly West, we could pass in front of the struggling Purgorites as they were slowed by the storm. For a storm it did become all too soon. The wind howled in our ears and the sheer amount of sand flying through the air in sheets made it hard for us to see more than a few feet in front of us. Bracing the brutal wind, I led my men due West, hunched down and shielding our faces from the worst sting of the flying debris. Each soldier had his left arm on the shoulder of the man in front and we moved like some huge twelve-footed insect. We must have passed not far in front of the Purgorites, for I heard shouted commands directly to my left, maybe not even twenty feet away. We struggled on as fast as the storm would allow, praying to lose our pursuers in that very timely sandstorm. After several tense minutes, I checked back over my shoulder and could only see sheets of flying sand. If I could not see our pursuers, hopefully, they could not see us.

Finally, I came to the valley, where we would at least escape some of the force of the storm. We would also be more exposed to keen enemy eyes, but at least we were that bit nearer to our defensible compound…and of course our bladed weapons. So down into the valley we travelled, still as one moving body. By that stage, we were pretty well exhausted, but the adrenaline of the chase was keeping the worst of the pain locked down. I did keep checking over my shoulder but could not see any Purgorite pursuers. Maybe they were going in the wrong direction, maybe they had let their prey go to simply return and find some shelter. I cared little as long as I did not see them hurtling down the valley side with weapons drawn, thirsty for our blood.

Chapter 17

Back in One Piece

It was a huge relief to arrive back at the gate of the compound. Our temporary home of Tol'Trevel. The gates were opened by 1Lt. Justain Smith.

"Good to see you all six of you back whole, Commander. Everyone else is back already. All accounted for!" Smith informed me, informed all of us really.

That was a second huge relief, to know that regardless of whatever difficulties each group had faced, we were all back in one piece. Still twenty living bodies. It was just a shame that, unbeknownst to me, it would not be long before that changed.

Our first port of call was the barracks, where we rested our weary legs, for we had been on our feet all day, other than the brief stop for food. Young Simon kindly fetched a large pail of drinking water and several mugs and brought them into the barracks so that our thirst could be quenched. We took turns in washing our bodies and re-dressing in more comfortable clothes, which were not covered in sand. We also took that opportunity to re-shave our faces and scalps. I was glad that our tribal markings had not washed off with the water or been blown away by the flying sand. As long as we could have them removed at some stage, I was content.

I gave instructions to my soldiers that we would hold a meeting at six of the clock, before the evening meal, to get the business part out of the way before we could enjoy food and some relaxation. Business before pleasure, as the saying goes. Perhaps I have that the wrong way around. It depends on who you ask, I would say.

That evening the meeting commenced at a few minutes past six of the clock, as some stragglers rushed in slightly late, red-faced and apologetic. I opened the meeting and provided my account of our group's activities. My words merely summed up our journey from start to finish, and what we had learned about the Communication Office and its potential areas of weakness. I finished of course with our very uncomfortable flight from the pursuing Purgorites through the fierce sandstorm. I made clear that the enemy was onto us, and we were ALL to carry arms at all times. I ordered the soldiers to be extra vigilant and always keep their guard up.

Darkwolf was the next to provide his account in his husky and mysterious voice. He advised that he and his team had been allowed access inside the training camp and spent most of the day there, seemingly taken as nothing more than hired swords looking for some extra training. He and his team had paid for several sessions of weapons training in different parts of the camp. During this time, the soldiers had made good use of their spare time to take note of the camp features, as I had instructed. We were told of guard numbers, the size and manner of the defensive perimeter, the number of potential entrances and exits, the highest lookout point and other useful information. I was impressed by Darkwolf and his team's depth of research. It seemed that no aspect had been left unchecked.

Finally, Major Heven began relaying how his day had fared. The most important feature the group had found was a bridge constructed primarily of wood and brick, which lay over a fairly deep and wide gorge. There were no other bridges covering this gorge for miles in either direction, so this only increased the bridge's importance as a throughfare. Major Heven's team had also identified a stretch of major road which ran over a series of underground tunnels and was more precarious than local engineers might have thought. If the tunnels could somehow be caused to collapse, then the road would fall in, causing all manner of disruption for wheeled vehicle traffic.

All this information certainly gave me something to think about. It was primarily up to me to decide which of these areas of interest we would focus on first. For I wanted to commit almost the entire force to any serious operation, rather than have three or so major 'attacks' going on at once with my team scattered about the land. Once the meeting was ended and any questions handled, I remained in the main Command room with Major Heven and De'Beresford, the two most senior officers below me.

"So, gentlemen, do you have any thoughts on which of these operations we should execute first, and how we should approach? I value your opinions as seasoned and capable Officers and would not want to do it 'my way' unless you were on board." I asked the two Majors.

"Well, Commander. I personally would prefer to start with what I believe to be the…errmm… 'easiest' task, or at least the least difficult. That is disabling the Communications Office. From all you have told us, it is most likely lightly guarded at night and not hard to breach." Ventured Major Heven.

"I am happy enough to agree with Major Heven. Let's start with a manageable task and see how it goes. I feel that whilst taking out the Office will not be easy, trying to disable a training camp will take some serious planning and carefully chosen equipment." Major De'Beresford said, quite wisely in my view.

"Thank you for your input, sirs. The Communication Office it is then. I am glad that you agree with me, for that was my first target the whole time." I told the Majors, grinning openly.

The evening meal was underway by half past seven of the clock. That evening we tucked into the fish stew, boiled potatoes, brown loaf and green vegetables that the soldiers on the cooking rota had been busily preparing whilst the rest of us were attending to other duties. The fish was called Green Kliver, which was odd as it did not look particularly green in appearance. It was of a fairly tough and chewy texture but still went down well and was much-needed sustenance.

It was 1Lt. Demetri, who broke a period of silence to talk about a possible new addition to the menu.

"I take it no-one has dined on Bletzvelt before. I'm just wondering what they would be like to eat." Demetri speculated during a pause in his eating.

"You and those bloody Bletzvelt's again, Bart. Please don't go and do what I think you're planning on doing. We are not here to hunt animals. If we need to supplement our food supply, then there are safer ways to do it." Remarked 1Lt. Smith, becoming agitated at his comrade's foolishness.

Demetri merely looked down and said nothing more, but I could see a certain glint in his eye, like he was not convinced that going to hunt a dangerous beast he knew nothing about was somehow not a good idea. I knew that I should have issued him with another stern warning as his senior Commanding Officer, but my mind was too focused on other more pressing topics. That was the last night we twenty men were all together as one companionship, for disaster struck early the next morning.

During the night, several bizarre and unwanted dreams dropped in on me to prevent me from true rest. Some dreams were odd, some horrific. My first dream was of some creature, maybe a dog, hiding in a ship's holding and sailing across a vast sea. I sensed that the dog was a little afraid but was going to rescue someone. The next dream was of some huge snarling wolf, standing some impossible thirty-foot high, with one of my men trapped in its vast fangs as his blood dripped to the ground. I couldn't tell exactly which man it was; I only knew it to be one of mine. The next dream was of the compound being overrun with scores of those hideous spiders we had seen at the port of Tol'mral. The spiders were scuttling to and fro, screaming and jumping at the soldiers. The soldiers were reduced to shivering wrecks, adopting fetal positions and screaming in terror. Many had voided their waste in a most shameful manner as a result of their extreme fear. The spiders even began pulling the screaming soldiers to pieces, limb from limb, as I watched on in shock. The final dream felt the most realistic and most harrowing. At first, I thought that it was just very dark, but as I looked around, I saw absolutely nothing. I felt like I was trapped in the endless abyss that the Mooden-thing had spoken of back in Halia, for there was just a void around me. I shouted "Hello" into the dark void, then immediately realised my error. For my greeting was quickly returned from behind me.

"Right here. I've been waiting a long time for you." Came an inhuman voice from right behind me.

Brutuck. I knew it was the monster without needing to look. I stood still and felt his immense bulk loom up behind me. I shuddered helplessly as I felt vast hands close over my shoulders, so large that the monster's fingers overlapped on my chest. I knew that the monster could rip me in two easily, but I could not move or react at all. My nightmare only ended as I felt someone shaking me and saying "Commander Kane" several times, to bring me back into the only slightly less nightmarish realm of North Utresh.

As my eyes focused, I saw the startled face of Captain Stire crouching down near to me in the gloomy room.

"Commander, it's my officers Demetri and Smith. Their beds are empty, and I cannot find them anywhere in the compound." Stire reported in a serious tone, his facial expression reflecting the concern in his words.

Chapter 18

The Beltzvelt and Lieutenant Smith

I arose almost immediately, still somewhat reeling from my sequence of formidable nightmares. I dressed properly before rousing a few of the other soldiers. I did not want to go scouring around in unfamiliar territory with only Stire and myself. As soon as 1Lt. Simon Fester and Darkwolf had readied themselves; we four left the confines of the barracks and walked into the courtyard. For a horrible moment, in the semi-dark of the dawn, I thought I saw several of those freakish spiders scuttling about between the buildings. But after another rub of my eyes and a few brisk self-administered slaps to the face, I saw that there were no spiders. I was allowing my dream to invade my waking hours, which was not on! I had to stay in command at all times, as my men were looking toward me for guidance. It would be no good if I was not fully focused on the task at hand.

I ordered four of the available horses to be untied and readied for travel. We would cover more ground in less time if all were seated ahorse. None of us knew how long each soldier had been gone, or whether they were together, or honestly, if they were even still alive. Once all four riders were ready by the main gate, Major De'Beresford, who was also up by then, kindly opened the gates, allowing our exit, before shutting and securing them behind us.

I immediately studied the ground for tracks, but could not see any markings betraying where the two men might have headed. I turned in my saddle and asked Darkwolf if he could identify any such tracks. Darkwolf nimbly leapt down from his horse and crept close to survey the ground for several metres in each direction. After a pause, which did not give me any reassurance, Darkwolf honestly told me that the blowing dust was making any footprints hard to locate. Not only that, but there were many existing prints from other animals and it was not easy to tell exactly which were fresh and which were older in the Utreshian dirt. Still, after Darkwolf had taken his seat again, we headed roughly West, into the open land, keeping our eyes peeled and checking in all directions.

It was Darkwolf whose keen senses first detected something potentially relevant.

"I smell fresh blood on the wind, it is coming from slightly to the South of us." The scout declared to the hunting party.

"Take us there Darkwolf, you lead," I ordered briskly.

Darkwolf did as he was bid and used his nose to guide him closer toward the odour. It was not long before we saw one of our missing soldiers running towards us in a state.

We slowed our horses right down as 1Lt. Demetri almost collapsed by our horses' hooves. The man was sweating profusely, and his reddened face was covered in tears as perspiration. He was gasping from sheer exertion but managed to bleat out some words of explanation.

"I'm…not hurt…its…its Justain. Justain…he's been…attacked…he's hurt!" Demetri gasped out, each word seeming to inflict further stabs of pain.

"Take us to him immediately, Lt. Demetri!" I growled, already feeling that Demetri was somehow the cause of all this.

I pulled Demetri up behind me onto my horse, so as to ensure that we got to 1Lt. Smith as hastily as possible. Demetri pointed over my shoulder to indicate our desired direction, so off we went.

We came across 1Lt. Smith leaning against a large tree, not far from a small grouping of trees. His sword was still in his scabbard, unused. The tree grouping was not large enough to be called a forest, but large enough to give shelter to some of the beasts that prowled those dangerous and harsh lands. I dismounted immediately, ordering my troops to do the same. Young Simon Fester held onto a horse's reins in each hand, whilst Darkwolf did the same, so that all four horses were temporarily secured.

Captain Stire and I rushed toward 1Lt. Smith to check the extent of his injuries. 1Lt. Smith was barely conscious, his eyes almost closed against the pain and his breathing laboured. He was holding both hands against his torso region, indicating where the worst of the pain appeared to be coming from. I slightly moved his bloodied left forearm to see what he was hiding. I tried to control my shock as I saw that the poor soldier had been badly mauled by either sharp teeth, or claws, or both. His stomach and chest were an absolute state, and he needed urgent medical attention.

"We can't do much here, even if we did have a medical kit. His injuries are extensive. We can't leave and come back for him, as he will likely die during that time. Can you carry him over your horse, in front of you? Try and make the journey as comfortable as you can, Captain Stire." I instructed the Captain, who was wide-eyed and ashen-faced by that time.

After the party had retaken their saddles, and the injured soldier supported as best he could be on Stire's horse, we all set off back to the compound as fast as was possible. Six men travelling between four horses.

Major De'Beresford already had the gate open as we travelled through into the compound courtyard at speed.

"1Lt. Smith has been badly wounded; he needs immediate attention. Major De'Beresford, get that infirmary room ready as quick as you can. We need clean water, towels, threading needle, any pain remedies if we have them." I shouted to the Major as I drew my horse to a halt.

I instructed Darkwolf and 1Lt. Fester to get the horses taken back to the stables and safely secured. I helped Captain Stire get the wounded 1Lt. Smith lowered from the horse. We both then carried the soldier straight into the infirmary room, before laying him on the inspection cot. Major De'Beresford was already in there, expertly assembling the necessary equipment. Captain Stire held his comrade's hand as I began to cut away the clothing so that the wound could be treated. I noticed that 1Lt. Smith was not wearing his mail vest, which may have saved his life. I use those words as I already knew that poor Justain Smith was not long for his mortal life, and there was little any of us could have done.

"Can you hear me, Justain? Stay in there. We need to patch you up." Captain Stire told the now unconscious Smith, using his first name rather than his fuller military title.

The two Officers were close, I knew. They had fought side-by-side in battle, drunk and sung in many a tavern, endured wounds together, travelled to distant countries together. Captain Stire was not just talking to another officer, he was talking to a friend, a brother in battle.

"I need to try and stitch up the wound, hand me that needle and thread, Major…Major?!" I ordered Major De'Beresford, feeling the need to repeat his title when he did not immediately hand me what I asked.

"Commander Kane, 1Lt. Smith's pulse is gone. Look at his eyes. He is already passed, I'm afraid." The Major said in a consoling and respectful tone, rather than with any kind of urgency.

My knee-jerk reaction was to refuse this truth and continue to try and save the soldier's life. He was under my command and thus I felt that his death was somehow my liability. I had seen plenty of men die though over the years, and I was seeing it again in that small infirmary block.

The Major and I stood quietly, as Captain Stire removed himself from the room with haste. At first, I thought that the Captain had merely taken some private time to vent his tears, until I heard his voice yell out in rage.

"Lieutenant Demetri, come here NOW!" roared Captain Stire from the courtyard.

By this stage, almost the whole company was in the courtyard to see what was going on. They had no doubt had their attention attracted by all the drama and raised voices surrounding our return. Demetri himself slowly approached his senior officer, his head lowered and his face fearful, as if he were a guilty dog expecting a reprimand from a furious master.

"Your friend Lieutenant Smith is dead, Demetri. He is dead. What happened, why were you out there at this hour of the morning? Tell me all!" Captain Stire growled, his eyes alight, his face contorted in fury.

All were silent as the assembled company awaited Demetri's account of what led up to this tragic death.

"I went out earlier, alone, Captain Stire. I...I wanted to hunt down one of those Bletzvelt things. Lieutenant Smith must have seen I was gone and followed me on foot to see where I had gone. I was near that outcrop of trees, staying quiet and trying to detect movement amongst the trees, when Smith caught up with me and yelled my name. The sound startled both me, and one of the large wolf creatures. The next thing I knew, one of the Bletvelfs had sprung out of the trees and hammered toward Smith. Smith saw the beast coming but couldn't unsheathe his blade in time. As the beast was attacking Smith I ran up and slashed at it with my sword, but it took several strikes before it ran off back into the woods. By then, the damage was done, though." 1Lt. Demetri confessed bleakly, his head hung low.

"Let me get this straight, 1Lt. Demetri. You left the safety of this compound alone, and waltzed off into the wasteland, without telling anyone, to hunt down a dangerous predator you knew nothing about, armed with only a sword you have barely used. Is that the measure of it?" I asked slowly and sternly, in front of the whole company.

"You have it correct, Commander Kane. I never thought it would come to this." Demetri responded remorsefully.

"Your reckless behaviour has cost the life of a good officer, Lieutenant Demetri." Interjected a distraught Captain Stire.

For several moments, we all just stood there in our new reduced company of nineteen men. The other men remained silent and just looked from 1Lt. Demetri, to Captain Stire, to me. Finally, I just walked off toward the command block to clear my head a little. The group seemed to slowly break up behind me as men returned to their various activities.

Breakfast was understandably downbeat that day. The atmosphere was tense after our first taste of group tragedy. The loss of one of our own company had hit harder than I expected. Still, there was work ahead which needed swift attention. Before we departed the dining hall, I announced that a full meeting would take place at ten of the clock that morning in the usual location of the Command block.

I prepared some plans for the meeting, whilst Captain Stire and 1Lt. Demetri attended to their comrade's body. They were to wash the body and wrap it in clean linen ready for a funeral service which would take place later in the day.

Whilst I was making plans for the meeting, Major Heven entered and nodded to me.

"Terrible shame about 1Lt. Smith. I didn't really know the man personally, but he seemed a good soldier, and brave. Can I ask if you intend on discipling 1Lt. Demetri?" Asked Major Heven delicately, hoping he had not overstepped a mark in questioning a senior officer as to his disciplinary methods.

"Honestly, I have not even thought how to punish him. His guilt may serve as punishment enough. I doubt he will be reckless enough to do that again, after everything that has happened. If he does, he is out of this company though." I told Major Heven.

Chapter 19

Trip to Beltreke

The meeting proceeded almost dead on ten of the clock. I alighted on that morning's tragic loss again and stated that a funeral service would take place in the afternoon within the confines of the compound.

Despite the tragic loss of a comrade, the operation still had to commence. My next topic was the plan to attack the Communication Office that night, as confident as I could be that we had done enough preparation work to guarantee a high probability of success. I could not of course guarantee success itself, only the fool would do such a thing. The plan was to gain entry and start several fires within the building at certain locations, before leaving the blazing inferno and disappearing back into the darkness. The plan was to split into smaller teams and break in through several different locations, on both floors. We were to take sturdy climbing ropes, extendable wooden ladders small enough to be carried by a strong soldier, as well as a range smaller tools used for removing windowpanes without issuing the telltale sounds of breaking glass. This was mostly gear that had been bestowed on us by the Higher Cadre back in Halia. I knew that the Office closed for business at six of the clock in the evening, but was still lightly guarded at night.

With regards to that morning's activities, I had devised something of a plan, which I then fed down to the assembled troops. Just under half of the group would be travelling South to Beltreke, still under the guise of Kazbarian mercenaries, to check what was on sale and see if there was any disruption to be caused there which could hamper the Purgorite war effort. I instructed the men to scope the place out, the various different stalls, shops, street vendors, stockhouses, piles of goods, services being offered, places of business and who their customer were. Anything and everything. Beltreke was not a small trading station, being laid out in a rough square formation with walls roughly one mile long. I would lead this party, taking with me Major De'Beresford, 1Lt. Fester, Captain D'Arten, 2Lt. Palos as well as four of the scouts; Darkwolf, Smoke, Wraithven and Creeper. I decided that we would travel on the eight horses due to the journey length and fairly flat terrain, as the trading post was on our side of the valley.

I instructed that Major Heven should take his turn to guard the compound during our absence, and that Captain McAdams should remain also. The remaining eight soldiers, to be led by Captain Stire, were to travel down into the dry valley floor and investigate the various cave formations and tunnels which could be accessed from the lower valley. The various cave and tunnels systems did not feature in any particular detail in any of our maps, and it had been decided that it would be very useful if we could at least scope out the various entryways that led off from the valley. I wanted to see where they led, possibly as an escape route, possibly as a way to access enemy territory from under the earth as supposed to over guarded walls. I realised that boring through solid rock was out of the question with our limited gear, but it was worth at least checking. The party could even have stumbled upon some useful goods down there. I made clear that they were to go in fully armed, with proper lighting and protection, and travel in groups of no fewer than three. Many of us in the party had already undergone experience of walking through dark tunnels that we knew little about and meeting some of the unpleasant "locals".

By eleven of the clock, my eight troops and I were seated ahorse by the main compound gate, packed and prepared for possibly a good few hours browsing the streets and paths of Beltreke. Once the gates were opened, we moved out and rode South at a canter.

We arrived at the gates of Beltreke in no time at all thanks to the good speed of our horses. The market was surrounded by twenty-foot-high stone walls, with a high circular tower built at each corner. From the ground I could see guards stationed in at least the two visible north towers. I had little doubt that both other towers were manned. The main entry way was in the centre of the North wall, in the form of a high rounded archway. A set of massive wooden doors had been opened to allow traffic in and out of Beltreke, which would no doubt be closed fast in the evening when business was over. No less than four stone-faced armoured troops guarded the entrance. Two were employed in the process of checking rucksacks, bags, cases or any other method of storage, whilst the other two stood stone still and starring, ready to step in at the first sign of trouble. The stationary guards both held long spears vertically, the wicked points facing the foul and gloomy sky.

We each dismounted our horses and held them by the tether as we led them slowly through the archway. We must have come at the right time, or on a slow day for business, as there was hardly any queue of patrons wishing to enter Beltreke. As I had anticipated, we were challenged by one of the two more active guards.

"What is your business here, and why do you carry weapons?" asked the guard, in very passable Halaze.

Clearly, these guards were slightly more professional, and most likely better paid, than the brutes who had guarded the Communications Office. Their linguistic skills were more polished for certain.

"We are Kazbarian mercenaries. We come here to buy supplies. We always carry our swords, if this be okay. We not look to start trouble." I uttered in my Kazbarian accent. Keeping my language clipped and short, using no more words than I had to.

"You may keep your blades about you, but we are watching. Take care. We will quickly search your travel sacks now," replied the guard, seemingly content with my explanation.

After some brief checking, and our sacks handed back to us by a rough hand and unsmiling face, we progressed into Beltreke proper. Patrons were not permitted to ride their horses through the fairly narrow streets, so our mounts were secured in the large stable just to our right as we came through the entryway.

I split the men into three teams of three, who were instructed to stay fairly close together whilst we were there. We were all to stay in the same quadrant additionally. We had already lost one man due to not sticking together and I would be damned if any of us lost our lives whilst essentially on a shopping mission. I took Lieutenant Fester and Palos with me. The Major took Captain D'Arten and Darkwolf with him, leaving the other three scouts to form their own group. I instructed that should any of our group come under attack and need support, they were to yell the words "Red Bear" loudly, until the rest of us could descend upon the scene of combat and lend support. I just hoped that there wasn't an overly eager vendor selling Red Bear meat by the pound!

Before we split and went our own ways, I made clear that as soon as the main Beltreke clock struck the hour of two of the clock, we were to make our way to the main North gate and regroup, hopefully as a team of nine.

There was indeed a huge range of goods and services on sale within the walls of Beltreke. Food could be bought in bulk for very reasonable prices. There were stalls selling warm fruit ale in large jugs, hot meat pies in thick pastry, dark bread loaves stuffed with cold meat, steaming bowls of fish stew and so much more. In truth, the wafting aromas of fresh food almost drowned out the stench of the unwashed bodies and dirt, and I felt strange pangs of desire. However, I kept my soldierly discipline and reminded myself that we were here on reconnaissance and business, not to indulge in hot snacks and potentially let our guard down.

As well as the food, Beltreke had a good supply of basic but sturdy and practical furniture for dwellings; be it floor rugs, mats, chairs, tables, sets of drawers, weapon racks or even suits of armour for slightly wealthier shoppers. Most of it was affordable gear that would not dazzle a visiting dignitary or be much of a conversation starter, but would last for years and serve its purpose.

As my little group moved further South, I noticed that there were not so many physical goods being sold. Instead, the ground space was more taken up by professionals advertising their services and willing to provide samples and demonstrations wherever possible. The services were varied; barbers who would provide haircuts and beard trims then and there for a small cost, medics and apothecaries who would listen to health concerns and even sell the apparently relevant treatment, building guilds offered to build patrons their ideal home from scratch for a sum they apparently would not find anywhere else, oddly dressed peasant women even proposed to onlookers that their very future itself could be revealed for a few coins, and so it went on. I had doubts about how many of these 'services' were some manner of scam, and the patron would regret parting with their money. The fact that so many of the service sellers had to basically scream at passers-by to get their attention was something of a sign as to how well their business was faring.

"Look at this, Commander Kane. You can even hire mercs here." Young Simon said to me, whilst pointing to a larger and better-established stall with several tables.

The three of us walked over together to take a better look at the place. It seemed that there were several mercenary groups advertising their services that day. Each had been allocated a wooden table, on which could be found informative documents detailing costs, qualifications of the soldiers you would be hiring, previous jobs they had done and other relevant information for any potential buyer. At each table sat a tough-looking grunt wearing light or medium armour, and a better-dressed gent with fewer scars and narrower arms, who most likely handled the "brains" side of the mercenary-employer agreement.

My eyes alighted on a wooden board listing the 'hierarchy' of mercenary groups available for hire in North Utresh. The lettering had been carefully stencilled on in black ink. Whilst groups at the bottom of the list charged a pittance and were likely only useful for forcefully retrieving sums of money from a neighbour who hadn't paid up, the groups toward the top of the list could afford to charge astronomical amounts for their services. These were the teams you employed if you were looking to win a war, take over a fortress, steal a heavily guarded artefact from a deep chasm, maybe even enter the depths of Lenfer itself. I made eye contact with one of the seated grunts, we nodded curtly to each other as one merc to another.

I moved away from the Mercenary stall, not knowing at the time that I should have taken a more in-depth look, as it turned out that I would be needing to hire mercenaries myself before even a few days had passed.

Beltreke also sold a good supply of weaponry and armour. Stalls advertised high-grade longswords, battle axes of various sizes and weights, spears of different lengths and different manners of tip, longbows made of a wood I was unfamiliar with, heavy-looking crossbows which could be loaded with bolts which looked thick and mean enough to punch through a five-inch-thick wooden door. The armour ranged from thin leather vests to ridiculously thick heavy metal plates, which looked so massive that only the strongest and largest brute would be able to move without exhausting himself. Right at that moment, another intrusive thought popped into my mind with startling clarity. I once again saw Brutuck wearing his heavy armour atop Mirgot's Pass, his fearsome Rhino-shaped helmet leering down at us. It had taken ten men to pick up and throw Brutuck's corpse off the top of the wall, and the same amount again to load the somewhat mangled corpse onto a heavy cart to be carted off to his new home of a hole in the ground.

From time to time, I spotted members of the other two groups and just hoped that we were all sticking to the same quadrant as agreed. We were going off the large clocks fixed into each of the four walls, which gave off a loud chime on the hour and half hour. Every half hour, we would move into the next quadrant in a clockwise pattern. The place was absolutely enormous, so it was not like we would run out of things to keep us occupied.

As we neared two of the clock, I was feeling despondent. Whilst our visit had still been worth it, and we had actually purchased some useful supplies we could and did use, I did not see any way we could disrupt the Utreshian war effort via Beltreke. How would destroying a few stalls and ruining some livelihoods stop a powerful demon from assembling an invasion force? I felt that we needed to think bigger and quicker, as time was of the essence. I did not want to find myself one day sharing a prison cell with one of the Higher Cadre in a new nightmare Halia ruled by Va'heash, explaining why I had failed in my duties.

Once the chiming clocks of Beltreke alerted us to the hour of two, my two soldiers and I made our way calmly North, to the entryway. After only a few minutes' wait, all nine of the party had reassembled, which was something of a relief. No-one had been arrested and I had heard no calls to arms. Any combat situation would not have gone our way, given how many armed guards patrolled the streets menacingly. Even if all nine Halians had assembled quickly, weapons drawn, we would have been outnumbered three to one before long by enemies much tougher and more ready than the unfortunate Pillards.

Once we had retrieved our horses from the stables and climbed into the saddles, I led my troop back north to the walls of Tol'Trevel. During the ride, I wondered how Captain Stire's party were getting on. Whether they had been able to trace out new maps, delve deep into the tunnels and caves to see where they led to, maybe find something useful hidden down there. I hoped that they had all managed to stay unharmed. Sadly, on that last hope, I was to be denied.

Chapter 20

A Double Funeral

As Major Heven opened the main gate, he informed us that we were the first group back and that he had seen no sign of Captain Stire. I updated the Major on our visit to Beltreke, and that it had sadly yielded little of use. We both retired to the Command block for a while, for not only were there funeral plans to finalise, but there was a raid to organise for that very night. I was just browsing the notes we had recorded concerning the interior of the Communications Office when my attention was broken by an update from Major Heven, who had just descended from the tower. His report was not promising.

"Captain Stire's group are returning. It looks like they are carrying a body between them. I cannot tell who it is, but even from this distance, they do not look in a good state." Major Heven informed me in a serious tone.

It turned out that Eclipse was already dead when we had seen his body being carried up the side of the valley. Captain Stire had provided an update shortly after his group returned and Eclipse was taken away to be cleaned and wrapped in the same manner as Justain Smith.

"It happened near the end of our mission, as we were planning on returning to base. We had trekked far into the tunnel systems, making adequate notes and sketches as we went along. We even found some ladders which led to heavy trapdoors, although we could of course progress no further, being unable to shift the doors. They may have been trapdoors into supply silos, concealed bases, who knows. Anyway, we had obviously startled something from its hiding place, something which felt the need to defend its territory. Eclipse was at the back of the group when the creature attacked. I do not know the name of the creature as none of it's kind dwell in Halia, but it was a large four-legged beast with thick matted fur, a large head and huge jaws. Each gigantic paw was tipped with thick, bone-like claws. The beast rushed out of the darkness at speed and bowled straight into Eclipse, before he had a chance to even ready himself. It sank those huge teeth straight into his neck, shaking its huge head in what appeared to be rage. We set to the beast with our swords, hacking and stabbing into its huge body, and whilst we did manage to put the beast down, we could not save Eclipse. He was already gone." Stire finished, his head bowed in a mixture of respect for the dead and shame at having let a man under his charge die.

"Two soldiers down and we have barely achieved anything," I said to Captain Stire in frustration and anger.

Captain Stire only listened mutely. I composed myself a little before continuing.

"Look, Captain Stire, don't blame yourself for what happened. This is a dangerous and hazardous land. I'm sure you were vigilant and took every precaution. We will bury Eclipse alongside our other fallen brother, 1Lt Justain Smith. Then, we will eat and drink to their memory."

I put a hand on Captain Stire's shoulder and leaned a little closer.

"Then, tonight, we will burn that damn building to the ground and go from there," I assured the Captain.

The funeral ceremony took place at four of the clock. Several of my troops and I had put our backs to work and dug fresh graves for the two bodies, side by side with a gap of maybe two feet between them. Each body had been carefully wrapped in a clean cloth and stitched shut. Two huge mounds of rough soil lay at the side of each pit, ready to be shovelled back in once the ceremony was over. The actual ceremony was nowhere near as elaborate, lengthy or official as a Halian military funeral would be due to several restraints, but we made sure to give the two fallen comrades whatever send-off we could. There was no trained cleric or holy man present, so as Commander, I took the service.

After a brief introduction to the service, I asked Captain Stire if he would like to say a few words about 1Lt. Smith, given that he knew the departed man better than most and had commanded him for some while. Captain Stire did indeed speak about Justain, his service in the military, his courage, his loyalty to his friends, how excited he had been to come on this trip and serve Halia. I then offered the same privilege to Darkwolf and invited him to speak a little of his fallen comrade, Eclipse. Darkwolf did as Captain Stire had done, and shared something of Eclipse's history, his achievements, his worthy attributes, and how much he would be missed. After a few minutes of silence around the graves, the service was concluded, and Major Heven and I filled in the graves fully before flattening the soil. We had no Halian gravestone to erect, so had to make do with fixing two long wooden stakes into the ground, each bearing a wooden placard marked with the soldier's name.

Then, as I had promised Captain Stire earlier in the day, we had a meal and good ale together in memory of Eclipse and 1Lt. Justain Smith. Several stories were shared about the two departed soldiers, some of which were humorous enough to even warrant a few smiles. 1Lt. Demetri fondly recounted a time when he and Justain had gone hunting for a huge wild boar, which actually began to hunt THEM, chasing them for miles across open countryside, squealing in rage. One of Eclipse's fellow scouts broke his usual silence to tell the group about a time when Eclipse had scaled a 500-foot-tall cliff using only his bare hands and feet, as it was slightly quicker than taking the long road round. I recall that meal fondly, even to this day, despite what had gone before. We were united in our grief. The life of a Halian soldier is not forever, eventually we must depart this life and return to whence we came.

Whilst it would have been good to remain there a little longer, there was business to attend to. I called another full meeting for seven of the clock, where we would finalise the plans for the assault on the Communications Office.

Chapter 21

Burn it Down!

My plan for the attack was that sixteen men, broken down into four groups of four, would approach the walls from each direction silently and crouched low. We did not need to be Kazbarian mercenaries for this task, so we clothed ourselves in dark armour and hoods. The men would quickly scale the walls, negating the metal spikes with a special wooden board one of the scouts had designed. This board should enable the men to climb over without being pierced by the brutal and sharp spikes. Then, the East and West teams were to penetrate the building via the ground floor window, whilst the North and South teams were to climb to the first floor and enter through the higher windows. Then, once each team was safely inside, one of the four would blow on a special whistle, designed to sound like a different bird. Each of the four teams had been given a whistle, which had been one of my purchases from Beltreke earlier in the day. Once all four whistles had been heard, we would set to our tasks. We would eliminate any guards as quietly and quickly as possible. We would set fires in several specially selected locations, which had been marked on each team's building layout. Then once the fires were underway, we would depart from the ground windows and head back to base with all due haste. That was my plan, but I was not foolish enough to think that all of this would just magically unfurl without any hiccups. We would have to think on our feet and change tactics accordingly if any unforeseen circumstances arose.

We set off from base at eight of the clock, fully clothed, armed and equipped, to begin our journey to the Communication Office. I only hoped that this effort would make a difference, and we were not just torching some random building when we should be trying to cut the head off the snake and go for Va'heash.

It was Major De'Beresford's turn to keep watch at camp, so he and Captain D'Arten stayed behind, missing the action but knowing there would be more. Around a quarter of a mile from the Office, we split into our four groups and moved into position. I would lead my team in from the West to break through one of the ground-floor windows. I had 1Lt. Fester, 2Lt. Palos and Darkwolf with me. Once we were at the wall, crouched, we all listened out for any footsteps or sounds of movement on the other side of the wall. I jumped up and grasped two of the vertical metal bars, before the point at which they became sharp, in my gloved hands. I then pulled myself up so that my hooded head was peering just above the top of the seven-foot wall. I looked in either direction to spot signs of guards and did notice a lone guard standing quietly some twenty feet away, to our left. I dropped back down and whispered to the group about the lone guard. We would have to eliminate him. Darkwolf immediately told me that he would take the kill; he knew exactly how to do it. I did not doubt the stern and capable warrior and agreed to his offer. Darkwolf moved to our left, still creeping low behind the wall, to the tune of about twenty feet. Darkwolf would have to be directly opposite the guard for his kill to work. Using hand signals, he asked me if this was the case. After another quick jump up the wall and a stealthy check on the guard, who was still totally unaware of our presence and had not shifted an inch, I indicated gently with my left hand that Darkwolf should move another foot to the left. Once Darkwolf had moved as such, I gave him the thumbs-up sign. Darkwolf, holding a long dagger in his right hand, seemed to race up the wall before nimbly grabbing one of the metal bars with his left hand and using this momentum to launch his body into the air. I saw his dark shape silhouetted against the night sky for a moment before he descended right on top of the guard. I heard no sound at all, despite the silence around us. After only a few tense seconds of waiting, I heard Darkwolf whispering from the other side of the wall.

"He's down, you can climb over now."

Once the special board had been fixed in place, I upped the wall again, this time climbing over the other side and dropping into enemy territory. Simon Fester and Jerome Palos followed quickly, so that all four of us were ready for the next step: the window.

The window began only five feet from the ground, so we would only need to stand on a portable wooden step to work. We could not just smash the window with force, as that would only alert any nearby guards to our presence. The panes would have to be removed carefully and with a special instrument. After looking through the window and seeing nobody on the other side, I stood side by side with 2Lt. Palos and began chiselling away at the edges of the glass panes. The panes were maybe one foot square, so we would need to remove a fair few before the largest of us, me, could squeeze through. I only hoped that the whole window would not collapse as the lower panes were removed. Before long, and after some serious chiselling away, enough panes had been removed and carefully lowered to the ground to enable people to start clambering through. I went first, as commander, believing that the man who went first endured the greatest risk.

So far there was no risk, and the four of us were soon inside the West ground floor corridor, kneeling, lying or standing in niches, corners and shadows. I crept to the window and blew on my whistle, emanating the sound of a nightbird. After only a few seconds, another call came back to my ears, that of a different nightbird. So, the East team had made it inside also. Good news so far. We would wait a few minutes longer for the other teams to make their sounds before proceeding. It was a tense wait as we four remained still, silent and sweating, hoping that a group of boisterous guards did not all come in for their night shift in one go. I knew that the guard room was nowhere near us, so it was less likely that we would be detected where we were.

We heard the call of the North team perhaps fifteen minutes after we had blown our whistle. This figured, as they had to ascend via an extendable ladder and did not have the ease of movement that we had enjoyed. After another five minutes came the sound of the South team. We were all ready and in place, good. I blew my whistle once more at the window, which was the signal for us to move to our next destination.

My team were to light our fires in the large main office. With all the paper, card, wood and cloth sacks in there, it was a prime location to get a good blaze going. We knew that once we lit the fires, the flames would spread fast. The heat and smoke would soon become hard to bear, so we could not dally. On our way to the main office, we continued to creep silently. We came across only one guard, whom I dispatched with a ruthless stab through the back of the neck. No room for fair fights that night. No room for chivalry.

We started our fires around the large room easily enough, constantly on the lookout for guards, who would no doubt begin to smell the smoke and come running. Once the room was beginning to really flame up, we headed slightly further west to light our second set of fires. This was a smaller office, mainly storing sacks of paper in large trolleys. The room also had a fairly low wooden ceiling, so the fire would spread up through onto the second floor with more ease. Once this room was well ablaze, we removed ourselves and headed back to our window. Before I climbed out, I thought about going back to see if I could do any more. I was tempted, I felt like setting those fires had been too easy; however, I decided against heading back deeper into the building. We would only be facing the heat of the flames, a lot of smoke, and potentially alerted guards. Plus, we would be going against procedure and may only make the operation more difficult. Instead, I led my men back out of the gap in the window and back over the seven-foot-high wall.

I could hear little else other than the sound of the growing flames from our rendezvous position a quarter mile West of the Office. No sounds of violent struggle, no screams and no bells or alarm clarions being rung. It was a painful wait, as I crouched down, wondering just how the other three teams were managing. We had heard the other whistles being blown into the night, so knew that we were all at least in place.

By this stage, flames could be seen licking up out of the windows, from both floors. If my troops were still in there, then how long until the heat and smoke made it unbearable? Where were they? The building was well ablaze, and our job had been done.

"That burning building is going to act as a beacon for any enemy eyes nearby. This whole area is going to be busy very soon. We cannot linger here waiting for that to happen, Commander Kane." Darkwolf spoke, close to my ear.

"I know, trust me, I know. Listen, just five more minutes and if still no sign, then we will at least move further towards the valley." I told Darkwolf.

Darkwolf nodded grimly. It was not just the mysterious scout who looked a little fearful. Lieutenants Fester and Palos were also looking decidedly uneasy, their eyes darting round in all directions as if expecting a troop of Purgorite brutes to come charging out of the darkness behind us. Just as I was about to give the order to move off, we saw eight figures come racing toward us out of the darkness. Even in our state of heightened nerves, we recognised the shape and look of our brethren and breathed a small sigh of relief.

As two of the three awaited groups neared us, puffing and panting, I could see that some had blood about their person, although due to the lack of visibility, I could not tell if the blood was theirs or from some other body. Major Heven, one of the small group leaders, spoke first.

"Commander, we cannot find Captain Stire's team. We were attacked by a unit of troops as we left and managed to fend them off, but we think that the other team may have been taken." The Major relayed, his tone beyond grim.

Taken? by the Purgorites? Already in that moment, my mind was cruelly conjuring up images of grizzly torture. I suffered disturbing and vivid images of my four comrades already being chained up and beaten whilst we stood there nearby. I was split between rushing back east to rescue our comrades and cutting our losses and heading back to base.

"How many enemy troops are there?" I found myself asking Major Heven.

"Errmm…we eight fought a group of maybe twelve or thirteen and killed a load, the rest retreated with wounds. I don't know the full numbers. It was hectic. We saw a scuffle a little further off into the dark, but there looked to be loads more troops. Twenty or more." The Major informed me, his sweaty face and bald plate shining from the reflection of the now roaring blaze behind him.

I knew that if I just ran off, leaving my men to be taken, I could never live with myself. The men would never forgive me or respect me as a leader if I did not LEAD, even if that meant risking my life to save even one of my comrades, my soldiers, my brothers in battle. Then and there, I made my decision.

"Men, our brothers are not yet lost. There is still hope. We take the fight to the enemy and get them back! On me!" I roared into the night, not caring how many enemies heard. How dare I even contemplate running back to safety.

Chapter 22

An Old Friend Appears

I started the charge east, just hoping that my eleven other soldiers were at my back. I did not even need to turn my head and look to know that this was the case. I both felt and heard the running feet all around me. I knew that we ran east as a solid unit of twelve fearless and capable Halian warriors.

I saw an enemy unit standing to the South of the roaring blaze. It was a group of fifteen or so milling Purgorite soldiers in medium armour, who were all too focused on the fire itself to notice us, until it was too late. They turned their heads to their left mere seconds before we barreled in from that direction. I only had time to see a series of stunned and shocked faces before our lethal blades began falling. I bowled straight into two, using my speed, powerful build and overall weight to knock them to the ground. I paid them no heed but cleanly beheaded the next standing Purgorite brute. I blocked a strike from a Purgorite to my right, before driving my sword pommel hard into his windpipe and finishing the attack with a mean overhead strike. Whilst the enemy brute was wearing a thin steel cap, the force of my strike was such that the blade still negated the brute's head armour and split his skull.

Not seeing any enemies directly before me, I turned to see how my men were faring. I was heartened to see numerous Purgorite corpses littering the arid ground. Any standing Purgorites were being finished off by Halian blades. I noticed that 1Lt. Fester was holding his side and wincing, a little dark liquid seeping through his fingers.

"Are you hurt, Simon?" I asked the Officer, forgetting to use his full title in the heat of the moment.

"Ughh.. No, Commander. Just a belly cut. Nothing I can't handle." 1Lt. Fester reassured me.

I nodded and turned back east. I could see little of whatever was out there in the darkness, as the roaring inferno was destroying any night vision I had built up whilst crouching in the darkness. The fight was not over as we still had Halian soldiers to rescue. I yelled my next order to my still-standing eleven comrades.

"Come on lads, follow me. Let's rescue the others." I screamed.

Once again, I led the charge East, my blood up and my sword seeming to cry out for more Purgorite lives to take. I heard a rousing chorus of war cries from behind me as I set off running again. It was insane really, twelve soldiers running out into the darkness of enemy territory to rescue friends who may not even be there any longer, but if sanity is always taking the safest and easiest option, then call me a lunatic!

It was only around one minute later that we came upon a 'good news, bad news' situation. The good news was that we saw our four missing brethren, who thankfully were still all alive. The bad news was that they were confined to a prison-like cage, being transported on a sturdy carriage. The carriage was also part of a company of some eighty or so armed and armoured enemy soldiers. Dozens of held torches lit the company up, as this moving snake of brutes had no reason to fear anything, apparently.

We were spotted, as many heads turned as we approached their snaking company. After some guttural shouted orders, some twenty or so enemy brutes broke off from the main body and started dashing towards us in a fairly compact group. It was too late to turn and run; we would only be chased and cut down like rabbits fleeing hounds, and that wasn't going to happen. I did the only thing I could in that moment, I formed my group into a driving wedge of flesh, steel and sword.

"Form a wedge, I take point. Five men to a side. Now!" I yelled to my team, the enemy rapidly closing in on us.

My men fell into position, whilst on the move and with minimal fuss. We were highly trained and mobile soldiers after all. A position amongst Halian soldierhood had to be earned, not given. We did not want the weak or unworthy amongst our ranks. Therefore, I knew that I was running with tough warriors at my back, who would not break rank.

We powered into that second serious group of Purgorite soldiers that night with more cohesion than we had the first. To do otherwise would have proved disastrous, as that second group were already focused on us and formed into a much tighter pack. I drove into the pack of Purgorites, my sword already swinging and hacking. Our wedge did some fair damage, and a good six or so enemy soldiers were knocked to the ground or outright killed with that first attack. Our progress was slowed almost immediately, as the Purgorites quickly reformed and pushed back. They fought using much the same big, ugly cleavers that so many of their invading brethren had wielded in Halia. In fact, some of those Purgorite soldiers we were fighting could have been from the defeated stock who had managed to flee Halia when things went wrong for them.

With a slightly wounded 1Lt. Fester to my immediate right and Darkwolf to my left, we found ourselves forming mini-battle lines and duelling face to face with our enemy for a few moments. Poor Simon Fester was tiring too fast, as his injury was clearly worse than he let on. His blocks were getting weaker, and each enemy strike he took was driving him back a little. He was not getting his sword high enough and would be in real trouble unless I stepped in. As his direct opponent powered up for a high strike that would have almost certainly brought Simon to his knees, I rapidly stepped in and skewered the brute through his exposed armpit, giving Simon some much-needed breathing space. Almost immediately after this attack, I unleashed a powerful backhanded strike that managed to all but hack off my immediate opponent's jaw. The brute dropped to the ground, enabling me to finish him with a sword plunge through the weak point of his chest plate.

"Midnight!" I heard Darkwolf cry in shock, but I did not have time to check what may have happened to Darkwolf's fellow scout.

My attention had to focus on the next Uteshian cleaver, which came flying low, as if to cut my legs out from under me. I backstepped in time and managed to deflect the worst of the strike, although the angle of my deflection hurt my wrist, and the strike that did connect still caused my knee to scream out in pain, although I had spared myself from what could have been a crippling blow. Damn, the Utreshian brutes packed a mean punch when you let them.

The brute I was facing actually went for the same trick again, hoping he would have more luck, slicing low with his wicked cleaver, hoping to take out one or both of my legs. This time I jumped back out of the blade's path fully and readjusted my footing, before driving a powerful armoured knee into his exposed and open face. The result was disastrous, for my enemy at least. The loud and sickening crunch that met my ears was probably the sound of half his skull collapsing in on itself. He dropped to the ground out cold. By this stage, that initial group that had broken off from the main enemy column were down or already dead. However, we could not rest long, as more brutes were breaking off to deal with the black-clad warriors who looked to have made easy work of their Purgorite comrades.

I then took an opportunity to check on the state of Midnight. I saw a Halian body lying still around fifteen feet away, with Darkwolf checking for the extent of injuries, maybe even signs of life. Darkwolf looked up at me after only a moment, his eyes full of pain in the darkness. He grimly shook his head and looked down at the ground. So, another of our brotherhood was gone.

I looked back to the snaking enemy column, which had kept moving during our little melee. By now the cage containing our captured fellows was almost out of sight in the darkness. I felt hopelessness close in, as much I wanted to stay strong. We were already tired. Another of us was dead. Simon Fester was injured and could barely fight. The brutes still had scores of men they could throw at us.

Trying to reach and rescue our fellows from the evil grasp of the Purgorites seemed like another insurmountable task.

I was about to swing at the next brute that came near me, with whatever energy and fire I had left, when something got there first. A long arrow with a bizarre tip seemed to just appear in the brute's neck, the metal tip coated in blood. The aim of the archer must have been true, for the big brute toppled forward almost instantly, spluttering and clutching his bleeding neck. Then, more arrows came flying out of the darkness to the north of us. Whilst many arrows missed and clattered to the desert ground, many more found their destination in Purgorite flesh. It was both uplifting and at the same time, harrowing, if that even sounds possible, to see the Purgorite column literally being torn apart with flying arrows from some unseen killers. Purgorites tried to run both toward and from the storm of arrows, only to be peppered with flying points of death. Many Purgorites took something of a stand and hunkered down with their swords held up like shields in front of their heads, but they died just the same. There was no escape. The arrows were too many, too well aimed and too relentless.

Whilst the arrows had been flying towards our enemy, my troops and I had quickly grabbed nearby Purgorite corpses and lay prone, using the dead brutes as invaluable meat shields. Once the sounds of whooshing arrows and Purgorite death screams had ceased, we deemed it safe to come out of cover and see just who had saved our skins.

I ordered Major Heven and a few men to check on the status of our captured comrades, whilst I walked north, cautiously. I sheathed my sword and held my hands up in something in a manner of a friendly gesture. The rest of my troops remained where they were, hands on hilts. We still had to be ready.

I saw a figure appear out of the darkness from the north, although the torch he carried cast a ring of light around him. He rode a strong-looking horse, which he brought to a halt only a few feet from me. He dismounted and looked right at me, before a smile broke out across his face. We embraced each other warmly.

"My friend, this is the second time you have come to our aid. One day I will have to save YOUR life." I told my South Utreshian friend.

"I look forward to that day." Responded Ravaise, still smiling.

"But, how…where…why were you out here in the darkness?" I asked my rescuer.

"I can explain all later, Commander Kane. There are more immediate issues to attend to now. I fear that the compound you were staying in may have been attacked." Warned Ravaise, no longer smiling but deadly serious.

Ravaise and ten of these troops agreed to accompany my men and I due north-west to check on the state of Tol'Trevel . The archers had purposefully avoided sending arrows too near to the prison cage containing our four comrades. Captain Stire, 1Lt. Demetri, Shadowprowler and Wraithven had been released from their confines all whole and beyond relieved at their freedom. Other than some minor cuts and wounds sustained during their violent capture, they were physically okay.

We travelled back fast, riding on borrowed horses until we reached the valley, whereby we would have to continue on foot, as to use horses would have proven very hazardous due to the terrain and darkness. Midnight's still body had been laid across the rump of a horse with as much dignity as could be allowed, given the current predicament. Two of his fellow scouts then agreed to transport their fallen comrade across the valley.

By the time we reached the east side of the long valley, we could already see fires burning back at the compound. So, the enemy had attacked whilst we were away. I only prayed then that Major De'Beresford and Captain D'Arten had somehow managed to escape.

Our temporarily increased band of warriors arrived at the walls of Tol'Trevel after a hasty traversing of the valley. We could hear no sounds of struggle from within, only the sounds of still raging fires. The apparently strong gate had proved not so strong, as it had been wrenched off its metal hinges and lay discarded in the entryway.

"Major De'Beresford. Captain D'Arten!" I yelled out loud as soon as I rushed into the courtyard.

We entered with swords drawn, eyes alert and ears straining. I immediately issued orders to some of the troops.

"Major Heven, take 1Lt. Fester to the infirmary to check on that stomach wound; he isn't getting any better. Captain Stire, take 1Lt. Demetri and check the barracks. Darkwolf, take Wraithven and check the kitchen and dining area. 2Lt. Palos, follow me to the Command Block." I bellowed.

The Command Block had been totally turned over. It looked like a tornado had hit the place whilst we were away. Maps had been ripped down from the wall and torn up, cabinets and desks had been flipped over, their contents scattered. Anything that could be smashed, snapped or crushed looked to have been attended to. Several smaller fires crackled around the rooms as piles of burning documents gave off red glows. However, the heat or smoke was not such that Palos or I struggled to remain in the room.

"I should have left more Officers to guard the place. Those men are probably taken and being tortured for info right now, as we speak." I said angrily, more to myself than to a stunned and pale-faced Palos.

Leaving the Command Block and walking at a trot back into the courtyard, I met up with Captain Stire, who advised that he had found no sign of the missing Officers during his check. He also told me that our personal belongings had been rummaged through and anything of use taken. My mind immediately fixed on a certain prized weapon of mine, a weapon I could not replace. Captain Stire saw the look in my eyes and solidified my fears.

"Commander, I am pretty certain that whoever raided this place took Mordak's Might with them."

I nodded in acknowledgement.

"That's only a piece of metal and wood, Major De'Beresford and Captain D'Arten are our battle brethren. They are my main concern." I responded.

In all honesty, Mordak's Might was far more than just inanimate material. It was NOT just metal and wood to me, but I had to downplay its significance when the lives of two fellow Officers were at stake. Though I had not really been able to establish much of a kinship with D'Arten, and I feared he still held his father's death against me, he was still my responsibility, and I would do whatever I had to get him back.

Darkwolf crossed the courtyard to join us and provide something of an update.

"Our food supply has been trashed, Commander, I am afraid. Barrels broken open and left to run dry. Food dumped onto the floor or hurled against the wall. Some animal even defecated on one of the kitchen counters. There is some potentially positive news, however. I saw that the wooden panel covering the trapdoor has been moved, as if someone has used it as a method of escape. I went down into the tunnels for a few minutes but saw or heard nothing, so came back. I can take some of my scouts down to do some tracking, if you wish." Darkwolf informed me.

"Not yet, Darkwolf. First, I need to speak with our friend Ravaise, and we need to formulate where to go next as a group." I said, both to Darkwolf and really any Officer within earshot.

Chapter 23

Romesh Agrees to Help

Within half an hour of arriving back at camp, some order had at least been established. The place had been thoroughly checked and the level of damage and theft roughly gauged. Any fires had been quenched. Simon Fester was being attended to by Major Heven and whilst Simon was in pain, he was at least not on death's door. Midnight's body was laid on a spare cot in the infirmary.

The meeting took place in the dining hall, which had mercifully not been too badly trashed. We could still sit around the long tables, which were probably too sturdy, boring and cheap-looking to appeal to the marauding raiders as something fun to destroy.

"Ravaise, tell me now how you knew how to find us," I asked the South Utreshian leader, eager to know the fuller story.

"I have been recognised as a friend of Halia, as you may well know. I was contacted by a certain Romesh, who I understand has acted as a contact for you. Well, we have been campaigning in the barren lands not far north of here, just over the border into Vak'akal. Romesh, as part of his occupation, has been keeping an eye on developments and movements in the area. Earlier today, his agents reported a large body of Purgorite troops travelling roughly north, with several empty prison carriages in tow. Upon hearing this, Romesh figured that your group was likely who they were looking for. He then fed this information to me to see if I could possibly lead my men south into North Utresh and intercept this movement of troops. I agreed and moved south with all haste. We approached just as the Purgorites were moving away from the Communications Office with their captives. It was then that I ordered the ranks of archers to silently ready themselves and shower the enemy column with arrows." Ravaise finished.

"We are eternally grateful for what you did, Ravaise. If not for you, four of us would have been taken away to face unspeakable torment, whilst the rest of us would be lying dead on the desert floor." I offered in praise.

"Believe me, the Purgorites are every bit our enemy as they are yours. Our bad blood goes back hundreds of years, if not thousands. But that is a story for another day." Ravaise declared.

"This place has been compromised. The Purgorite leadership will soon know that their troops failed in capturing us and that the bulk of us were not at the compound. We cannot defend the place, send messages, feed ourselves or even rest properly. We need to find somewhere else." I declared.

"Commander Kane, I can take you directly to Romesh. He can help you and find new accommodation and supplies. After all, it is part of his job. After that, though, my troops and I cannot continue to fight with you. We have our own duties elsewhere. We can only wish you luck." Ravaise advised me.

"That sounds great, Ravaise. I cannot ask anymore. It is best we leave as soon as possible." I said.

Before leaving Tol'Trevel, for the very last time, it turned out, we packed up what little we had left and fixed it onto the backs of the eight horses, who I would not just leave to starve. Then, we filed out of the compound in order, our heads still held high and our dignity still intact. The body of Midnight had been buried in a hastily dug pit, and some quiet words said over his body before the soil was replaced. We could not afford to be carting a fourteen-stone dead body around with us.

Instead of crossing the valley straight away, Ravaise took a different path. The man knew the land well and led us due north for some miles, before crossing the valley via a large, raised stone walkway that the horses could easily manage. Once on the east side of the valley, we continued on for another five miles or so before we came to our destination.

Ravaise and his small entourage of troops led the way, as Ravaise knew how best to approach Romesh's headquarters and make his request, on our behalf. I saw Ravaise speak quietly to a uniformed guard through a window opening by a large, heavy outer door. After some spoken exchange and positive nods of the head, the heavy door was opened. Ravaise turned and indicated that I should bring my troops forward, now only fifteen of us. I trotted my horse forward, Simon Fester sitting directly behind me, as we had ridden two to a horse wherever possible. There was no separate outer defence wall to the building, however the walls of the structure itself were high and looked thick and strong. The lowest windows were barred with iron and the building was surrounded by a deep ditch, which we had to cross via a fairly narrow walkway.

I found myself following Ravaise and his troops through the high doorway and into another courtyard, slightly larger and grander than the one at Tol' Trevel. The courtyard was enclosed on all sides by two-story high buildings, so the compound itself resembled a hollowed-out square. Shortly enough, Romesh himself appeared, dressed in a fine ankle-length robe and unarmed. It was ten of the clock by this time, so Romesh may well have been either preparing for bed, or already in bed and asleep. He and Ravaise exchanged a handshake and dropped into a conversation I could not really hear. Hearing it would have proved of little use though, given that they were most likely conversing in a more familiar local dialect and not the Halian that they both spoke so fluently. Again, nods were exchanged, and the discussion seemed to be progressing in our favour. Ravaise then once again signalled for me to approach. I did so swiftly, dismounting my horse and leaving a stable but still pained Simon Fester still seated.

"Our friend Ravaise has told me what happened tonight and about your current situation. I will gladly accommodate you here for the time being and offer you whatever support I can. First, your men can wash and rest a little and settle themselves. Then I will order my cooks to prepare some food and drink. You look awful, Commander Kane, if I may be so bold as to say so, one fighter to another." Romesh told me, smiling a little.

As offered, the rest of my troops clambered down from their horses in the courtyard. I helped Simon down from our horse as gently as I could, taking care not to disturb his still fresh wound any more than necessary. We were ushered into the building via a main door directly opposite the entryway, before being led down a series of corridors to our accommodation. The interior building walls were of stone and had been painted a brilliant white, however the place was obviously cleaned regularly as I could see no mark or blemish disgracing the walls. The floor was polished stones slabs graced with long thin lines of red carpet. We passed several of Romesh's agents during our journey, all dressed in knee-length belted tunics with some manner of badge pinned to their right breast, who all nodded respectfully as we passed.

Our accommodation was slightly more luxurious than it had been at Tol' Trevel, being that the rooms been designed for the comfort of higher-paid officials rather than armed grunts and hired blades. The beds were slightly wider, softer, and there was much more privacy between each sleeping station. I was thrilled to discover that the washroom in Romesh's outpost was not just as good as any washroom in Halia, but better. There was even a design whereby heated water was pumped through a thin metal funnel which sprouted from the washroom wall some seven feet above ground level. A person could stand below this funnel and wash themselves as hot water poured from on high! As soon as I had some privacy, I tested out this usual contraption and allowed the hot water to wash away the blood, sweat, dust and filth from my body. After drying myself with a clean towel, I felt much better. Once back in the dormitory, I dressed in clean garments before making my way downstairs to rejoin Romesh.

When I left the dormitory, it was still a hive of activity. Troops were once again choosing beds, stripping off their dirty war before going to wash off the day's filth in the washroom. There were several conversations about what had happened during the day in progress; Captain Stire was relating to Major Heven how he and the three other men had been bundled into the cages. 1Lt. Fester was trying to assure 2Lt. Palos that his torso wound wasn't that bad and that he was already on the mend. Darkwolf and Wraithven were discussing the subject of trying to track down where Major De'Beresford and Captain D'Arten may have gone. It was that last discussion which gave me the greatest concern. Two of our number were still missing and could be anywhere. Were they still at large and trying to find other shelter? Did they get attacked by one of the gruesome beasts that stalk the lands once darkness falls? Were they already in chains and being dragged back to some Purgorite Lord to be brutalised for information? I feared that soon enough we would know, and the answer would not be encouraging.

I found Romesh in the compound's spacious dining hall. Similar to the dining hall at Tol' Trevel, several long trestle tables and benches occupied the centre space of the room. Through an opening in the wall, I could see into the kitchen section, where wooden counters and stacks of pots and pans. I could also hear the din of cooks barking orders, the sound of what seemed to be knives hitting chopping blocks, the sizzling of food being cooked in a frying pan and footsteps moving about the place. I felt my stomach growl as the first wafts of food smells hit my nostrils. I did not realise how hungry I was until that moment, given all else that had been going on. My mind had buried the desire for food as other, more important things had to be attended to.

Once the rest of my troops had arrived, washed and dressed in more comfortable clothing, much of which Romesh had kindly provided, we sat down around the tables and the food was brought out from the kitchen. It was only the fifteen Halians and Romesh, as Ravaise had departed with his troops once we were safely inside. Standing in the courtyard, he and I had shaken hands as comrades and hoped that we would meet again. I owed him several times over for his timely interventions and would be devastated if I never got a chance to repay his kindness.

The food was delicious that night. It was roasted Bull, boiled potatoes, steamed green vegetables covered with a rich type of gravy. To follow was a hot sponge pudding with treacle. It was clear that Romesh was a man of the world and had tailored this meal to appeal to our Halian palates, rather than stagger us with an unfamiliar and potentially unappealing cuisine when we primarily just needed sustenance and a hearty meal.

Once we had satisfied ourselves with the food and rehydrated ourselves with fresh drinking water from Romesh's private well, we sat and talked a little of general things. We had not yet spoken of our next move, or our losses, or the fact that we were likely being hunted at that very moment. Right then, we were safe, well fed and amongst brothers. We just took some moments for relaxation and to recover ourselves, not knowing when the next relaxation would come.

"I will excuse myself now Commander Kane, my Officers. Feel free to use this dining hall for further discussion. You may also use a more private meeting room just across the hall if you wish. Remember that I am a friend of Halia, the Cadre has instructed me to assist you wherever possible. Please do not be afraid to ask for anything you may need."

With those words, Romesh bowed once again and departed the dining hall, whilst several of the Officers and I voiced our warm expressions of gratitude.

"I am tired and cannot be the only one. I would suggest that we rest now and hold a private meeting tomorrow after we break our fast, where we plan our next move. There is still the matter of the bridge, the roads and the training camp to attend to. Not to mention trying to find Major De'Beresford and Captain D'Arten. I feel bad about sitting here eating and drinking whilst they could already be in enemy hands, but it would be folly to rush out now into the darkness looking for traces. But enough for now, take your bed as soon as you are ready. We have had enough for today and tomorrow will only bring more." I told my soldiers, on what would turn out to be our last night together as a coherent company.

Chapter 24

A Harrowing Nightmare

That night, the nightmares came again, only worse and more intense. Even during the nightmares, I knew that Va'heash was behind it and bragging to me that he didn't even need to be anywhere near me to trouble me. I will try and replay the nightmares, painful as it is.

The nightmare began by taking me back to Halia. It seemed that Carnagon Castle had been overthrown and the inhabitants mostly slaughtered. Bloodied and mutilated corpses littered the ground. Poor Brother Abel's severed head had been fixed on a spike atop the castle walls. His rotted-out eyes seemed to be staring directly at me, as if to ask why I, Marcus Kane, let this happen. His jaw hung open in a frightening rictus of pain. I was then dragged to Gutvast Palace against any will I had. I saw two gibbets, each containing Lord Vincent Harbrandt and his lady Vivian. They were in a terrible state of decomposition, although still recognisable. Crows pecked at their rotting flesh and wild starving dogs tried to snap at their hanging lower limbs for a much-needed mouthful of meat. Next, I was rushed through the foul sky to Mirgot's Pass, where a huge giant in Purgorite armour was smashing the fortress to pieces like it was a sandcastle on a beach. The giant was grotesque beyond description and no words would convey the hideousness of its appearance. It stood so tall that the top of the pass only reached its chest. I looked slightly south and saw the golden city of Farchester in flames. I could hear the screams of pain, agony and fear. I strained my sight, although I did not want to, and saw monstrous fleets of Purgorite warships along the South coast. I felt myself struggle to leave the nightmare but could sense a force forcing me to keep looking at the chaos around me. Finally, I seemed to hear a blood-curdling and deeply sinister voice say, "Enough for now, let's try something else."

I was suddenly back in the dining room of Romesh's compound, listening to the cooks preparing the meal. Only, something was very wrong here. The sounds coming from the cooks were more like animalistic barks and growls. The sounds were laced with gleeful wickedness and insanity and were spine-chilling to hear. I could hear the sound of a knife hitting a chopping block, only the sound got louder and louder, and louder still until the whole room seemed to shake. Then, I heard the sound of heavy lumbering footsteps approaching the opening between the kitchen and the dining hall. I saw the shadow of whatever was making the sound, and even the shadow seemed to be exuding malice and evil. The huge figure of Brutuck came into view.

Due to his towering height, he had to bow his head a little to get through the already high doorway and stepped a little closer to me. He was grinning wickedly, displaying yellowed fangs. His eyes were pure black, just darkness. I can only describe his face as that of Lenfer itself; anything less would be a disservice. The thing spoke, it's voice easy to understand, but incredibly hard to actually experience.

"Marcus, little Marcus. There had been a slight change to the menu. Tonight, you will be feasting on the bodies of De'Beresford and D'Arten. You cannot let their flesh go to waste." Growled the creature.

"I..we…we killed you. You were buried. You're dead." I felt my voice say, although I cannot recall actually wanting to speak.

"Not here. Not in your nightmares, you little shit. Here I can come and go as I please. Here, you are my toy, my plaything." The creature responded with dark relish.

The Brutuck thing, still grinning, held up the severed heads of De'Beresford and D'Arten. Each head was grasped in a massive, armoured fist. In my dream, both men still had hair, and it was this hair that was being held tightly. Their necks were spilling fresh blood to the dining hall floor. I found myself being forced to look at the two dead men's faces. At first, the faces were still and motionless, then, both dead faces sprang to life (or a mockery of life) and began screaming hysterically. They were both looking at me with deep rage and bloodlust, their heads shaking with the sheer force of their screams. The Brutuck thing then simply let go of the heads. In any sane world, the heads would have dropped to the ground due to the forces of gravity, but my dream was not sane; it was taking place in a world of chaos with no rules or reason. Instead, the heads remained floating horrifically in the air, still screaming uncontrollably. I stood and tried to ask them to stop yelling and told them both that I was sorry they were dead. That was when their eyeballs burst out of their skulls due to the force of their screaming. The two hanging skulls, now starting to break apart totally, flew toward me at shocking speed. By this stage in the nightmare, I was screaming as well, although as soon as the flying skulls were about to hit me, I was transported from that hellish dining hall yet again to somewhere else alien and saturated in evil.

I found myself floating alone on the surface of what I knew to be the vast Palmorian Ocean. I felt an intense fear of being such a small thing in such a vast area. I felt a crippling vulnerability I had never before come close to experiencing. I then felt myself pulled under the surface, into the inky darkness of the ocean. Only, my sight was somehow much improved, and this unfortunately allowed me to see for miles in each direction under the water. I could almost see the ocean bed, fathoms below me. I saw the outlines of huge sea monsters swimming around the deep waters. I saw the wrecks of lost ships stuck forever on the ocean bed. Nearer to me, I saw the floating corpses of sailors. Forever belonging to the watery depths that they now inhabited. One of the nearest sailors, a bloated corpse with an arm missing, turned what remained of his head to gaze at me. Other dead sailors followed suit, until I saw dozens of dead eyes gazing at this intruder. I tried to swim away from them, but there was nowhere to swim to. One of the corpses grasped my flailing ankle with his rotten hand and began to pull me down into the deep void of the ocean. Into the abyss. I looked up, desperate to escape, but only saw the light of the surface getting darker and further away as I was pulled further down.

I awoke with a start from this horrific sequence of nightmares. Even when I was awake, I found myself alone and in a strange location. For a few insanity inducing moments, I could not tell dream from reality. I was sweating and breathing heavily, looking about me to get my bearings. Finally, I managed to come back to the present. I told myself I was safe in Romesh's compound, and that my nightmares were only Va'heashes efforts to try and hurt me. I steadily reassured myself that they were only nightmares, that they were not real. I tried to tell myself that they were only images in my mind, and I should pay them no heed. I tried to tell myself that…and failed.

Chapter 25

The Mission Continues

I was understandably a little shaky the next morning when what passed for daylight began to pierce the gloom of our dormitory, through one of the six plate-glass windows the room boasted. The vividness of the nightmares was hard to shake, and I was almost expecting to see those horrific severed heads floating in the air as I went downstairs with some of the troops to break our fast. Thankfully, no Brutuck, no blood, no screaming severed heads. Just a plain old dining hall with a selection of food being laid out on the table by Romesh's kitchen staff. There was a delicious-looking selection of fine bread, smoked fish, poached eggs, slices of meat on a platter, fresh fruit, heated oats and even some local cuisine I could not name. I picked up a wooden plate and began helping myself and tucking in, hoping that the sensory pleasure of the fresh food would at least distract me from my whirling thoughts for a few precious minutes.

It was during breakfast that one of our number broached the subject of nightmares, which I was relieved to see that I was not experiencing alone.

"I don't know about you fellows, but I've been having the most awful dreams recently. The most intense nightmares. I don't want to go into detail as I don't want to relive them at all. But they were just evil dreams." Captain Stire confessed to the seated group; his face severe.

"You are not alone, Captain Stire. I had a particularly nasty batch during the night. I could really do without them to be honest." I admitted out loud.

Other Officers then piped up, saying that they had also been experiencing awful night visions but did not want to be seen as 'weak' for complaining about them. 1Lt. Schmidt even gave some details of his hideous nightmares as he told the table about gigantic floating snakes and being inflicted with hideous bodily deformities.

"This is Va'heashes doing, I am certain. Unfortunately, there seems to be little we can do. We must sleep, and whilst in that space, we are extra vulnerable to the demon's talons. Just try and remember that none of it is real. They are meaningless visions sent to scare you." I told the assembled soldiers.

I held the morning's meeting at ten of the clock in the private meeting chamber that Romesh had kindly loaned us. There were now a mere fifteen of us around the large wooden table. Of the original twenty, three were dead and two were currently missing. Young Simon Fester was of course still wounded, but much improved from last night and out of any danger, for the time at least.

"Right, despite everything that happened last night, the mission was still a success. The Communication Office was torched and taken out of commission. That Office was an important post in terms of relaying Purgorite directions and orders, so we have just made communications between Va'heash's army hopefully much more difficult. That was our first true step in stalling the Purgorite invasion effort, even if it felt like a small step. So well done to all. I would next like to tackle the issue of the bridge, which has already been surveyed and weak points identified. There is a substance available for purchase on the market in North Utresh, a powder which will explode…so to speak…if it comes into contact with naked flame. It is called 'Tok-porokh' in these parts, but for reasons of ease, I will just call it…'firepowder' to make things easier. Cases of this firepowder can be placed at both ends of the bridge, and lit with a fuse, to give the men on the far side of the bridge time to get back across the bridge before the powder is set off! As per last night, I would propose to execute this duty during the hours of darkness. The bridge traffic is fairly heavy during the day, and whilst North Utresh as a nation is our enemy, I do not want to inflict needless civilian casualties. Many unarmed merchants, tradesman and messengers use that bridge, and I do not wish them harmed. This mission is about disrupting the flow of troops from one place to the next, not about murder. I will speak to Romesh about procuring at least six cases of this firepowder. It is not in his business to ask exactly what I need these items for, he is only obliged to assist me.

Darkwolf, would you be good enough to take maybe three of your scouts and travel back to the ruins of Tol'Trevel? Then follow that secret route from the larder to see what tracks you find. I am sorry that we could not do this last night, but I did not want to split the group right then, as you would not know where to meet us. So, follow the tracks and report back as and when you have detected anything of interest, or Lord forbid, our comrades fallen bodies.

The rest of us will not sit here idle today, as there is plenty of work to still be done. I will take a unit down to the warren of tunnels and holes beneath the road, which Major Heven identified, to see for myself the best plan forward. I would also like a team to head west a little to scout out that deserted farm. See if there is anything we can scavenge for use, any information or money hidden, or even if it is somewhere we could establish as a temporary base of operations. It at least has a defensive ditch and a good-sized wall of wooden spikes. It may even have some arable soil and a water source. Captain Stire, I would like you to lead this party and report back later today with your findings." I instructed.

After fielding some of the usual questions about supplies, weapons, timescales and travel, I ended the meeting and stood as the men began to shuffle out of the room.

I had luck with Romesh about the cases of firepowder, as these were items available on the special market that he had access to. This special market was not available to the underlings who tended to roam the filthy lanes of Beltreke; instead, these were items only available to military, higher officials and certain political agents. I went ahead and ordered six cases of the goods, hoping that would be sufficient. It was hard to gauge necessary amounts, given that I had not seen the powder in action and could hardly conduct a 'test run' on some other random bridge, given our time restraints. I filled out a purchase order for the goods, meaning that the Halian banking system would be obliged to refund Romesh as soon as possible for the cost of the six firepowder cases, which was not cheap.

At around half past the hour of eleven, we all set off on horseback to ride toward the low-lying road which Heven had scouted out earlier in the expedition. The riders consisted of Major Heven, 1Lt. Fester (who claimed he was fine and insisted on accompanying us) 2Lt. Palos, Captain McAdams and I. We were once again dressed as Kazbarian mercenaries, complete with freshly shaven heads and appropriate weapons and armour. Whilst a lot of gear had been stolen from Tol'Trevel by the raiders, Romesh had been good enough to provide us with some of his stored equipment and clothing.

After an hour of riding, during which our eyes were constantly peeled for any signs of enemy movement, we reached the strip of road we were looking for and drew our horses to a halt. We knew that our unwanted presence had been detected around those lands, multiple times, so were always ready to leap ahorse and scarper if we felt that we were in more danger than we could handle. Even if we engaged with a Purgorite mob and defeated them, the conflict would still result in a load of dead bodies, noise and missing troops. Better to not engage unless we truly have to. For obvious reasons, we did not want to go anywhere near the ruins of the Communication Office given the drama that had unfurled the previous night.

We had dismounted our horses and were moving down the slope so that we could access the tunnels that ran beneath the road. Major Heven, having been there so recently, was doing most of the guiding. He took us deep into the tunnels and using the light of a torch, showed us the potential weak spots in the rock. I nodded in understanding, already planning out where to set the firepowder cases for maximum effect. At the time, I did not realise that my speculations and plans were in waste, for we would never get a chance to carry out that particular act of disruption. Staying together as group of five, we walked deep into the tunnel system, making our plans. We must have been in there for some time, as when we emerged back into the daylight, I could tell that the position of the sun had changed in the sky, even behind the cover of the ominous yellow clouds. We climbed back onto our mounts with our new knowledge, before heading back toward Romesh's well-defended outpost.

Upon getting back to base, I enquired with the door guards to see if either of the other groups had returned from their missions. Their response was in the negative, and I could only hope that both groups were still well and not in enemy custody, which was now a constant worry.

I had a chance to catch up with Simon Fester and Jerome Palos in the Dining Hall over a mug of ale, as we waited for our comrades to return.

"How is the wound, Simon?" I asked the young Officer, using his first name as it was only the three of us alone in the room.

"Not bad at all, Commander. Still a little painful, but I can move okay and the sickness is gone. It wasn't a deep cut, just wide. Will leave a nasty scar, but what is that to a fighting man?" Young Simon asked.

"I'm glad that you are on the mend, Simon. What about you Jerome, are you well, given everything that has been going on?" I enquired of the quiet but reliable Officer.

"I am well, Commander. This is the toughest campaign I have worked on, if we can even call it a campaign, but I am still standing and ready for whatever comes next." Responded the Lieutenant, putting on a brave front as possible.

"Still no regrets about agreeing to come on the mission?" I asked both of the Lieutenants.

"Absolutely not, Commander. If I wanted a boring life with no risk, I would have stayed in Halia, mending shoes or delivering sacks of food. I feel like I am where I need to be, odd as that sounds." Replied Simon.

It was then that one of Romesh's guards appeared in the Dining Hall doorway with news.

"Commander Kane, Darkwolf has just arrived back."

I immediately rose from the table and made my way to the courtyard to meet up with the lead scout and hopefully receive an update. I could not see any 'good news' option, but as long as there was hope that the men were still alive, that was something. Simon and Jerome accompanied me.

"Commander Kane, we went back and followed that tunnel from the larder. We detected at least six sets of recent footprints on the ground, which indicates that if our comrades did escape via that tunnel, they were pursued. We followed the tunnel all the way through the rock until it exited out of the valley's side. There, we found signs of a scuffle and spatters of blood. We also noticed wheel tracks leading away from this scuffle, I'm afraid, south down the valley. We followed these tracks for a few miles but lost them when the vehicle must have crossed a shallow stream before hitting harder dusty ground where the tracks were all but destroyed by blowing sand." Darkwolf informed me as soon as we met in the courtyard.

It did not take a master philosopher to put together that information and reach the grim conclusion that one or both of my Officers had been detained and transported away in some manner of vehicle to Lord knows where. At least their corpses were not found, so there was still hope in that moment.

"Thank you, everyone, for your efforts. If the men have been taken, there is no way of knowing exactly where. I only pray that they have not been taken to this infamous Balostroma, as a rescue would most likely be out of our scope. Although it pains me, there is little we can do for them right now. I will, however, speak with Romesh about the situation and ask for advice as soon as he is available." I told any troops within earshot.

Before we dispersed, I reminded the team that we would assemble at eight of the clock in the private meeting room we had used earlier in the day, to go over final plans for that evening's exercise. I did not go into any further detail, as even around Romesh's agents, protocol still had to be respected, and sensitive information kept sensitive.

Chapter 26

The Bridge, the Battle and the Bletzvelts

By that stage, it was only a matter of hours until the hour of eight. My troops spent the time by resting, taking some refreshment, sorting out their gear for the upcoming mission, sharpening blades, writing in their personal logs or just talking amongst themselves. There was definitely no small anxiety amongst some of the men, which was understandable given what had occurred only the previous night. Were there legions of Purgorites just waiting out there in the shadows for us to leave the safety of the outpost? Did they have eyes on us even then? These were fears we entertained but could not let dictate our behaviour. Our work HAD to be done, danger or no danger. We were not in North Utresh to enjoy a holiday.

The meeting at eight of the clock went ahead without a hiccup. Fifteen men sat around the table listening to my final instructions. Looking back, I recall the faces staring back at me. They still stare back at me in my dreams to this day, many of them ghosts long in the grave. I cannot even recall the exact date, only that it was that night when the expedition basically came to pieces.

We set out soon after half past the hour of eight, all on horseback, to travel in a roughly south-east direction toward this particular bridge spanning the deep gorge. We rode fast through the darkness, putting faith in the enhanced night vision of the horses we rode. The fifteen of us reached the bridge unmolested and unchallenged after pushing our horses for 90 minutes or so. Bringing the horses to a stop and giving them a chance to rest, at least for a while, we all dismounted and approached the bridge in question. No wheeled vehicles or people in sight. All looked good so far. I ordered for the six cases of firepowder to be removed from the backs of the horses on which they had been transported. Although no expert on this certain chemical, I had been assured that rigorous motion would not set the powder off, only direct flame.

Major Heven took Captain McAdams and 1Lt. Schmidt, each carefully carrying one box of firepowder each, across the bridge to the other side. I gave firm instructions that they were not to light the extra-long fuses until I gave the signal, only place the cases in the agreed spots amongst the bridge's lower supports and wait. Captain Stire and I placed the other three cases on our side of the bridge, carefully fitting them in amongst the supports where their combined explosions would hopefully cause maximum damage.

Once I was as confident as I could be that all six cases were in place and ready to be lit, I gave the specific arm signal to Major Heven, indicating that the long fuses were to be lit. The three Officers on the other side of the bridge all lit a fuse each, in tandem, before rising and quickly recrossing the 60-foot-long bridge. Once they were back on our side, our three shorter fuses were lit. It was my plan that the six cases of powder would explode as simultaneously as possible. As soon as our three fuses were lit, I ordered the entire team to get well back from the bridge and cover their ears whilst crouching.

I felt like I was waiting a surprisingly long time for the inevitable loud boom to occur, and for a dreadful moment, I had a feeling that the fuses had somehow sparked out and we had wasted our time. I was reminded of those tense moments back in the tunnels underneath Halia, when the sea of flammable oil had taken a moment to catch light. Then, I felt the ground shake, indeed I felt my whole body shake. I looked up and saw two huge balls of fire rise into the ugly gloom above. Chips of brick, wood and dirt were sprayed through the air, although we were out of range and most of the detritus seemed to be spraying either up in the air or to the sides. The landscape itself shielded us from the worst of the explosion.

Using a cloth face covering to protect my mouth and nose from the cloud of smoke and dirt hanging in the air, I approached the bridge to survey the damage we had caused. I had never blown up a bridge before, so I did not really know what to expect. I then saw that whilst the bridge had not simply ceased to exist, which was a very idealistic prediction, it had at least been taken out of commission. Our end of the bridge had been shifted down a good six feet and was hanging loose, with huge chunks of brick and wood blown out. The bride itself was mangled, misshapen and afire. I knew that no weight could be put on the bridge and no heavy wheeled vehicle would be crossing anytime soon. Plus with all the intense heat and burning, there was every chance that the bridge would start to fall away piece by piece. As I stood there I pondered over some questions, some relevant, some no longer relevant. Could we do more with our weapons to destroy the bridge then and there? Should we have brought more cases, or grouped them at just one side of the bridge? I soon felt that it was futile to ask such questions as the job was done.

"Commander, that explosion will have alerted any ears or eyes for miles around. We need to move." Warned Major Heven, showing no hesitation in essentially giving his senior officer a command.

Move we did, for our job was done. It was time to head back to Romesh's compound. Sadly, fate determined that we would not all make it back.

We had been riding at a good pace for only around twenty minutes when we first spotted signs of enemy movement. A small sea of lit torches seemed to swim out of the darkness, not far in front of us, barring our path.

"Turn to the right, hard right, head north-east as fast as your horses can go!" I bellowed to my fellow riders around me.

We all broke to the right to try and move around this enemy formation. Although we could not see what was really behind all those torches, it was quite clear that they were not friendly pilgrims looking for shelter. In heading north-east, we only seemed to run into more torches, these moving much quicker through the darkness. Of course, the fast-moving torches indicated only more bad news: mounted enemy riders.

"Drive through them, stay together. Keep moving!" was my next order to the riders, who had all by then drawn their solid Kazbarian blades, which many of the troops even seemed to prefer to the slightly smaller Halian blades.

I drove my trusty Stallion toward the horseman directly in my way, just wishing that I had the power of my friend Palladin underneath me. The horseman was a big brute in solid-looking armour, astride a powerful horse not much smaller than a Drutzer. As I passed him, I hacked my sword high, aiming for his helmeted skull. He raised his own blade in time to block mine, although with the sheer weight and force behind my blow, he was knocked entirely out of his saddle. My own arm rang with pain at the impact, and I came close to losing my only main weapon, but luckily, I managed to reestablish my grip for the next enemy horseman. This enemy actually came at me with a long spear, the mean-looking spike at the end reflecting the torchlight. I just about parried the spear thrust, using my empty but fisted left gauntlet to viciously hammer the brute in the side of his head as I barreled past. So far, my riders were keeping up the pace and managing to drive through the enemy pack, but our fortune was not going to last.

It seems that the enemy cavalry had been more of a ploy to slow us down a little and distract us, for after managing to break past another challenging horseman, I was shocked by the sight of several long, spiked wooden barricades being hastily positioned by teams of straining foot soldiers. The barricades looked to be only around four feet in height, and I knew that with Palladin I would have powered straight over the obstacles, but the Stallion beneath me was no Palladin. Instead, the horse panicked and reared at this mass of spikes in front of him. The panic seemed to be contagious, as the other horses followed this example, refusing to go any further. This meant that we were trapped between the length of barricades and the furious enemy horsemen we had so recently broken through. I was about to yell for the men to turn around and head back, but never got the chance, for everything went dark just then.

I awoke groggily, my hand immediately moving to inspect the bleeding cut on my forehead. It seemed that I had to move both hands, as they had been tied together. As I grudgingly came back to the world of misery around me, I saw that my troops were all seated and unarmed in the dirt. Their hands had also been tied with lengths of sturdy-looking rope. Many of my men were injured and bloodied, and for a moment, I thought that we were all at least still breathing.

"Don't kill any more of them, Va'heash wants the bastards alive." Roared one of their leaders, a towering brute garbed in some manner of plate armour.

"Any more of us?" I asked out loud to the group, the question hanging painfully in the air before anyone wished to answer.

"It's Captain McAdams, Commander. He's gone," uttered Major Heven, not meeting my eye.

My eye then found the dead Captain, slightly further away in the circle of torchlight. His body was slouching, whilst his eyes were closed and his bloodied head lolled forward onto his chest. Even in death, he had not been allowed to assume a respectful position of rest. *'Fourteen now'* I thought to myself, already fearing the worst for our still missing comrades De'Beresford and D'Arten. I looked up and saw that we were totally surrounded by a ring of enemy flesh, steel and sword. Grim faces and feral eyes glared back at me, as if goading me into being foolish enough to speak again. I merely lowered my head and did not give them any more satisfaction than they were already savouring.

The sound of a cage door being unlocked drew my attention. I then noticed the three transport cages being readied just beyond the circle of torchlight.

"Right, take these five and put them in this first cage. Barbak, take these four and put them in your cage. Veshel, take the last five of these dogs and kennel them up in your cage. Leave that dead bastard for the

Bletzvelts and desert beasts." The big leader instructed, pointing out the prisoners in question with his large, mailed hand as he barked his orders.

Several of the stationary Purgorite troops then broke into action and started manhandling the first batch of five troops toward the sturdy prison cage. I knew that once I was locked in that cage, it was all over. I, alongside the rest of my troops, would be taken to somewhere highly unpleasant from which escape would not be an option. My escape had to be right then, and right there, in the dark expanse of the wild deserts.

Once more, I focused and found myself desperately searching for nearby lifeforms. I could hardly expect our friend from the depths of the Palmorian Ocean to come bursting through the hard ground, but I knew there were animals out there I could call to. I felt the pressure in my head increase and my pulse rise as I started detecting many smaller minds out there in the darkness. Once again, I felt a connection and sent out a pulse to all listening.

"Help us…help us…come to our aid…help us…come to the light…kill the brutes" were words I did not speak, but communicated, nonetheless.

I focused hard, trying to blank out all the movement around me, as I kept sending out pulses from my mind. I was aware that the first transport cage had already been filled, locked and was moving off at speed into the darkness. I could now feel some of the animals getting closer, sense their hot breath, their bloodlust, and even see through their eyes.

"What's that out there!? Are those Bletzvelt's coming towards us? What are they doing?" An observant Purgorite grunt yelled out in panic.

The second loaded prisoner transport was moving off as well, in a different direction from the first. This was something that I sensed rather than saw with my own eyes.

"Yes…attack…all of you!!" I called out, knowing that my friends were closing in hard and fast.

I opened my eyes fully, my chest heaving, my head pounding and my vision a little hazy, as the first snarling and slavering Beltzvelt seemed to fly out of the darkness and sink his fangs into a Purgorite throat. The wolf-like creature was followed by a whole pack of his friends. They attacked from all directions, without mercy. They knocked over and mauled Purgorite guards, they sank their teeth into the enemy horses' legs, scaring the beasts, which in turn spilt the riders from their seats. Within moments, there was chaos all around us. Whilst many Purgorites did fight back and slay a few Bletzvelts, they were soon swarmed and brought down. The Bletzvelts attacked with wicked efficiency and sharpened predator instincts. They sought out weak points in the most brutal fashion, before powering toward the next hapless Purgorite whilst their previous victim's blood had barely started spurting from an arterial wound.

Whilst the Purgorites had been distracted and kept occupied by the unexpected attackers, the five remaining free Halians amongst us began frantically sawing our ropes against some of the several Purgorite cleavers that had dropped from the hands of dead or dying Purgorites. Captain Stire was the first to cut through his bonds and immediately began helping his comrades, happy to leave the wolf creatures to their feasting and slaughter.

Within minutes, we were all unfettered and picking up discarded weapons. It seemed that other than having to cut down a handful of still-standing Purgorites, the battle was over. All around us lay a macabre sea of messy corpses, both of the two-legged and four-legged variety. We saw some movement and heard some pained groans from the severely wounded or dying, but had no time to go round finishing enemy troops off in the dark. Let those bastards suffer where they lie.

"The transports, where did they go?" Yelled 1Lt. Fester, who was one of the final five of us not currently in a cage.

"I think the first one went South, not sure about the second. I was watching all those eyes appearing from the darkness." Answered Darkwolf.

"Shall we track the vehicles?" asked Smoke, the fifth and final member of our new, much-reduced unit.

"How many troops were guarding each transport vehicle?" I asked my troops.

"At least six armoured riders with each transport vehicle, plus two drivers." Came the response from Darkwolf.

I thought about our options right then and there, surrounded by a sudden quiet following those several moments of intense sound, chaos and movement as the battle had raged between Bletzvelt and Purgorite. Even if we all pursued one of the vehicles, it would be a fight of five against eight, if we could even find the vehicle out there in the wasteland. Tracks would be hard to detect, given the mess around us and the absence of even the semi-light of North Utreshian daytime. I knew that to just ride out into the dark wastes hoping for the best was folly. There could be hordes of Purgorites out there waiting for us. We had been rescued from the clutches of our enemies, at least to some degree, several times by this point on our journey. First was the sea monster, next was the very timely sandstorm, next was Ravaise charging to our rescue, and most recently, the horde of furious Bletzvelts. I knew that our luck must be running out. It was not easy to leave troops behind, but they were already gone.

"We will not give chase. Take a good horse and follow me back to base." I ordered the four troops, struggling to meet their eyes.

I climbed up into the empty saddle of one of the horses that had not bolted in fear. The still body of our comrade Lane McAdams was lifted onto the back of Captain Stire's horse. As soon as we were all ahorse, we started back for base.

Once back at Romesh's compound, we dismounted from the horses and carried Captain McAdams's body to the infirmary room on the ground floor, where he could at least lie in peace. We wrapped him carefully in a cloth sheet. I felt that we should attend to yet another burial service, but knew that such a thing may have to wait with so many of our comrades missing. Instead, I went to find Romesh, as with only five of us left, the mission had basically come to pieces. Even a Commander sometimes needs advice and assistance.

Chapter 27

Daegon's Division

Romesh met me in his smaller meeting room on the first floor of the compound. It was a room roughly twelve feet square, with a fine circular table acting as a centrepiece for the room. A fine woven rug covered most of the otherwise bare stone floor, whilst maps and charts decorated the walls. Romesh took his seat in a high-backed wooden chair, facing me across the table. Also at the table were Captain Stire and one of Romesh's close agents. Ule' Trelleck was a cold-eyed, grim-looking man with braided hair and scars who had clearly seen and likely done some brutal things in his time.

"Thanks for meeting me at such short notice, Romesh. I know it is late and you were most likely in bed. As I'm sure you have been informed, only five of us made it back tonight. We lost one of our troops during the Purgorite attack, and the other nine were taken off in cages. We managed to carry out our mission, but with only five of us left, I'm not sure where to go next. Can the Cadre send any reinforcements? I know that you have methods of contacting them which I do not." I enquired of Romesh.

"It is highly unlikely that the Cadre will organise another expedition, another ten or so chosen Officers to be removed from their duties, equipped and sail out here. That all takes time, effort and coin that the Cadre would rather place elsewhere. No, the next step is up to us, in this very room. I was made a friend of Halia for a reason. I am here to assist." Responded Romesh in a reassuring tone.

"What do you advise as our next step?" I asked Romesh.

"You will need more soldiers, that is clear. It is just a question of where to source them from. Luckily, there are possibilities. Trelleck, maybe you should take it from here." Romesh said, turning toward his fearsome-looking colleague.

"We have close contact with several mercenary groups. Bands of fighters that can be hired for a certain task for a pre-arranged fee. They do not come cheap, believe me, but they are worth the money. Do not worry about the price, that can be worked out between Romesh's treasures and the Halian bank. There are several options to choose from, but personally, there is a certain team I would like to recommend. I know how effective they are and what they are capable of." Trelleck smiled grimly, his eyes seeming to shine.

"I know, because I used to be one of them. They are known as 'Daegon's Division'." Continued Trelleck.

Captain Stire and I were then given the rundown on this notoriously tough and lethal team. Daegon's Division were a brotherhood of some fifty in number, although this would obviously fluctuate as soldiers were killed and new soldiers recruited.

In terms of recruitment, Daegon's Division did not just accept random soldiers on the basis that they could fight and had endured the horrors of battle. The Division instead selected carefully from amongst members of a war-like and notoriously fearsome tribe who inhabited the harsh lands just north of the Kromos Mountains. This was a tribe where you either grew up tough or did not get to grow up at all. They were born hunters, fighters and killers. Boys would begin martial training at a young age and were usually lethal warriors by the mere age of sixteen, with numerous enemy kills to their name. Even the tribe's bodies were different; due to the quality of the air, elements in the regional water sources, the food they were fed early in life, the unforgiving atmosphere of the lands they grew up in and even their very genetics, the tribe was stronger, faster, more durable and more resilient than most of the known world. Any fear in them was burned out early. Pain was not something that bothered them.

Once a warrior from this tribe had been selected, they were then put through further gruelling tests and advanced training of all types.

This training was so tough that it filtered out the 'weaker' of the tribe, leaving only the strongest to rise to the ranks of Daegon's Division. The training could even prove fatal, as recruits could succumb to death by bodily wound, heat, cold, animal attack, falling from heights, drowning, being crushed or being buried alive, amongst other grizzly fates. Even once inside the brotherhood of Daegon, life continued to be brutal, comfortless, bloody and hard.

Daegon's Division could not just be recruited by any fat merchant offering handfuls of coin. The Division only hired their services to certain parties, such as Romesh's office.

There was a moment of pause as I weighed up what I had just heard.

"Right. So, say that I agree to employ Daegon's Division, how soon can the men arrive?" I asked the two agents.

"I can send an order to the Division's chief. We will have to agree on exactly what and where their mission is, and certain details like troop numbers, probable length of the task and of course what we offer in terms of fee, which can either be accepted or refused. We tend to aim for a high pay offer if we are trying to employ them. They know that people will pay just about anything for their services, which can be frustrating sometimes." Came the response from Romesh.

My issue right then was that I did not know the answer to many of the queries raised. Where was the mission, what was the mission and how long would it take? I did not know where my soldiers had been taken, or really what to do if and when we discovered their location.

"I would like to keep the idea of hiring this mercenary group very much on the table, but truly, Romesh, I do not presently know what I would enter on the order. We cannot hire mercenaries if we do not even know what their job is!" I said, my voice rising higher than it should have.

In truth, I was tired, angry and confused. I felt like my mission had failed. Plus, I had the extra weight of eleven Halian lives bearing down on my thoughts. How many of the men were even still alive as we sat there planning the next stage?

Captain Stire then spoke up for the first time since the basic introductions, choosing his words carefully.

"Romesh, thank you for all the help you are providing. It is most appreciated. The Commander and I should speak privately with the other three members of our team and work out exactly where to go next. We will get back to you tomorrow morning, if that's okay." Captain Stire proposed to Romesh, as if my frustration somehow negated my position as his senior officer.

I let his proposition go unchallenged though, as he spoke sensibly. There was further discussion to be had amongst the Halian contingent before we committed to involving a third party in what was supposed to be a clandestine operation. We all stood and made our farewells before Captain Stire and I left the meeting room first.

We found our remaining comrades sharing a drink in the Dining Hall. By this stage, it was around two of the clock in the morning. All three raised their eyes in expectation and became quiet as we walked in, as if to await whatever our update was.

"Gentlemen, we have a fair bit to discuss tomorrow, in private. It is very late now, and we have all had a rough time. I am struggling to think straight and cannot be the only one. I suggest we get some rest now and hold the discussion as soon as we have broken our fast together in the morning." I told the soldiers, even though it was already morning.

What followed was another restless night of dark and frightening dreams. The next always worse than the last. Always new fears to probe into and mental screws to turn. I had no choice though, none of us did. The nightmares were just something we were going to have to endure as part of the job. It should come as no surprise that I awoke sweaty, edgy and in low spirits.

After a subdued breaking of our fast, during which the five of us chewed away on bread, ham and oats that seemed to have no taste, we assembled at nine of the clock in our now familiar private meeting room. Without further delay, I began the meeting.

"Okay, listen. I have already been in touch with Romesh, and asked if he can do whatever is in his power to try and locate where our comrades are being detained, if they are even still alive. He has agents working within the Purgorite command structure, although Romesh can hardly stroll into enemy territory and casually ask for an update. This request for information will have to go via several agents in between. This will take time, which I know is very frustrating whilst we sit here talking. I can only advise patience, however. With only the five of us left to conduct this mission, I do not know what more we can do. The enemy knows that we are here, and no doubt has troops scouring the land for us right now. We are in no state to become involved in open battle out there. We have already destroyed the Communication Office and a primary bridge, which will have caused what I truly hope is significant disruption to Va'heash. That bridge was part of a major route for the movement of Purgorite troops and supplies. Now, the enemy will find travel much more difficult, as they will be forced to make a major detour through rough terrain which is nigh on impossible for wheeled vehicles. That was the only bridge for many miles in each direction, and our maps show the bridge crossed a vast gorge which stretches for mile after mile in each direction. But going forward, I fear that this mission is drawing to a close." Came my opening speech, before we were interrupted by a knock at the door.

Chapter 28

An Unexpected Appearance

One of Romesh's agents entered after I had given the invitation, before bowing smartly and speaking.

"Excuse me Commander Kane, but I bring an urgent message. There is a Halian Officer only one mile west of here, he has requested to speak to you at once. He is alone and can be found at Kho'Bore," Delivered the agent.

I was taken aback by this news. A Halian Officer all the way out here? Alone?

"Did the Officer give his name?" I asked the agent.

"Yes, Commander. The Officer introduced himself as Commander Vorgo when I spoke to him at Kho'Bore. He had been seen waving a green flag from the top of the building, a sign in North Utresh that a peaceful discussion is sought. Our guards spotted him through their eyeglass and several of us rode out to meet him." Responded the agent.

"I see. I do know the man, I had better go out and see what he wants. Thank you for the message." I told the agent, who once again bowed quickly and left the room, closing the door gently behind him.

"Commander Vorgo? What is he doing here? I know that he is senior in rank to me, but…that man is a snake. If I may speak amongst brothers." Opined Captain Stire.

"Off the record, I agree with you. But still, I should go and see what he wants. 1Lt. Fester, will you accompany me?" I asked young Simon.

"We will all go, Commander Kane, if that is okay. If this turns out to be trouble, all the better to have four swords at your side as supposed to only one." Captain Stire spoke up.

Darkwolf, 1Lt. Fester and Smoke all nodded in agreement at the captain's proposal. I sighed and shrugged. It seems that we were all riding out as one, win, lose or draw.

It was only a matter of minutes later that the five of us rode out west, fully armoured and armed, toward the then derelict and abandoned outpost of Kho'Bore. I will not deny that I felt fear twist in my guts. My instincts were screaming at me to turn back, yet I kept on riding. As we got closer, I saw a figure standing alone atop the highest point of Kho'Bore. The figure was indeed dressed in Halian armour, as if not fearing if he was seen by enemy eyes. I found myself taking my horse from a gallop to a canter, to a gentle walk. The other four riders noticed that I had dropped back and decreased the speed of their horses as well.

"What is it, Commander?" Asked Captain Stire, his voice anxious.

By now, we had all brought our horses to a halt.

"We will go no further. I do not like any of this. We are returning to the compound right now." I told the men, my voice deadly serious and commanding.

Whoever was lying in wait for us saw that we had brought our horses to a standstill and figured that we had smelled the ruse. They knew what we were thinking. They acted.

"Commander, look, bands of riders!" Simon yelled in horror, pointing North to bring focus to a group of armed riders emerging at speed from below the crest of a slope.

"They are south of us, too, more of them!" This time from Smoke, yelling and pointing.

The snake Vorgo had never been alone. This had indeed been a trap. One that we had responded to far too late. I knew then, in that moment, that we should have instructed Vorgo to meet us inside the relative safety of the compound. Too late for regrets, though. The two groups of riders were approaching at speed, as if to join forces east of us and block our route back to Romesh's compound. In a heat-of-the-moment decision, I chose to continue riding west, well clear of our original destination and away from the horsemen. Maybe we could lose them in the valley if we rode hard and fast enough.

"Ride west, keep riding and don't stop. May Halia herself give you speed!" I yelled at my riders.

So, the five of us dug our spurs deep into our horses' flanks and began barreling west, away from the two groups of enemy horsemen at our backs…and into another group of horsemen at our front! I knew then that escape was not on the table. The group in front of us was spread in a formation ten wide and two deep. Twenty mounted warriors against our meagre five. The beast had us.

Still, I rode hard to our left, to try and outmanoeuvre the approaching cavalry. It was a good effort, but the enemy cavalry merely steered their reins to close in on us. Even if we had somehow managed to fight past the cavalry in front of us, the riders to our rear were right on our heels and would have hamstrung us from the rear. There was no escape this time.

I heard the sound of arrows, or bolts - for I could not tell which in my state of panic and adrenaline rush - whizz through the air. None of my men were armed with such projectile weapons, so I deduced that these were weapons being loosed by the enemy. As my horse buckled and staggered beneath me, fast losing speed, I looked down and saw three or four long shafts of wood protruding unnaturally from his side. I turned around in my saddle to see that the other four horses were also adorned with lengths of flying wood. They were also hampered and struggling to do much more than writhe in agony and make an awful din of neighing and screaming. It was then that I felt myself fall from my saddle to strike the ground painfully on my right shoulder. Luckily, I did not feel or hear anything break. That was about as far as my luck extended though.

I looked up to see the Purgorite horsemen staring down at their captured prey with looks of malevolent glee distorting their ugly faces. Their heads all turned, though toward something happening just behind me. They suddenly became silent, and their grim smiles softened a little, as if even they were afraid of what approached me. I heard not only heavy footsteps but also the thing's animalistic, low growling. I took a deep breath and turned my head to witness the approaching monster. I almost felt my bowels loosen and my heart stop as I saw what came toward me.

I knew, without being told, that I was looking at Va'heashes new champion. I was staring with wide eyes and a dry mouth at Brutuck's even more fearsome and infamous replacement. The champion was not quite as tall or wide as Brutuck but appeared every bit as horrific. The thing seemed to radiate menace from every pore of its body. It towered over me, wearing heavy, fearsome-looking armour that I doubt even a Greatsword could penetrate. Its eyes were deep pools of black hatred and its mouth was a gaping hole of jagged teeth. Its helmet boasted a set of mean-looking horns, although the horns could have sprouted directly from the monster's head. I immediately had the sense that this new champion was smarter, more capable and somehow even more evil than Brutuck. The thing then spoke, its awful voice seeming to come from all around us.

"So, you're the whelp that managed to kill Brutuck? I am almost impressed. You honestly look like you're about to shit yourself down there." Growled the dark champion, to the amusement of his hunting pack.

In truth, the dark champion was right. I was scared witless in that horrific moment. The larger part of me wanted to curl up and just die, to melt away in fear and come apart. But a deep part of me surfaced, and I remembered that I was Marcus Kane, a Halian Commander and leader of some of the toughest and bravest troops in the world. I would not be intimidated by this thing that was basically still a huge errand dog.

I forced myself to look the towering monster in the eyes, right into those dark and soulless chasms. I took a deep breath and found my voice.

"We killed that piece of shit Brutuck and threw you people out of Halia. I'm not afraid of you." I stated through gritted teeth, urging my heart to believe in the words of my mouth.

The beast looked untroubled and just kept staring down at me.

"Good for you. You're all going to go to sleep for a while. You'll wake up somewhere you really won't like, and then, you're going to learn what fear is." The dark thing leered from up high.

The last thing I remembered was a bottle of some liquid being dashed across the ground, releasing a strange green smoke which made me feel very suddenly sleepy and helpless.

I then fell into what felt like an endless cycle of delirium, nightmares and hallucinations. I could not tell vision from reality, or fiction from truth. I knew vaguely that I was tied up and being transported in some manner of cage, but that was about as far as my awareness went. I would wake up for a few moments, look about me through bleary eyes, see that I was surrounded by mounted troops, before dropping back into my terrible state. I saw things I cannot even begin to put into words, nor want to. It was like I was being exposed to a relentless montage of every obscene, shocking, repulsive and just plain wrong thing my deepest and darkest mind could conjure up. I was vaguely aware that I was sweating, thrashing and moaning during my fits of terror. Of course, the Purgorites could see all of this. They got to laugh at and mock the apparently mighty Halian, who had helped kill their champion Brutuck, as he sweated and moaned like a lunatic in his cage.

Chapter 29

Captured by the Enemy

Wearing only my undergarments, I felt myself dragged from the cage by large hands, before being thrown roughly to a cold stone surface. I heard voices around me, speaking in a strange tongue. The voices sounded cold, brutal, mocking, dangerous, even and full of dark hate.

Gradually, as the effects of the chemicals wore off, I began to feel myself regain my senses. The dullness and confusion in my head started to fade. My vision and thoughts became clearer. I was offered water by someone; I will never know who, as I did not even look up at the face. I grabbed the cup of water to slake my thirst, downing all of it. The water was cold and felt cool and refreshing, even though I coughed a little due to trying to down it so fast.

When I felt ready, I sat up and began to take in my surroundings, bit by bit and at my reduced speed. I was alone in a stone cell, maybe eight feet square. The cell was basic and included only a wooden cot and a small bowl, which I assumed was for bodily waste. I was sitting with my back against the rear wall, facing a strong-looking wooden door with a small opening. I felt myself taken back to that awful time in Carnagon Castle, when I had been knocked out and taken into Purgorite custody, which was EXACTLY what had happened again. Sadly, there was no hole in the ground for me to escape from. I was trapped this time, for good.

It was not long before I heard the sound of several sets of footsteps progressing down the corridor, toward my cell. Instinctively, I felt my body crouch even further down, as if to hide within itself and try and appear invisible. I knew that whatever came through that cell door would not be anything pleasant and did not wish me good fortune. Thankfully, I managed to resist this urge and instead forced myself to my feet. It was a painful and draining act, and I almost passed out in the physical effort of doing so, but I would not greet my fate seated and helpless. I kept my eyes on the door, forcing myself not to look away.

When I saw the face that appeared at the door, I was for a moment confused, until elements of the past started creeping back into the front of my mind. For the stern face of Commander Vorgo looked at me through the opening. Now I remembered, the man was a snake who had betrayed us!

Vorgo unlocked the strong door before opening it wide and stepping within. He continued to look at me, still not speaking or showing any emotion in his set features. He then stepped to one side, as if to give room for someone more important. I felt my heart momentarily stop, as I knew exactly what was about to make its hideous appearance. The demon's face looked different to what it had looked like the last time I had seen it over a year previously during that unforgettable night of chaos. It was like another layer of human disguise had been peeled away, showing me something slightly closer to what Va'heash actually was.

"Marcus. Been sleeping well lately?" Va'heash said mockingly, a cruel grin spreading across its terrible face.

I felt tongue-tied and did not offer any verbal response. I only continued to stand and stare mutely, in shock. At least it was better than sitting in shock, or even cowering in shock like a whipped cur.

"Not in a talking mood, I see. As you will. I will be back to see you later, I have some…entertainment…planned, and you will be taking centre stage. I will explain more later on, don't worry. For now, though, your comrade Commander Vorgo will update you a little as to your predicament." Va'heash told me.

"Vorgo is no comrade of mine. He is another of your pets, an utter disgrace." I said, finally finding my voice.

Va'heash just laughed mockingly at this, a dark light dancing in its inhuman, deep-set eyes.

"Yes, you are probably right on that count. But Vorgo and I have something of an arrangement. He is useful to me at present." Va'heash confirmed, before turning and leaving the room.

I could not help but notice that the air seemed lighter and warmer as soon as Va'heash left the cell. It was truly as if the creature was surrounded by a constant air of dark energy and menace.

Two large armed brutes stepped into the cell and stood quietly, as if deterring me from trying to rip Vorgo's treacherous head off. In truth, I would not have dared to do such a thing. Vorgo was not only armoured and well-armed with naked steel near his hand, but he was also a very capable fighter. Whilst I knew little of the Officer personally, a man did not reach the rank of Commander in Halia without serious battlefield experience and skill. His prowess with a sword had actually been backed up by Major Heven, who had fought beside Vorgo several times and could attest to how deadly he was. I was barely clothed, unarmed and still a little groggy. If I wanted revenge, I would have to bide my time and wait for the right moment, which was not then.

"Commander Kane, believe me, I take no joy in doing what I am doing now. I know you will think of me as a traitor for siding with Va'heash. Maybe I am, call me what you will. This may sound odd, but I am only thinking about Halia's future, her very survival. Va'heash will conquer Halia whether you or I like it, or not. I would rather Halia is not reduced to ash in order for that to happen. This takeover can go ahead with minimal bloodshed and needless slaughter. Sometimes, when a strong enemy is at your door, you do not try and keep him out fruitlessly, you open the door and ask him what he wants. This may sound insane, but if your "enemy" is halfway reasonable, it's incredible what can be worked out. I want to be on the winning side of any war that is to happen. Call me selfish and foolish, I call myself practical." Vorgo explained, as if trying to appear like he had all the answers.

"Traitor. Insane. Selfish. Foolish. I have used none of these terms, Vorgo. YOU uttered those words, as you already know what you are. Real Halians do not make deals with monsters and foreign invaders. I do not know what you are now, Vorgo. I will not call you 'Commander' as those days are over. Do not try and justify your treason to me." I spat at Vorgo, my face red with my newfound anger.

Vorgo merely looked at me in silence for several long seconds, as if to formulate a clever and witty response. I could see his cogs turning, but to no avail. Instead, he gritted his teeth as his facial expression switched quickly to one of rage. He swung his right fist into my face without saying another word, knocking my head back and stunning me. I dropped back to the ground, holding my hand up to feel the bloody damage. The bastard had burst my lip open and made my nose bleed. I also felt a dislodged tooth and my head began feeling much like it had during my drug-induced haze. Still, despite the pain, I laughed up at the traitor. Vorgo knew that I was right, so his only response was anger and violence.

"Leave this idiot to stew with his foolish thoughts for a while, let Va'heash have him," Vorgo yelled to the guards as he stormed out of the cell.

Ironically, I could have said exactly the same thing about him.

It was maybe two hours later, after I had been fed a meal of meat, bread, cheese and strong ale, that the sour face of a guard appeared at the opening of my cell door. The brute unlocked the cell door before throwing a pile of clothing and armour into the centre of the cell.

"Get dressed now. I'll be back in a few minutes to fetch you." Barked the brute, before his footfalls receded away into nothingness.

I had been fed, watered and had now just been provided with what looked to be fairly good quality armour. It was not the chainmail or plate that I would have worn back in Halia. Instead, it was a bizarre mismatch; a heavy metal helmet which seemed to cover most of the skull, two armoured and spiked gauntlets, a single shoulder guard of tough leather, which seemed to be attached to a wide leather belt.

Strips of reinforced leather hung from this belt down to my knees. As for my lower body, there was a pair of knee-high leather boots complete with metal shin guards and knee plates. Whilst this armour was sturdy enough, it only protected part of the body and offered plenty of exposed skin. It was armour unlike any I had seen before.

I knew that I would be expected to fight, and soon. It was just a question of who, how, and where. The 'why' I had already been told. It was for entertainment, just not entertainment for me.

When the Purgorite guard dutifully came back after the given few minutes, I was already fully dressed and as ready as I could be. The door was unlocked once again and opened, and without further ado, I followed the guard out. As I walked down the corridor, I felt like a warrior again. I was no longer hiding behind the guise of a Kazbarian mercenary any longer. If I was to fight and die, it would be as a Halian. I kept my chin up and my shoulders back. I took deep breaths and tried to steady my pounding heart. Most importantly, I remembered who I was. I passed several cells as I walked the corridor, but did not stop and look through any of the openings. I knew that I was still being watched. I would have to wait a little longer to see what had become of my comrades, who I was pretty sure were now all either detained or dead. None had escaped as far as I knew.

The guard guided me into a large windowless stone chamber. As I walked in, the first set of eyes I met were that of 1Lt. Fester. He was dressed similar to me, in bizarre armour which covered only part of his body. He did wear a full chest plate though, so at least most of his internal organs were somewhat protected should any offensive weapon be hurled his way.

"Commander Kane," Young Simon said, offering me a curt nod.

"Quiet!!" Snapped one of the several armed Purgorites standing about the room like statues. I followed their request and merely nodded back at Simon.

As I took a seat on one of the wooden benches, I looked around the room to scan for any other familiar faces. I was gladdened to see

Captain Stire, looking better than I felt. In addition, the grim faces of Darkwolf, Wraithven, Captain D'Arten and 1Lt. Schmidt could be made out in the glow of the burning torches fixed around the room. So, at least seven of the team were still alive. All the soldiers were clad in the same manner of combat armour. As I sat there composing myself and just wanting to get the wait over, our host arrived.

"Gentlemen, welcome to my home. Welcome to Balostroma. I know that you are here against your will, but what do you expect? You sneak into my country and try and cause me all manner of trouble. Burning things here, blowing things up there, killing my troops all the while. And don't think I didn't hear about that very expensive warship I lost. You, Marcus Kane, are truly a thorn in my side. Not only did you escape from me at Carnagon, which was humiliating, but you brought down my champion and played a large part in ruining my plans of conquering Halia." Was the introduction from Va'heash.

"Why weren't you there at the final battle?" I ventured to ask the demon, knowing that it could have my tongue removed for even speaking without being invited to do so.

Va'heash merely paused and looked at me oddly, as if he was shocked by my boldness and defiance. The Demon's facial composure almost indicated what it was thinking, most likely 'How dare this human filth ask ME such an audacious question?!'

"I was wrong. I admit it. I put too much faith in my generals, and especially in Brutuck. I left Halia to travel back as I had other business to attend to. I underestimated the resolve of your country, a mistake I will not repeat. Believe me. Brutuck was big, strong and a brute in battle, but he had very little rolling around in that big dumb skull of his. He was never more than my attack dog. My new champion though, he is of a different sort. He is cunning, clever in all the right ways and the best tactician I have ever had work for me. You may well be meeting him again later; he will show you what he is capable of. He will show you what he can do and the pain he can inflict. I will enjoy watching him do it, although for you it will be most horrible.

Marcus, do you know why I have not just had you all tortured and executed brutally?" Asked the demon, its eyes shining.

I shook my head and shrugged, as if not caring why this creature made the choices it did.

"Because you are a warrior. You are all warriors." Va'heash said in an almost complimentary tone, as he looked about the chamber at the rest of my comrades.

"You have proven yourself in battle time and again, and several of my scouts and troops who managed to escape have spoken of your prowess in combat. I am not without a small degree of mercy, so I have decided that you have at least earned a chance to die a warrior's death. But die you shall, believe me!" Spoke the sinister being, its voice becoming more menacing still on that final harrowing sentence.

"One last question, my Lord. If I may be so bold," I asked the Demon, using an appellation it did not deserve, even in its own wretched home.

"One question, yes. Speak it!" Allowed the Va'heash thing.

"Where are the rest of my men. I only see seven of us sitting here?" I enquired boldly.

"Oh, I will not lie. Not when you are all so close to death. The two named Creeper and Parcher were killed whilst foolishly trying to escape. I cannot blame them. They saw an opening and took it. Sadly, for them, the opening was not wide enough. I fed their bodies to my hounds, as they do like the taste of fresh meat. The others are still alive and being held around my palace." The demon responded.

I was about to try my luck with a further question, but managed to stay quiet. I had, after all, only been allowed one question. I was in no position to haggle and barter. We were prisoners who would soon become fighters.

"Hopefully, I will not be seeing any of you again. I would ask that you at least stay standing for a while and make this show worth our while. There is quite an audience watching!"

With those final words, the demon turned on its heels and disappeared into the darkened corridor. I mean that quite literally, Va'heash just seemed to vanish into the darkness like a ghost. I could not even hear footsteps or movement.

My attention was refocused by the rough shouting of one of the Purgorite brutes.

"Right, you vermin. Grab some weapons from the table and head up those stairs to the metal gate. Right now!!" Yelled the brute.

It was time to fight again. I took a deep breath and smiled broadly.

Chapter 30

Few Against Many

There was actually an impressive range of weaponry on display for us to choose from. There were long spears, heavy battle axes that looked like they could chop a man in two, shields of varying sizes and shapes, maces, long daggers, longswords, gigantic two-handed swords that looked like only a giant could wield them and grizzly-looking weapons that I didn't even recognise. Whilst I had fought with a spear before, both on horseback and on foot, I was most adept and fluent with the combination of sword and shield. The shield was of course not just for blocking but was a lethal weapon in its own right. A good smash into an enemy windpipe or skull would put them down fast! I thus went for a strong-looking longsword and a square wooden shield reinforced with animal skin and strips of metal. Looking about me, I saw that whilst the army Officers had also gone with a sword and shield combo, the two scouts had selected the much longer spears. *'Each to his own'* I thought to myself, I was not going to decide how each man would meet their fate.

I grew increasingly aware of the growing roar of the crowd, which was sounding from the end of the tunnel we were about to walk. The audience was hungry for sport, for a spectacle, for raw combat, for the spilling of blood. It was time to give it to them.

"Right, up to that gate and wait for it to open. Now!" yelled one of the brutes.

I led my soldiers up to the gate, all of us armed and as ready as we could be. The roar of the crowd was so loud now, the ground itself seemed to vibrate with their combined screams and shouts. Through the gaps in the gate, I could see that the fighting arena we were about to enter was large. It looked to be circular and maybe 100 feet in diameter. The ground was of dirt and sand and littered with old yellow bones and pools of drying blood. The bones were of varying sizes, some so large that they must have belonged to some gigantic beast killed as part of the dark entertainment Va'heash clearly liked to put on for his guests. I could smell the stench of old death from so close. Then, with a grinding sound, the sturdy metal gates slowly began to rise. It was time.

At a jog, we entered the arena that I was sure was going to be the last place we would ever see. I stopped at what I believe to be the dead centre of the arena, as I figured that wherever our opponents spawned from, being in the centre as a group was the 'best' place to stand. The opponents could come from several of the gated openings around the arena walls, from one gate or all of them at the same time. I swivelled my head around and took in the roaring crowd around me, many now standing and waving their arms. I was not even sure if they were cheering for us directly or merely for us to be killed. Maybe they just wanted death, whether Halian or otherwise. I then regarded my soldiers around me, before offering some words of encouragement, for what they were worth.

"Right, let's give these fuckers a good fight. Fight back-to-back and show them what Halians are made of. If it comes to it....I'll see you all on the other side, my brothers." I said, grateful for all they had done so far. For their bravery and courage.

"It's been quite an adventure, Commander Kane. I am still glad I came. Better than sitting around polishing armour." Said young Simon stoically, his head nodding.

The other troops all murmured in agreement. Maybe this was where we were meant to be. We had done what we could. We had done our duty as Halian Officers, as warriors, as patriots. Our moment together was broken by a harsh roar coming from up high.

"All rise for the Lord Va'heash." Yelled a Purgorite official from the large box, which we now looked toward.

The animated and noisy audience became suddenly very quiet and stood smartly with their heads bowed as the demon led a procession of his underlings towards his grand seat in the high box which overlooked the arena. We did not bow; instead, we kept our gaze on the demon as he seemed to glide toward his destination, wearing his long, fine robes. Once Va'heash had taken his place, he began speaking in a voice that seemed to reach every corner, nook and cranny of the large space. It seemed to come from everywhere at once. There was no hiding from it.

"My people, welcome to my home of Balostroma. As is my due, I have organised some true entertainment tonight. Cast your eyes down into the pit below you. There you see a group of Halian invaders. They smuggled themselves into our lands under the guise of foreign mercenaries, then promptly indulged in terrorist activities and flagrantly murdered our brothers, seemingly for sport." Came Va'heashes' opening.

The demonic Lord let the crowd vent their rage and anger at the purported crimes of the villainous wretches standing below them. Then, at a sharp hand signal from Va'heash, the booing and hissing seemed to stop dead. It was clear that Va'heash had full control of his audience. I had a dark feeling that if Va'heash ordered the audience to slit their own throats, that many would do so blindly and without a further thought.

"I was tempted to merely execute them in a slow, painful way, like I usually do. But these particular invaders have proven that they fight like the hounds of Lenfer. So, they will fight again, right now in front of you. They will fight until they drop! For die they shall! LET THE GAMES BEGIN!!" yelled the demon, it's eyes glowing red and it's voice a banshee-like shriek as it longed for the joy of spilt blood and death.

'Okay you fucker, if you want blood and death, I'll give it you!' I thought to myself as my hand tightened about my longsword and I held my shield high.

It was then that not one, not two, but three of the gates around the sides of the arena slid open. We Halians formed a tight unit with our backs together and our blades and spears facing outwards. For a brief moment, all we saw were three gaping black holes. We all held our breath, bracing ourselves for whatever may emerge to meet us. Then, the first enemies dashed out into the arena and came straight for us.

As I looked around rapidly, I saw that each of the three openings seemed to spawn five or six lightly armoured fighters. They were not as big or tough-looking as some of the larger Purgorite brutes and wore armour similar to ours. Probably rank and file pit slaves sent as a warm-up to get us ready, I recall thinking.

"Stay together in the centre. Don't break rank and get separated!" I ordered the soldiers, still their Commander, even in that perilous situation.

Darkwolf took the first unlucky enemy with an expertly aimed stab through the chest, which powered right through his torso and out through his back. Darkwolf immediately yanked back his messy spear, ready for the next victim. I blocked a wild swing from a hand axe using my shield, before hacking off the combatant's head with a strong swing of my longsword. I quickly checked to my right to see D'Arten actually slice up two enemies almost at once. He was slicing from left to right, both high and low, with vicious speed and precision. Soon, both enemies were down and out. I shield barged an enemy from the side whilst he was engaged with Simon Fester, knocking him brutally to the ground, where Simon quickly finished him off by slicing his exposed lower neck wide open and painting the dirt with his blood.

Many of the first wave of enemies were already down, but we were still outnumbered and could not take a breath yet. I heard Simon yell in pain as an enemy spear found his still unhealed torso wound and ripped it back open. Simon managed to slice down into the attacker's right arm, severing his hand from the rest of his body, as part of a knee-jerk reflex response. I knew I had to check on my young comrade, but could hardly spare the time. I blocked a heavy overhand strike from a frantic and strong slave wielding a two-handed sword. The blow was severe and almost drove me to my knees, but I recovered in time and struck out low at my opponent, driving the point of my sword into his lightly armoured right knee. His knee buckled painfully, and he fell back screaming. I immediately stepped forward and smashed my wooden shield rim down into his still screaming face until his screaming stopped.

D'Arten finished off the last opponent with a brutal downward stroke that cleaved the poor slave from skull to groin, spilling his entrails onto the dirt. We stood there panting, temporarily relieved to still be able to pant, to be able to breathe. I then checked poor Simon's wound and almost wished I hadn't. The wound was deep and bleeding seriously. That breastplate clearly wasn't of the best quality. Simon was already pale in the face and sweating. Yet, he gritted his teeth and kept his steel.

"Don't worry….Commander Kane… it's…not t-t-t-t-that bad." Simon stammered out, his face straining to keep composure and hide the pain.

"So, that was the first round over. Now our little band are warmed up, for something a little tougher. But we cannot let these seventeen useless corpses litter the ground, can we? There will be a minor pause as the carcasses are removed, so that the fighters can move freely." Va'heash spoke, almost sounding like he was doing us a favour.

"Is anyone else hurt?" I asked the group of Halian warriors around me.

"My right hand is as good as useless, I'm afraid, Commander," Wraithven informed me, sounding guilty, as if he should have known better than to let a weapon touch him.

The study scout held up a bloody and mangled-looking hand, which had evidently taken a nasty pounding. I could only agree that he would not be wielding a weapon with that hand anytime soon.

"Well, fight with your left as best you can. Best of luck, Wraithven." I said to the scout, who turned out to be the last words I would ever speak to him.

We stood regaining our composure and preparing for the next battle as the dead bodies were carried out by more of Va'heashes' never-ending army of slaves and dogs' bodies. Simon still stayed on his feet despite his pain, as to sit would be to act like it was already over. I knew that if he sat, he might never stand again. He knew it too.

All too soon, the mess of dead bodies and severed body parts had been cleared away and the feverish din of the crowd was picking up again. Then, a loud clarion sounded. The gates opened once again, and more enemies began pouring into the arena. Time for round two.

This time, the enemies were the larger Purgorite brutes clad in tougher armour. From our own experience, they were several levels tougher than the pit slaves we had just cut through. Not only that, but the numbers were still very much against us. It was seven of us, one wounded grievously and one with only one useful hand, against a good fifteen brutes. Still, we kept our backs together and formed a circle of steel.

The combat began with me parrying a sword blow from a snarling Purgorite wearing a half-helm, before ramming the top rim of my shield up into his jaw, rocking his head back on his shoulders. I took advantage of my enemy's dazed state to drive the sword straight through his face and skull, killing him almost instantly. As soon as I pulled the gory sword back, I had to immediately block another attack from the right. Once again, I responded with my shield, this time swinging it in hard from my left into the brute's neck. I heard the sound of a horrible snap, as the brute swam to the hard ground. I could hear the clashing of steel, the grunts of pain, of effort, of rage behind me, but could not stop to check on our progress.

It was then that Simon gallantly saved my life, at the cost of his own. Whilst I was fending off the fast strikes of one brute directly in front of me with both sword and shield, the brute's comrade moved in fast from the side, trying to skewer me with a snake-like dagger strike. Simon saw this side attack against his commander and moved in low to deflect the blade, which would have plunged deep into my exposed mid-section had it found its target. But in doing so, Simon left himself exposed on his right side, which was where the fatal attack came from. It was a fast and ruthless overhead strike from a battle-axe which went straight through Simon's upper body armour and deep into his flesh and blood. Poor Simon immediately went to ground, his eyes wide in shock and his hands already clutching fruitlessly at the gaping wound. I roared in rage and hatred, using both my hands to swing my longsword into the killer's wretched head with such beast-like energy that I not only cleaved his skull in two, but sent his body flying sideways. Given that there were no longer any enemies in front of me, I turned to see how my comrades had fared. I saw that fighting with his left hand had not gone well for Wraithven, as he was bent double and holding his mangled right hand to a bleeding leg wound whilst desperately trying to fend off two brutes with a spear. Wraithven, using a final burst of strength, drove his spear directly into the chest of one of the brutes. That was sadly the scout's final kill, though, as the other Purgorite merely cut him down with a powerful diagonal slash which Wraithven could have done nothing to prevent in the moment. I ran to Captain D'Arten's side to help him fend off three brutes who were driving the captain back with strong and hammering blows from swords and axes. D'Arten was once again giving a good account of himself, his sword and shield moving fast and being where they needed to be. His footwork was amazing as he danced, dodged, parried and snaked his way around his multiple opponents. I quickly took the left arm off a brute at his burly shoulder, leaving only a spurting stump. D'Arten then ended the life of another opponent via an expert horizontal neck slash. We both took the last of the three brutes together, moving apart and hacking the brute down from each side, where he would struggle to fend us off at the same time.

Darkwolf was still standing strong and working well with his spear. I saw him send the weapon slicing through the air straight into a brute's muscular upper chest. The lead scout then seemed to fly through the air like a pouncing cat, before grabbing the spear handle and driving it deeper in, causing the Purgorite to yell some impressive death screams. Captain Stire was winning a duel against an already wounded Purgorite, chopping and slicing his sword like a maniac. I then spotted 1Lt. Schmidt lying still on the ground with his skull caved in. He had been wearing a helmet, but like Simon's breastplate, it had failed to offer much protection when it was most needed. Another good Halian soldier was gone from our ranks.

Now down to four of us still standing strong; Captain Stire, Captain D'Arten, Darkwolf and I. Poor Simon, rest his soul, was already gone and could not be helped. I tried to turn my sadness at his death into rage, a rage I would turn against those who had killed him. The last of the second wave had been hacked down, or so it seemed. We allowed ourselves a quick breath as we foolishly thought that the round was over. Of course, the demon was not going to let us off so easily.

"This looks way too easy. Not even half of the Halian fighters are dead yet. Send in the rest!" Yelled the demon from his position of power, looking down at us with malicious glee.

"The rest?" asked D'Arten frantically, looking at each of us in desperation.

I did not even need to know how many enemies we would be against; this was the end. The four of us could not stand against wave after wave of fighters. They would just keep coming until we were felled. There was no escape and no chance of victory. Va'heash was never going to allow it. Still, I kept my head high and held my weapons ready as the enemies started to pour from the arena gates. My three remaining comrades did much the same, ready to give their last. I lost count of the enemy number; there were dozens already in the arena and more following behind. An insurmountable number.

"Commander Kane, Commander Kane!" I looked up to where the sound had come from, but at first, I did not see the caller.

Then, I saw him. My old friend and comrade Major Ralph De'Beresford was standing at the edge of the arena seating, looking down at me over the stone barrier. He was injured and bloodied, and I knew that he had fought his way to us through Lord only knows what.

"Please, call me Marcus," I yelled to the sturdy warrior, despite the fact that the Purgorite enemy were closing in fast.

"Marcus, I believe this belongs to you." Roared the Major.

Then, with what remained of his strength, the Major hurled something long and heavy into the arena. At first, I saw only a large piece of metal flying through the air. Then, I saw that it was not just a piece of wood and steel, it was not just a weapon, it was a symbol. I found myself racing across the blood-soaked arena ground to intercept the flying weapon. As soon as my hand closed on the familiar grip of Mordak's Might, everything seemed to change.

I was no longer afraid. I no longer feared death or even felt in danger. I immediately felt the power of the weapon flow through me. I felt myself on fire, although it was not painful. I felt rather than heard the voices of departed Halian warriors whispering to each other from the afterlife.

"Is that Marcus Kane?"

"He's got his hammer back!"

"He's ready, it's time!"

"We are with you Marcus!"

Then, the voices were speaking directly to me. They were close. They were louder.

"Marcus, my brother. I like what you've done with my hammer. You do us proud!" From my fallen comrade, Mordak.

Then, as one deafening voice of fury, the combined shout of ten thousand dead Halian warriors roared at me across the ages, across the lives, across the worlds.

"Yes Marcus… it's time… let's FUCKING GO!!"

Later on, after reflection, I would come to understand that my link to Mordak's Might was not magic. Instead, the hammer was somehow my link to Halia, to her people, her strength, her spirit, even her very soul. It was my belief and my faith that could direct Halia's immense power THROUGH the weapon and make it so much more than wood and steel.

And so I went. Or should I say WE went.

I felt the hammer almost as another limb in that arena. We were united as one. The hammer screamed for enemy blood, and I was going to ensure that it was given. I started swinging the hammer in large sweeping arcs at the approaching horde of enemies, not even caring about numbers. I started swinging, and did not, could not stop. The furious lump of flying steel cleaved through enemy after enemy at frightening speed. Dark blood was spraying through the air in every direction as enemy body after enemy body was mauled, smashed, torn, broken, mangled or just plain obliterated. I vaguely knew that I was walking over a gory carpet of enemy corpses to reach the still living enemies. The enemies attempted to block Mordak's Might with their feeble weapons, but the mighty hammer merely broke through whatever resistance they offered and sent them screaming from their mortal lives. The force of the hammer alone was incredible; even enemies a clear two feet from the swinging beast were knocked messily to the ground from the lethal shockwave. I felt like an unstoppable hurricane of death in that arena as Halia's enemies were laid low.

Meanwhile, my comrades had not been standing idly. Whilst I had been tearing into the main pack of the enemies and keeping the heat on me, they had all been taking advantage of the chaos I was causing and picking off stragglers and smaller groups.

Eventually, I found that I was swinging at nothing but thin air. Purgorite bodies and barely recognisable body parts covered almost the entire floor of the arena. Some of the poor bastards had hit the ground many metres from where they had been struck, such was the ungodly force behind my swings. Others had been splattered against the walls of the arena. I looked down and then noticed that I was plastered in foul, dark blood. Mordaks Might seemed to be sizzling and smoking, as if needing a rest after all that effort. I let Mordak's Might hang loose at my side, coming back to myself a little. That had been one wild ride of a battle.

As the sound of the crowd started coming back to my ears, I looked up to see their response, to see what they had made of the bloody chaos I had just unleashed. I took some strange pride that many of the spectators nearest the edge of the area were standing and cheering at our efforts, despite us being the enemy. However, there was another movement in the audience seating behind the cheering crowd, as agitated Purgorite guards paced to and fro, exchanged hurried words and angry looks. I looked again to see if the Major was there, but of course, my friend was gone. I only hoped that he had managed to once again escape the guards, and I would be seeing him soon.

"Commander Kane, these bastards are cheering for us now! You must have slaughtered dozens! Did you see what happened to De'Beresford?" I heard Captain Stire say from behind me, his voice grim.

I turned then and saw Stire, a little wounded but still whole and standing. I allowed my eyes to drop and see Simon's still body lying bloodied on the ground. It was not rage I felt in that moment, so much as guilt and devastation. I had recruited the promising young Officer and brought him over here on a mission he wasn't ready for. My protégé was dead, and I had no one to blame but myself. Through my wave of pain, I dimly noticed that alongside Stire, D'Arten and Darkwolf still stood, all of us slathered in enemy blood.

My focus was immediately riveted back to the present moment as the sound of the demon's voice hit my ears.

"Quite a performance. I did tell you that these Halians can fight. Now, enough of the rank-and-file grunts. Time for a REAL opponent. MAL'VADAR!!" Screamed Va'heash, so loud that the whole arena shook, and I felt my head spin for a moment.

Chapter 31

Against the New Champion

Even though I had not heard that name before, it could only be the towering creature I had seen earlier after being tricked into meeting with the snake Vorgo. Once again, I hefted closed my hands tight around Mordak's Might and prepared to intercept the next of Va'heashes' pets. My three comrades closed in around me, their swords at the ready. We did not know from which of the gated openings Mal'vadar would emerge, so we had to keep turning our heads and scanning all possible points of entrance.

When Mal'vadar arrived, he did so with terrifying speed. He did not so much as run into the arena as *materialise* in the arena with a swish of displaced air. He appeared so fast that my first solid swing of my hammer missed him by a good foot. Captain D'Arten directed a flashing sword strike at the champion's head, but D'Arten's sword was simply deflected with a huge armoured fist, as if the champion was doing no more than batting away a pestering fly. Darkwolf darted in and launched his spear point at the dark champion's right knee. Whilst this expert move would have incapacitated any standard foe, Mal'vadar saw the move early and deftly shifted to one side before stamping down hard and snapping the wooden spear like it was a twig.

Whilst the dark champion was engaged in his spear snapping stamp, D'Arten saw an opening and aimed high at his opponent's neck. Whatever D'Arten was visualising in his head sadly failed though. The dark champion simply lowered his armoured head and took the blow on the strongest part of his metal helmet, which seemed to have no effect at all. The dark champion then drove his armoured right knee up and into D'Arten's side, causing a horrific snapping of bone. The blow was so powerful that D'Arten's whole body was lifted clear off the ground and any air in his lungs was expelled in a painful wheeze.

D'Arten promptly dropped to the ground, gasping in shock and unable to move.

Looking for any weak spots as the one-sided fight went on, I had aimed for Mal'vadar's left leg whilst he was kneeing D'Arten. Only my swing was clearly not quite quick enough, as the dark champion smartly dropped his large rectangular shield in time to block my blow. The blow did stagger the dark champion a little, which was encouraging; however, the champion recovered his footing almost immediately, before striking hard and fast with his primary weapon, a gigantic claw with four long and nasty-looking spikes lancing out to the tune of one and a half feet, which enclosed his right fist. I just about managed to stop myself from being skewered by the spikes by deflecting the worst of the strike with my reinforced hammer shaft. It was a dangerously close call, though, as the spikes had come within mere centimetres of my exposed chest, and the effort to deflect took everything I had.

The dark champion Mal'vadar was tanking everything we had with enviable ease. It was now only three of us standing against this monster of a fighter, as D'Arten was still immobilised on the blood-soaked ground. The new champion had expert technique, fast reflexes and instincts that Brutuck did not. Truly, Va'heash had chosen wisely. I tried to move to the side of the towering opponent so that I could attack from the rear. This of course was nothing but foolishness, as I was quickly checked with a fast and brutal shield barge which drove right through my inadequate hammer block and knocked me sprawling to the ground. Whilst I was grounded and trying to roll quickly aside to avoid a follow-up strike, I saw Mal'vadar actually ignore me for the moment and instead launch a vicious, unstoppable strike at Darkwolf and Stire, who were standing desperately shoulder to shoulder. Whilst Darkwolf managed to dance out of the path of the speeding claw, Stire was not so lucky. Instead, the dark champion's wicked claw caught his right hand full on, slicing it to pieces. Stire instantly dropped his sword, no longer able to hold anything, sword handle or otherwise. The Captain screamed in shock and pain, clutching the bleeding mess that was his right hand and dropping to his knees. It was now only two of us against this seemingly unstoppable instrument of pain.

I remembered then what Va'heash had said earlier, about his new champion inflicting pain on us and making us suffer. The huge thing clad in heavy armour and wielding the claw was merely toying with us, breaking some ribs there, mangling a hand there. Mal'vadar had orders to make us suffer and not give us a quick death. As if to confirm this point, the dark champion brought his heavy foot of steel crashing down onto D'Arten's right ankle, causing both an indescribable crunching sound and an agonised wail from an already injured D'Arten.

I knew that I could not give up, I would fight this creature until one of us died, even if that someone would most likely be me. I tried my luck with a strong overhead strike with Mordak's Might, giving it my all and wanting to at least go out strong. Mal'vadar once again took the worst of the blow on his shield, right before twisting his shield and driving it up into my chin. The sharp blow rocked my head back painfully, knocking me down so that I landed on my backside in the filth and gore of the arena. Mordak's Might dropped from my slack hands as I struggled to hold onto consciousness. I looked up dimly to see the dark champion towering over me, his claw raised in what looked to be a killing blow.

'Don't let me face death sitting unarmed in the dirt!' I called out internally to whoever may be listening up there.

I forced myself to reach out and grab hold of my hammer, so that I would at least leave this life with a weapon in hand. With my head still spinning and my vision blurry, I gritted my teeth and painfully tried to force my body to stand. I would face the end standing, at least. As it turned out, that end wasn't to come. Not there in that arena, deep in enemy territory.

A figure seemed to appear from nowhere above Mal'vadar's monstrous head of dark metal. At the time I could only see a fast-moving blur due to my stunted vision. The blur powered down right onto Mal'vadar's head though, instantly distracting him from me, his prey. I felt strong hands lifting me to my feet and turned my head to see Darkwolf helping me. I looked about to take in what was happening and saw that alongside the figure that had leapt down to attack the dark champion, two other figures had magically appeared in the arena with us. I did not know who they were at the time, but even through my dizziness and fog, I knew that they were not foes.

It was then that I heard a familiar voice from one of the open portals in the arena wall.

"Commander Kane, follow me. We need to leave. Demetri, can you help carry Captain D'Arten? Shadowprowler, can you help Captain Stire, he's bleeding!" Came the yelled instructions from Major Heven.

I had so many questions in that hectic moment, but knew that they would have to wait for a more opportune time. It was time to escape, to fight free of that horrible place.

"Wait, what about Simon's body?!" I said fiercely to Major Heven.

"1Lt. Fester's dead?… Look, I'm sorry, Commander. We can't afford to take the bodies with us, we need to move fast!" Declared Major Heven.

I was about to argue and insist that we had to take Simon's body with us and give him a proper burial, however, I held my tongue as Major Heven and Darkwolf both took firm hold of me and guided me out of the arena at a fast jog. My giddy legs seemed to obey my brain a little more and we all picked up speed. I glanced over my shoulder before leaving that horrible arena and saw quite a sight. The three newcomers who had dropped into the arena from on high were lashing about them like Lenferspawn. Two were battling the huge dark champion with much more skill and ability than we had been doing not long before, whilst the other was making easy work of any Purgorite guard foolish enough to enter the arena. I was devastated at having to leave Simon's body behind, but I was at least thankful that Mordak's Might was still in my hands.

Chapter 32

Escape from Balostroma

I tried to ignore the din of the crowd behind me as we hastily made our way back down the corridor we had ascended earlier, into the armoury in which Va'heash had addressed us. The rescue operation had by this stage likely caught the attention of the whole fortress, and I knew that no shortage of armed Purgorite brutes would be trying to close us off within the network of corridors, tunnels and pathways that could be found within the confines of Balostroma. Time was of the essence, and we could not afford to stop moving. As I entered the armoury, I was encouraged to see some familiar faces staring back at me. Alongside Major Heven, I saw Smoke, who was still clad in the armour in which we had been captured and was brandishing his familiar Kazbarian blade. Dark blood dripped from the tip of his blade to the stone flags, indicating that Smoke had not played a passive role in the escape operation. Unseen was present, standing strong with two razor-sharp foot-long daggers grasped in his fists. Finally, I saw Jerome Palos standing at the armoury doorway with his weapon at the ready and his eyes alert. He was turned slightly away from me, clearly keeping his eyes open for incoming intruders.

"Where's Major De'Beresford?" I heard myself ask hurriedly, as I knew that he was the only living soldier from the original group that was not present.

"De'Beresford is still alive, I hope. But he's injured and got separated from us during the struggle. Listen, Commander. We need to keep heading down; that is our way out of this nightmarish pit." Major Heven instructed me.

Although I was hardly up to advanced mathematics in those hectic moments of fast movements and panic, I did still find myself figuring that we were down to half numbers after the intense arena battle. There were now only ten of us still alive, assuming that Major De'Beresford had not yet perished.

So, our new party of ten continued driving roughly downward. The tenth addition was a newcomer, a mysterious and powerful figure who led the way and acted as our guide. I could only hope that he knew where he was going and was not running as blind as the rest of us. He was a muscular figure clad in bizarre armour which almost seemed to be made of different bones interlaced with metal and leather. In each of his thick arms, he wielded a long war-axe. Any Purgorites we encountered were quickly and almost effortlessly dispatched by the guide by means of fast, well-aimed and brutal strikes. He did not even stop moving forward when he killed, as if huge Purgorite brutes charging at him with weapons aloft were merely an irritation to be swatted away.

The guide continued to lead us down dimly lit stone corridors, through turn after turn, then down several sets of roughly hewn stairs. Never stopping and barely checking over his shoulder, he was like an unstoppable force of motion. He had the eyes of a hunter, of a predator, of a monster. We could hear the sound of angry footsteps and yelling all around us, as it seemed to come from beneath, behind, above and in front. The sound alone was disorientating and terrifying, let alone the threat it brought. I had escaped Va'heash multiple times by that stage. I could not even fathom what he might do if we were taken alive. I knew in that moment that I would turn my own blade on myself before I let that happen. After maybe ten solid minutes of racing through corridors, I heard the clashing of steel on steel and the roars of battle coming from up ahead.

Our group darted round a right-hand bend into a slightly larger area where several corridors met. The light there was better due to numerous burning torches fixed to the walls. It was by that light that we saw our gallant comrade Major Ralph De'Beresford fiercely fending off three Purgorite brutes. The Major looked to be seriously injured and was having trouble even holding his sword properly. I wasted no time in dashing in to lend support, rage once again rising in my chest. One firm swing of my hammer saw one of the Purgorite's heads messily removed from his thick neck. Our mysterious guide handled another of the brutes with a series of lethal axe strikes into vital organs. The third and final brute had his neck sliced wide open by D'Arten before dropping to the ground to bleed out. The Major, now with his opponents dead and his friends nearby, finally seemed to realise the extent of his injuries and how much damage his body had taken. He sat down hard as his face twisted in pain.

"Major De'Beresford!" I yelled in a mix of concern and shock.

"Please, call…me…Ralph" The Major asked me, making a heroic effort to smile despite all he was going through.

"We cannot halt. That man is already dead. The enemy is closing in as we speak!" Commanded the guide in a deep and stern voice, obviously referring to the seriously wounded Major.

"Don't halt. Keep moving. I will catch you up, I swear. GO!!" I yelled at the guide, whose name I still did not know.

The guide nodded grimly before turning back toward his original direction and resuming his fast pace. Most of the soldiers followed the guide after a few seconds, although some lingered with me, not wanting to leave Major De'Beresford behind.

"Comman….Marcus. I saw you briefly with that hammer before I had to run. That was…truly..th…the…the stuff..of legends!" The Major managed to splutter out, finding it increasingly hard to speak.

"Remember what…I said…on board that ship…over here? I… I want to die…sword in hand, pref…. preferably covered in m…m…m….my enemy's blood. Well…here I..am." The Major said with a choked but audible chuckle.

The Major then pulled a packet of something from under his armoured vest. I knew immediately that it was a packet of the firepowder we had used earlier to destroy the bridge.

"Ralph, what, how…what do you…?" I asked the dying old soldier, already knowing what he meant to do with the volatile substance.

"I…I…managed to take a sample of…the…s.s.stuff back at Romesh's compound. I kept it back, kept…kept it h..h.hidden. Thankfully, it has not gone off yet. It will not be enough..to…blow this wh…whole damn b..building..dd.down…but it will…give you time..to..escape. Marcus…pass me..o…one of those torches!" The Major asked of me.

I did not speak; instead, I nodded and stood, wiping the tears from my eyes. I was not going to deny this brave Halian soldier his chance at the manner of death he wanted. I promptly moved to the nearest torch and removed it from its bracket before returning to my comrade.

"It's…been..an honour…Marcus. Now go….fight your way free. If you get h…home. Find my bo…oy, Nath…Nathaniel. Send h…him my lo…love. Oh..and make s..s..sure to tell B…Brother Abel…that his….herb…herbal tea…is the best I've ever tasted!" Said the Major, forcing himself to laugh at his final sentence.

I clasped hands with the Major one last time as he held the torch. We both heard the heavy thump of footsteps, an ominous signal of multiple groups of soldiers coming toward us at some speed.

"I'll see you on the other side, Brother. Thank you for everything!" These were the last words I ever said to my friend, comrade and battle-brother Major Ralph De'Beresford.

I ran fast and hard in the direction I had seen the rest of the troops go. I did not look back when it happened, but it was a mere fifteen seconds later when I heard an almighty boom and felt the floor shake. I knew that the Major had done his final duty. His was another brave and selfless sacrifice which Halia would never forget. After running hard for a few more moments, I caught up with the rest of my pack. Whilst the explosion behind us would cut off enemy reinforcements from that direction, we were still far from clear, given that the enemy seemed to be closing in from several other paths. The noise was as disorientating as it was frightening. It sounded like the roar of a thousand furious beasts thirsty for blood.

Our tireless leader took a hard right and led us into the darkest tunnel I at least had come across since waking up in that palace of pain. I found myself staring into nothing but darkness, and beyond twenty feet or so, I could not make out a thing. Despite this, our guide seemed eerily confident that he had the right track.

"Trust me, if you are able to do so. This is the fastest way towards our exit." Our guide told us.

I noticed that his eyes had taken on a strange shine, as if they were seeing something that us Halians were not. Then, I realised without needing to be told that our guide was able to see in the dark, that he was graced with the night vision of a cat. It was not like we were in much of a position to argue. It was either follow this mysterious guide into total darkness or just choose our own way and run the very high risk of running into large bodies of enemy brutes. So, into darkness we went. Some of the party did carry torches, but they lit only the immediate patch around our feet, meaning that the sea of nothingness began after only a few measly feet from the light source. The darkness in that place seemed to be more than just the absence of light; instead, it seemed to be another enemy trying to thwart and disarm us. Still, we stayed as a group as we ran, trying to make sure that no one fell out of the moving ring of light to get swallowed by the malevolent blackness. I feared that if anyone fell into the darkness, we would not get them back. The rest of the group did their best to support their comrades D'Arten and Stire, whose wounds meant that they were not able to move as fast as they otherwise would have. We also had to try and keep up with our guide, who had still not slackened his pace. Soon enough, we heard a monstrous sound from somewhere ahead of us. It was a din of numerous roars and shouts combined. I was actually glad that I couldn't see what was making the noise. I felt that we had already seen more than enough blood, guts and death for one day.

Our guide was totally unfazed and just shouted over his shoulder to us.

"I can see what it is. Keep moving, I'll race ahead and deal with the problem."

Without uttering another further word of explanation, our guide seemed to double, then triple his speed. He went powering off into the thick blanket of darkness, clearly not bothered about whatever was up ahead of us. Just before he left my limited range of vision, he seemed to adopt the four-legged motion of a racing wolf, and even his bodily form seemed to change into something more bestial.

Quickly enough, we heard the all too familiar sounds of combat from up ahead. A deafening ruckus of screams, roars, yells of pain, shouts of anger, heavy bodies hitting the floor. We could still see nothing of what was going on up ahead, which was undoubtedly a good thing. As our circle of firelight lit up the stone floor ahead, we found ourselves running into a pool of dark blood. Mangled enemy corpses littered the floor and bodily fluids had been splattered all over the walls and even the ceiling. The place looked like an abattoir after a very busy day of slaughtering. The enemies were not all dead though, as our torches lit up a most intense scene. A large, heavily muscled wolf-like creature was in the process of tearing an enemy's head from their shoulders. The wolf's strong teeth were sunk deep into the flesh of the helpless brute, who had already given himself up to a brutal death. After finishing his prey off, the blood-soaked thing looked at us with glowing yellow eyes, eyes which seemed to be burning, before speaking in a half-man, half-beast growl.

"Keep moving!" Our ferocious shape-shifting guide ordered us, given that we had come to a halt and were gawping both at him and the mayhem he had just caused.

The guide darted back off into the darkness ahead of us. So, we gathered our wits again and remembered just how urgently we needed to be free of that horrible place. We carried on running, and running….and running. The tunnel seemed endless, and I lost track of time. It felt like we had been running for hours on end, but that could not be true, as the tunnel was dead straight and even in my mid-forties, I could run comfortably at six miles per hour for prolonged periods.

Just how large was Balaostroma? Finally, though, our endless nightmare of running through darkness seemed to be coming to an end. Remember that I was still carting around Mordak's Might, which was a considerable weight. Yes, it would have been easier to leave the hammer, but like heck that was going to happen. Like I have said earlier, it was more than a piece of metal and wood. Ultimately, carrying it all that way was worth every extra ounce of pain. The life of a Halian warrior was never meant to be sunshine and roses.

We found ourselves at the end of the corridor and up against a brick wall. I can imagine that most of us were probably surprised that the corridor even HAD an end to it. By this stage, our guide had retaken his man form and was back on two legs. Although his eyes still glowed an unsettling yellow in the gloom.

"The wall here is particularly weak. A few good hammer strikes in the right place should do the trick. Just here." Our guide advised, pointing to a particular spot on the wall and looking directly at me.

I looked around at my troops, who were all looking right back at me with expectant faces. Their commander. The man who was supposed to get them out of this mess. So, once again, it was time to use Mordak's Might.

My first strike seemed to do nothing. I felt like I may as well be blowing on the solid brick wall. In fact, it only hurt my arms. My second strike seemed to do even less, if that was even possible. I tried not to let my disappointment show to the men around me. They were relying on me. If I could not break through that wall, then we were doomed. We all knew it as well as the next man.

"Take your time, Commander. Keep trying." Were Major Heven's words of encouragement.

I felt like turning around and telling him to try his bloody self rather than stand around watching, but I held my tongue. I had to master myself. I had to succeed. So, I swung the hammer again at the same spot. Surprise, surprise, nothing happened but the metal head bouncing off the brick wall. Where was the Marcus Kane who had carved through all those enemies in the arena not long before? Where was the Marcus Kane who had made easy work of those foolish Pillards who tried to take over Oceanwolf? It was time to find him.

It was then that we heard the sound of incoming enemy voices once again. It would have been nothing but foolishness to believe that we had outrun them. We all looked around to see where the sound was coming from, which I know sounds odd, as sounds cannot be seen to the naked eye. After a few seconds, I felt pretty certain that the sounds were coming from down the endless tunnel we had just finished traversing.

I set to the wall once again with renewed vigour. I had to tell myself that I was doing something a lot more than swinging a hammer against a wall. I had my homeland to save, a people to rescue from the clutches of a relentless demonic lord, many dead comrades to avenge, even stories to tell many years later. But first, I needed to get through that brick wall and free of Balostroma.

My strikes seemed to be doing more then. I felt less pain in my arms and the wall seemed to shift that bit more under my strikes. I dug deep and tried to regain that focus as the sound of enemy voices got louder and closer. I dared not stop to look behind me. My sole purpose was to break through that wall, so I spared nothing. I hammered with everything I had, again and again. It was just me versus the wall, a battle of opponents. I felt my spirit surge as that first brick fell out of the wall, allowing weak light to filter through. I kept swinging hard at the surrounding bricks, each strike throwing dust and small chips into the air. The sound of enemies was scarily close by now, but I could not spare even a glance over my shoulder. Then, a second brick fell loose. I took a deep breath, knowing that I would have to summon up everything I had to perform one last strike that would burst the wall wide open. I grasped Mordak's Might firmly in both hands, feeling its power run through my body like ice, like fire, like energy, like life itself. I half laughed, half roared as I swung the hammer in one last epic strike, which hit the once solid wall with such force that it totally gave way outwards in a shower of flying bricks.

I stood to the side of the new exit, allowing my men to move through first. My chest was heaving as I took deep gulps of air. My eyes felt like they were about to force themselves from my sockets.

"You'll have to jump, I'm afraid." The guide said, as Captain D'Arten stood at the newly created exit, looking uncertain.

I turned my head left to look through the opening I had just created. It seemed that breaking through the wall was only part of the challenge, for there was only a sheer drop on the other side. It was a drop into darkness. It seemed that the options were to either jump into nothingness or fight and die as our enemies closed in around us.

"You will hit water after around sixty feet or so. Just jump and keep your body pointed downward with feet together." Yelled our guide.

So D'Arten led the way by jumping first. I watched his body disappear into the darkness below, and said a quiet prayer that he would land safely. Demetri went next, then Darkwolf, then the rest of the men in fairly rapid succession, until it was just the guide and I on that side of the hole in the wall. By this stage, the enemy was in clear sight and a matter of feet from us.

"Jump now!" The guide ordered.

Grasping my faithful hammer firmly, I moved to the edge of the gap, only briefly looking down. Then, without further thought, I let my body fall into nothingness as enemy screams filled my ears from right behind me. The sound of screams soon faded into insignificance as I descended at a startling speed. Under different circumstances, I might have enjoyed the feeling of unhindered freefall, but with danger on all sides, enjoyment was not on the table. As I looked down, I could make out other dark shapes hurtling downward with me. Soon enough, the surface of the water seemed to rush up to meet me. There were a frightening few moments when I felt myself in a dark underworld of water, immediately following my plunge. The water felt shockingly cold, and if that wasn't enough of an issue, I realised that I was still wearing armour which threatened to drag me down unless I got moving fast. So, I forced my body into action and began powering myself towards the surface. I looked up and could see the dim light of the surface calling out for me. I swam hard with all I had. Even with the armour, reaching the surface would not have been much of a problem, but I was determined to keep hold of Mordak's Might. The hammer seemed to weigh triple its usual weight at just the time when I could have done with it weighing a third of its usual weight. My lungs were burning for air as I expended all my energy in powering the hammer and I toward the surface. I felt my vision starting to close in around the edges, as if the underwater world was getting darker still. *'Please, don't let me die now.'* I pleaded to anyone willing to listen. Just when I felt myself fade out and was about to cave in to my lungs' increasingly angry demand for oxygen, I was aware of strong hands lifting me up toward the surface.

Chapter 33

Heading for the Coast

Sounds came back to my ears as I broke the surface, mercifully only semi-conscious as supposed to something more extreme. Still gripping the hammer, I was ushered toward the nearby bank of rock and dirt, where I lay face-up and getting my breath back. After a few more moments and deep breaths, I sat up properly and looked about me.

"Are we all here?" I asked of the dark outlines standing or sitting about me.

"The ten that are left. Yes. We didn't lose anyone in the fall. Captain D'Arten put all that swimming practice to good use. It was him who managed to go back and pull you out." Major Heven confirmed.

I immediately looked around in the gloom to find D'Arten. I found him a mere six feet away, standing and looking back at me.

"Thank you, Captain." I offered the young Officer.

"Ah, think nothing of it. You have saved the rest of us a few times now and it was time for me to return the favour. It was that bloody hammer holding you back. I can understand why you carry it though. The Purgorites must be pissing themselves whenever they see you with that thing by now." D'Arten returned.

"The Purgorites will not be far behind at all. We need to keep moving. Va'heash will not be happy that his prey has escaped, and that he has been made to look like a fool in front of high-ranking comrades." Our guide instructed.

"Just who is 'we'?" I asked the guide, standing as I uttered the words.

There was a brief silence as my troops looked toward the shadowy warrior, as if to await his response. I for one needed to know who he was and what events led up to him flying into the arena before leading us to safety, or at least leading us out of immediate danger.

"You can call me Teras. I work amongst the ranks of Daegon's Division. I was employed to locate you and enable a rescue…and here we are." The guide revealed.

"So, you rescued us, and for that you have our thanks. But why are you still here now that we are outside of the fortress?" Enquired Major Heven.

"Currently, you are only partway free. We are still very much in enemy territory. We need to move west. I will continue to lead the way. Unless of course you fancy choosing your own path and likely ending up back in a cage. Va'heashes' eyes and ears are everywhere this close to the fortress walls. Let us move now!" Teras more ordered than suggested, before beginning to head west.

"I thought the walls to this place were supposed to be super-thick. How is it that the Commander only had to break through a thin wall to make an opening?" Asked Demetri, craning his neck up in an effort to see the opening from which we had jumped.

I disapproved of Demetri's use of the word 'only' in his question, given what I had put myself through to actually break through the wall, but held my tongue, instead awaiting the response from Teras.

"I directed us to a fairly newly built section of wall. It used to be an outflow pipe for waste before there was some reconstruction within Balostroma. The builders had only seen fit to build the wall back thinly at that spot. Maybe cheap and unskilled peasants were hired for the labour who didn't really care what they were doing. So luckily for us, the wall was only around six inches thick, not seven feet thick, like it is for most of the outer wall." Teras informed us.

What other choice did we have but to follow Teras and hope that not only did he know where he was going, but also that he had no devious intentions to trick us or hand us back to the enemy? Who knows what really goes through the mind of soldiers who have no real allegiance to any master but coin.

Still grasping Mordak's Might in my right hand, I followed Teras west, into the mouth of a narrow gorge between two groups of rock. My soldiers followed suit behind me, all of us being led by this still mysterious mercenary named Teras.

After maybe twenty minutes of silent marching through the bleak-looking landscape of rock, dirt and sand, I pulled up level with Teras and asked him to explain how he had found us in more detail. Teras was a large and powerfully built man with the look you may expect from a lifetime of hard and dangerous living. He barely blinked and his face appeared to be chiselled from stone. He continued to stare forward with a disquieting shine to his killer's eyes.

"Soon after you were captured outside Romesh's compound, his scouts told him what they had seen. That was when Romesh contacted the Division to update us and seek our immediate employment. I gathered a small team of warriors and headed south over the border into North Utresh. We received intelligence that you had all been taken to Balostroma. So, that was our destination. Here we are now." Teras responded.

Whilst I now had a better picture of the story and was grateful for the information, I still had questions to ask, perhaps too many for Teras' liking.

"I mean…how did you actually get inside the place? What about those other warriors you were with, who we left fighting in the arena? How did you know where to go?" Were the multiple questions I asked Teras, without awaiting a response before moving on to the next one.

"Commander Kane. None of those are questions to which you need to know the answer. I was not hired to field irrelevant questions. Who we are and exactly how we operate is not your concern. We are due to meet two other members of The Division later today. I have little doubt that they escaped Balostroma successfully. If you have no further questions…" Teras said firmly whilst still looking straight ahead, clearly not in a chatty mood.

I dropped back, content enough to walk on in silence for a while longer. It was not long before Captain D'Arten stepped up beside me.

"Thank you again for rescuing me, Captain D'Arten. I know that the hammer was dragging me down, but I cannot let go of it. In a strange sense, I would rather die than live without this hammer. I know how crazy that must sound." I said to the young Captain to whom I owed my life.

"Ah, I understand. Many of us have prized possessions which we would be loath to part with. Back in Halia, I always wear a pair of bracers that my father gave me for my eighteenth birthday whenever I go into battle. I would have brought them with me, but with the strict stance of uniform, I had to leave them at base." D'Arten told me.

There was an awkward pause, as once again the thorny subject of Henry D'Arten had been raised. I was about to speak, however, D'Arten beat me to it.

"Commander, about my father. I don't blame you for what happened to my father, or even Captain Stire. After much thought, I can only come to the conclusion that whatever happened to my father began and ended with him. He did something or even several things, which were totally unbecoming of him, and sadly paid a heavy price." Said D'Arten, his tone serious.

"I did not know your father well, although I did meet him and speak a little. I cannot believe he was ever a truly bad person. By the sounds of it, he got involved with an entity he could not understand and was used like a puppet. What's done is done though. Your father is gone. We all weave our own tapestries. Yours and mine is still in progress." I told the Captain, feeling much better after we had cleared the air.

Our moment of silence was interrupted by the sound of Major Heven's raised voice.

"When do we stop to rest again, and to eat or drink? Captain Stire's stump is still bleeding, and he is weak from blood loss and all the exertion. We are not all as strong as you, Teras."

"One mile ahead, there will be a chance to rest, eat and hydrate. Just keep moving if you will." Said Commander Teras, not even looking over his shoulder.

I had the impression that Teras could walk at that pace for hundreds of miles, without taking food, water or even rest. I would go one step further and entertain the thought that Teras would even enjoy the pain that it would bring.

True to his word, Teras did allow us to halt after another mile. We were led into a small clearing surrounded by thick dry vegetation, the like of which we never saw in Halia. I saw eyes glaring at us newcomers from the depths of the twisted roots, trunks and plants, but whatever creatures the eyes belonged to chose to stay hidden and observe from their position of relative safety. Teras walked into the centre of the clearing as the rest of us found suitable places to sit and rest our legs. I wasted little time in checking up on Captain Stire. The bandage that had been wrapped around his wrist earlier at the enemy fortress was already a dark maroon colour. The soldier's face was pale and sweat rolled lazily down his face.

"How are you faring, Captain Stire?" I asked my comrade.

"I've been better. I've been worse. I could do with some sustenance and a fresh bandage though." Stire responded, gritting his teeth and clearly trying to cloak the worst of his pain.

"Absolutely, just rest and I will see what I can do," I told Stire, already turning to walk back towards Teras.

Teras was standing silently and still in the centre of the clearing. I was about ten feet away from him when he spoke to me in a stern voice, which brokered no argument.

"Get well back. This will only take a moment."

Slightly startled, I did as I was bid and stepped back. Teras then took one deep breath and issued a wild howl into the air. The howl lasted maybe four seconds, then Teras was silent again. I looked over my shoulder at my resting troops and saw by the looks on their faces that they shared my confusion. The silence was broken by the sound of heavy incoming steps. I looked to my left and saw a large and fearsome four-legged creature come stampeding out of the vegetation and into the opening. The beast was moving at speed straight at Teras's back. It was a huge hairy creature, standing as tall as a horse but more solid. It was roaring as it barrelled forward, displaying two rows of mean-looking fangs. Teras must have heard it, but remained totally still and looking ahead. I could only watch in horror as the beast closed the distance, ten feet, five feet, then one foot.

With insane speed, Teras turned at the last second and braced himself for impact. The hairy beast barged into him at a speed which would have smashed a Halian man to pieces, only Teras was something totally different. Instead of giving way, Teras grabbed the beast by its head and dug his own feet into the ground. Teras was only pushed back some four feet before the beast's momentum came to a halt and both fighters were stationary and facing each other. Teras then grabbed both the beast's upper and lower jaw in his two hands, seeming to ignore the danger of the teeth. Using some incredible strength Halian's could only long for, Teras then prized the huge jaws wide open to breaking point, before using one final burst of power to push well past the point and break the thing's neck. Teras stepped back, barely fatigued, as the hairy creature dropped to the ground and lay still.

Teras then turned to look at a small sea of incredulous faces and open mouths.

"We need to skin it, gut it and then we can cook the flesh. You can use those blades of yours. I am not doing everything." We were instructed.

The creatures' flesh was tough, tasted unpleasant and felt like something we shouldn't be eating. I would not have served it to prisoners or vagabonds. But it was sustenance and would give us energy and there was lots of it to share between us. Teras told us that the animal was called a 'Bersk'. It was generally a feared and savage animal that even Purgorites preferred to keep at a distance. I could never imagine that its flesh fetched a high price in the food market!

As we were chewing away at our meal of cooked Bersk, two imposing-looking figures emerged out of the dark green foliage and approached us. After only a quick inspection, I recognised them as Teras' two fellow mercenaries I had seen fighting with such skill in the arena.

Teras rose and went to greet them, before a few words were exchanged in a foreign tongue. I was grateful to see that one of the mercs carried a heaving waterskin and several cups. I could imagine that we all felt parched and in need of liquid.

As my soldiers and I slaked our thirst, I took a gamble by asking the two newer mercenaries how they had escaped Balostroma and if they had managed to kill Mal'vadar. Even if they turned out to be as taciturn as Teras, I had lost nothing by asking. One of the hard-looking mercs identified himself as 'Kameal the sleepless' and revealed that sadly they had not managed to slay Va'heash's champion as they soon became overwhelmed and had no choice but to escape. Mal'vadar was too tough even for the two of them to put down and they would have certainly been slain if they had simply stood and exchanged blows with the towering creature.

The other merc, who went by the name of 'Haephtol the fierce' told me that Va'heashes' hunting pack were not far behind, and we could not dally for long. The three mercs had apparently done all they could to confuse the efforts of the Purgorite pursuers; however it was only a question of buying time. Va'heash was understandably furious and would stop at nothing to have us back in his torture chambers.

As soon as we had finished drinking, Teras stood before us and gave his longest public speech yet, which still wasn't very long.

"Listen, Halians. Our group has received updated instructions from Romesh, who has been in recent contact with your Higher Cadre.

Your mission here is over. We are to escort you to the nearest port, whereby you will be transported back to Halia. According to our maps, that port is called Tul'Voor and lies around thirty miles Southwest. The trek will have to be on foot, I'm afraid. By now, the warning has gone out. Vaheash is offering a huge sum of coin for your capture, even for your dead bodies. Messengers carrying your details and description have been riding at speed to almost every corner of North Utresh. We cannot afford to stop at even smaller settlements or use main roads. I know a good route, but we need to get moving. We can stop again later."

We got moving again, although at least then we knew what direction we were going in and roughly how far it was until we reached this port of Tul'Voor. We could all put thirty miles into context and knew that we were in for a long trek, especially that it was all on foot and we were all tired despite our brief rest.

I walked alongside Captain Stire, who was sporting a fresh bandage by that stage and was better off for some food and water. He was still weakened though from the blood loss and was struggling to keep pace with the rest of us. The Daegon Mercenaries seemed to keep forgetting that even at our fittest we would struggle to keep pace with them. They pushed tirelessly onward, grim-faced and speaking only when they needed to. As we marched, I tried to distract Captain Stire from his pain with conversation about food, travel, music, arts, anything other than battle and war. Stire even managed to open up about some of the campaigns he had been on with our departed friend Kurt Winters. He told me about a training exercise they had been on together in the far-off land of Freastel. Whilst there, David, Kurt and the rest of the soldiers had crossed mountains so high that they found themselves above cloud level and having to wrap head to toe in furs to be able to bear the merciless cold and evil winds. Some nights the soldiers had sampled the local cuisine, usually the cooked flesh of one of the mountain beasts. Whilst some soldiers seemed to like the taste, the food had sent others amongst them grabbing their belly and racing for the privy! This even brought out a laugh from David and I, the first laugh I had heard in what felt like forever.

Gradually, though, the conversation slowed back to silence, and both of us resumed our quiet marching and went wherever we needed to in our heads to make the long walk easier. It was another ten miles before we paused for another rest. I know this as our guide, Teras informed us. He knew the land well, and I had no good reason to doubt his information. I was grateful to rest my weary legs and my even more weary head and had no doubt that this relief was shared by my comrades. Once again, some much-needed food and water was passed around. This time it was dry bread and smoked meat, not quite as interesting as the fresh and steaming Bersk we had found ten miles back. It was something to put in our bellies though. It was energy and that was what mattered.

"Teras is there any chance we can ease off the pace a little? We are all tired and are simply not as resilient as you three. I know that we need to reach the port as soon as possible, but at the same time, we do not want to drop dead from exhaustion." I asked our guide.

Teras glared at me for a few seconds before answering what he seemed to think was a stupid question.

"If you were as…'resilient'…as us, then our services would not have been requested in the first place. I acknowledge your point. In recognition of your reduced abilities, we will move slightly slower and stop every five miles instead of every ten. Will this be enough?"

I did not appreciate Teras' condescending tone one bit, especially in front of my men, but I knew that he was there to guide us and keep us alive, not to be nice to us.

"Thank you, that will make it a little easier," I replied smartly, trying to hide my relief.

We did indeed stop roughly five miles later, as Teras had agreed, and the pace had been slightly more manageable. We just set our heads forward and continued walking quietly towards our destination. I was trying to think positive thoughts and even planned what I would do when I get back to Halia, not IF, but WHEN, for I forced myself to keep faith and remain hopeful.

For our third rest, we just took water, as the remaining food supplies had to be rationed carefully. There was some muted conversation between the soldiers, but it was clear that we were all focused on just getting back to relative safety, and if everything went well, sailing home. By this stage, we had roughly fifteen miles of our journey left. It was almost the distance of our deep tunnel trek the year before, although at least this time we were above ground and had more chance to see the enemies coming. As a negative side, we were much fewer in number and equipment, so had much less capability to deal with those incoming enemies.

The walking continued, foot after foot, mile after mile. We had our five-mile rests and at each stop, I asked about the group to make sure that none of us were suffering too much and could at least put one foot in front of the other. I tried to put wind into the men by telling them that we were almost there. Although even when we got wherever "there" was, there would still be a lot to worry about. It seemed that D'Arten's foot injury was not as bad as it had originally looked, as his armoured boot had protected his flesh and bone from the worst of the strike. He was not moving as well as he could, but he was gritting his teeth and keeping up with the pace.

It was just as I was transferring the weight of Mordak's Might from my left hand to my right when Teras held up his hand and ordered us to halt. It took a few seconds for the order to register in my mind, as I had almost put myself in a trance just to make the constant and painful walking easier. This resulted in me almost knocking into Teras, as he had come to a total halt.

"Crouch down and wait here," Teras ordered the group, turning his head over his shoulder so that his voice would carry down the line.

I grimaced and winced as I dropped my tired body into a crouch. My legs were stiff and my muscles were screaming and protesting like never before. Teras seemed to melt into the semi-darkness ahead of us, for night was starting to fall. The rest of us waited quietly in our crouching position, our hands never far from our hilts. Teras returned after a few minutes, bearing ill tidings. After beckoning us to form a group so that he would not have to repeat himself or raise his voice, he informed us that an enemy pack had already beaten us to the port and closed off that path. We would have to move to the next port along the coast, which was another ten miles or so.

"But what if that port is being monitored as well? We cannot keep marching forever." I said to Teras, wanting to say more about our lack of food and the fact that we were almost dead on our feet, but also knowing that Teras was not the kind of person who would want to hear whinging and problems at that moment.

Teras was about to answer when his comrade Kameal crept up close and spoke to Teras quietly in their foreign tongue. Teras looked hard at Kameal before turning back to us.

"Unfortunately, another pack of enemies has closed in not far behind us. The route to the next port is about to be cut off as well. I suggest that we stick to the original plan and aim for Tul'Voor. If we move quietly and stay low, then there is a chance we can creep up on the enemy and get the drop on them. Just follow my instructions at all times." Teras commanded, for there was no discussion to be had.

Chapter 34

The Battle of Tul'voor

So, still crouching, we moved forward slowly and as quietly as we could, our eyes and ears switched to high sensitivity and our nerves were in a state of high tension. Soon enough, we came to the top of a slight rise and were able to look across the land between us and the port. Numerous Purgorite guards patrolled the area with lit torches and could be seen scanning the land in every direction. There was little doubt as to exactly what, or whom, they were looking for. Whilst the land in front of us was mostly flat, there were luckily still groupings of trees and outcrops of rock large enough to conceal a small group such as ours.

"Follow me closely, continue to stay low and stay quiet," Teras told us, in little more than a whisper, before moving off to the left into the path that provided the most cover.

I followed our sturdy guide and could hear the next man moving just behind me. There was a grouping of rocks around thirty feet from where we had paused to survey the land, and it was behind those rocks that our party of twelve paused for a moment. Teras stealthily poked his head around the corner to see if the path to the next potential hiding spot was clear. He must have felt that this was the case, as he turned his head back to me and nodded in confirmation. I turned to look at the rest of my men in the growing shadows, and that was when I saw how close our pursuers were. There was another party of enemies nearing the slight rise in the land where we had paused only minutes before. Luckily, at that moment, we were partially hidden from their view, but I knew the closer they got, the less our temporary cover would conceal us. We could not stay where we were.

Teras led the way once again, crouching low and moving toward a clumping of ugly-looking trees. The trees were only twenty feet away, but I can tell you that it was a painful twenty feet, where I am sure we all felt exposed and vulnerable. The Purgorites outnumbered us well over two to one in that area. Not only that, but we were hardly in top fighting form, plus at a signal from our enemy, enemy reinforcements would no doubt descend upon the area rapidly. It was therefore prudent to try and avoid open battle.

"The port is not far now, maybe a further one hundred feet. I can see three armed guards directly blocking the main port entrance. There is no getting past them quietly. I can see a side entrance. It will be a longer journey, but 'safer' or at least slightly less dangerous." Teras murmured, pointing the way to this side entrance.

After another quick check with his keen eyes, Teras moved off swiftly towards the side entrance to the port. By this stage, we were moving through almost waist-high undergrowth, which almost concealed our crouching forms. Even if we had crawled on our bellies, any watching enemy would see the telltale signs of movement as the undergrowth was disturbed by twelves shifting bodies. As we got nearer the cover of the port walls, which would hide us from the view of the Purgorite guards patrolling in front of the port, I felt my spirits rise. I allowed myself to think that we might be able to climb over the walls, creep into the port and steal away on a ship. Just cruise away from this horrible place and head home.

I was a fool to think it would be so easy.

The first arrow whizzed within an inch of Teras's head, and I believe it was only his super keen reflexes which saved his life. Another arrow flew over my shoulder and sank into the flesh of a soldier behind me, causing the poor man to cry out loud. I turned quickly to see 2 Lt. Palos with an arrow shaft sticking out of his upper chest. He clutched at the wound as his face contorted in pain. I looked forward again to see that we were never to have entered the port stealthily via a supposedly lesser-known side entrance, as a team of three Purgorite brutes emerged from those same shadows, all armed with bows.

It seemed that our enemies had selected a poor choice of weapons though. Teras, grasping his two killing axes, sprinted straight toward the enemy archers. He was sprinting fast but still keeping his body in a semi-crouch. He held up his arms in front of him, using his forearm armour as some manner of shield. The archers seemed to be focusing their arrows on him as a fast-moving, immediate threat.

"On me!!" I yelled to my soldiers as I followed Teras whilst desperately trying to avoid any flying arrows.

As soon as Teras was within around twelve feet of our enemy, he leapt through the air, his axes held out in front of him. He was still airborne when he beheaded the Purgorite archer directly in front of him. The two other hapless archers were frantically trying to nock fresh arrows with shaking hands as Teras rapidly slashed the life from them with startling speed and accuracy. I looked behind me and saw a horde of at least twenty-five Purgorites charging towards us, most holding a torch in one hand and a blade or blunt weapon in the other. It seemed that once again, the only way was forward.

"Toward the port wall, follow me!" Teras yelled as he drove past the three corpses he had just made.

We raced toward the port wall; the wounded Palos being supported on either side by the strong arms of a comrade. Soon enough, we reached the wall, which was only around seven feet high and was luckily not adorned with any manner of defensive spikes or wire. Teras numbly leapt up to poke his head above the top of the wall, to check for immediate danger. Unluckily, the danger was indeed very immediate, as Teras had to jerk his head back to avoid being skewered by a spear tip. So, the enemy was lying in wait on the other side of the port wall. We should have known. Climbing over would not be an option, as even Teras would likely be hacked apart as soon as he hit ground on the other side.

"Head east along the coast!" Teras yelled, beginning to run in that direction.

We of course all followed Teras, with nowhere else to go. We could have just run into the cold sea and tried to escape that way, but even in my panic, I knew that only death lay that way. I could see only open ground ahead of us and knew that it was only a matter of moments before the enemy behind caught up with us. They were fresher and there were many more of them. I dared not even look over my shoulder though. When the enemy had caught up with us, we would know regardless. Once again, the fear of dying whilst running away came into my mind. I did not want to be felled with an arrow in the back after all this effort, all this pain, all this fighting, after the loss of so many battle brothers.

"Keep running, we'll hold them off," I heard Kameal roar from not far behind me.

As I ran, I heard the sound of fierce combat behind me. The din of screams, steel crashing against steel, the loud grunts of effort. So, two of Daegon's heroes were making their fearless last stand. Part of me wanted to join them, but I knew that my ultimate goal was to get back to Halia. I am sure that Kameal and Haephtol fought like legends and took many enemies with them to the afterworld, but even their battle prowess could not stop the waves of enemies closing in on us. As I ran, I tried calling out to any nearby wildlife for assistance, but could detect nothing. Either I was too weak to focus, or the animals had decided to leave us to our fate. I could hear charging footsteps right behind me, but did not know if they were from friend or foe, from Halian or North Utreshian. It was when I was pushed messily to the ground, that I realised that the pursuer was most likely a Purgorite brute wanting to claim his prize and be the one that captured Marcus Kane. For a moment, this Purgorite scum believed that he was about to take me prisoner and gain favour and applaud from his demon of a leader.

I quickly rose from the dirty ground and showed the brute that I would be the one doing the taking. I swung hard with my hammer, and whilst the brute did try and mount a defence with his cleaver, my heavy swing crushed his skull in as if it were a giant egg being thrown against a wall. I looked about me and saw that the rest of my soldiers were mounting a defence as well. Captain D'Arten was carving his blade through the air, each swing and slice sending dark enemy blood flying in all directions. The huge Major Heven beheaded one enemy, then pivoted expertly and impaled another Purgorite brute right through his middle. So, it seemed that my troops and I were not that tired at all. I found myself standing shoulder to shoulder with Darkwolf, who already had a well bloodied sword. I drove my hammer low into an enemy knee, destroying it in an explosion of bone and blood, whilst Darkwolf took off an enemy arm at the shoulder.

We were managing to stand our ground and mount something of a defence, but it was not to last, for reinforcements were approaching from the north, from the direction of Balostroma. I took in my surroundings and saw that we were no longer outnumbered well over two to one, but more like six to one, even with the piles of dead Purgorites carpeting the ground. All I could do was continue to fight well, to lay about me with Mordak's Might and claim some more enemy lives before it was all over. It was then that I sensed an animal. Oddly, it was an animal I was familiar with, an animal that was already a friend. During this momentary distraction, I was knocked back to the ground by a huge blow. From my new viewpoint on the ground, I looked up through slightly blurry eyes to see a huge form towering over me. Even though my vision was not the best in that moment, I recognised the huge form of Mal'vadar looking down from on high. It was then that I once again heard the thing's horrible voice.

"Va'heash wants you alive…..But I am going to pretend that I misheard him. My loyalty has its limits after all. He will have to be happy with what I leave of your corpse."

With those words, the huge thing put its gigantic, armoured foot on my chest and began to slowly apply pressure. Even though most of Mal'vadar's weight was still on the ground, the force he exerted felt immense to the degree that my ribs felt like they were about to give way. I could not breathe, let alone grab my hammer and try and defend myself. I tried to push the champion's foot off my chest, but it was like trying to move a deeply rooted tree. In my pain and desperation, I again sensed the apparently friendly animal. I was detecting them more strongly, as if they were getting closer.

Mal'vadar and I seemed to turn our heads at the same time, as a familiar and friendly face came hurtling toward us. At first, I thought that my eyes were deceiving me. But it all became real when all 150 pounds of Morse flew through the air, teeth first, straight at Mal'vadar's neck. The dark champion was unprepared for such an assault and actually stumbled to his knees. He totally lost his footing on my chest in the process. Whilst my faithful Bullhound was sinking his huge jaws into our enemy's neck, I forced myself to rise. It took a few moments for me to regain my regular breathing patterns after having the wind crushed out of me. I knew that I had to help Morse, though, even his formidable strength and ferocity would not be enough to overpower a creature such as Mal'vadar. So, I quickly picked up Mordak's Might and prepared to bring it down on my distracted opponent. Mal'vadar was not going to prove so easily dispatched though, as using his insane strength, he managed to dislodge Morse's vice-like jaws and hurl him several feet through the air. My hound had managed to sink some serious damage into Mal'vadar's neck, but despite bleeding, he was still very much alive and dangerous.

I swung a hard horizontal blow at Mal'vadar, who simply danced back, missing the blow entirely. I had already fought against this monster earlier, only then I had several comrades around me, and the monster still managed to get the better of us. One-on-one, I felt like I was finished. Morse bravely returned and tried to bite at Mal'vadar's lower legs, but even Morse's strong teeth could not do much against his tough armour. I pressed forward again with my hammer, trying a combination of high and low blows. Mal'vadar simply dodged the blows or blocked them with the heavy shield he was carrying. I dug deep and swung with as much force as I could, but felt myself draining. Mal'vadar saw my weakness and pressed his attack. He slashed at me with a long, curved blade which looked sharp enough to cut water itself into thin slices. I just about managed to block these blows with the long handle of my hammer, but each block was driving me back and even my strong arms were tiring, and worse, starting to fail. As he had done during our earlier battle, Mal'vadar delivered a crushing armoured kick to my chest, sending me crashing helplessly to the ground. I craned my head up, once again as good as helpless, to see the dark champion bearing down on me. I saw him lift his armoured right foot high, as if powering up for one brutal stamp which would doubtless see my end.

Mercifully, that kick never came though, for a lone arrow sailed through the air to find its home in Mal'vadar's neck. This assault was enough to distract the dark champion from his heavy stamp and caused both him and I to turn our heads to see where the arrow had come from. It was then I saw another unexpected friendly face, in the form of Brother Abel. Abel wasted no time in nocking another arrow and drawing back the string, as Mal'vadar simply ripped the arrow out of his huge neck, as if it were a minor annoyance. Brother Abel was clearly better with a bow than I had known, as a second arrow was driven deep into the dark champion's cheek. Rather than wait for Mal'vadar to charge at Abel and get in close, I rose with a scream and once again took hold of Mordak's Might. My next blow was worthy, as the heavy metal head smashed into Mal'vadar's knee, causing the bones to break with a horrific crunching sound. For the first time, I heard the dark champion roar in pain. The champion was still not done though, as he viciously lanced up with his blade, straight toward my exposed face. I still believe that strike would have killed me, only that strike never found its target. For Darkwolf intervened at the last moment, kicking hard at Malvadar's outstretched arm and deflecting the blow. Darkwolf immediately dropped low and used his blade to stab deep into a gap between Mal'vadar's armour plates. The blade was driven handle deep into Mal'vadar's armpit, allowing a shocking eruption of dark and foul blood to shoot out. Yet another of Abel's arrows raced through the air, this time to sink deep into the dark champion's left eye socket. The shot would have been fatal for a lesser creature, but it was clear that Va'heash had chosen his champion wisely, for Mal'vadar seemed to just take the arrow to the brain as another injury. Mal'vadar switched his blade from his right hand to left, as to be able to keep swinging at enemies. He slashed at Darkwolf, who managed to dodge out of the blade's path before driving his blade deep into Mal'vadar's neck. The monster was finally tiring. Despite its huge size, strength and ability, it was still made of flesh and blood and hence had certain biological laws to follow. Holding Mordak's Might, sweating and shaking with effort, it was I who delivered the killing blow. I swung at Mal'vadar's head with all I had left. The impact was devastating, as the innards of the dark champion's head sprayed messily in all directions. As my hammer came to a rest, there was no head left.

Chapter 35

Time to Leave

I dropped to a sitting position, exhausted, but not so much so that I could not raise a hand to stroke a happy Morse as he came over to make a fuss of me. Brother Abel also approached with a warm smile on his face. I took a moment to look about the field, to see how the larger battle was faring. The battle was as good as won, given that I saw barely any Purgorites still standing. Any remainers were being finished off by soldiers wearing Halian colours. So, a relief force had come to our aid, and not a moment too soon it seemed.

"Brother Abel, thanks for your aid. We would likely have been corpses if you hadn't shown when you did. But what are you doing here in North Utresh?" I asked my old friend.

"Romesh got in contact with the Higher Cadre some days ago. He told them what had happened and that your group would need assistance and most importantly, extraction. So here we are. It is beyond lucky that we managed to find you when we did. I'm just sorry that we could not rescue you earlier. As a technical non-combatant, I did not have to join the relief force, but I opted to. You are no longer alone, Marcus." Brother Abel informed me.

I churned over Abel's words 'some days ago' and figured that I had been in that awful drug haze for longer than I had originally though. The relief force must have travelled on an impressively fast ship to arrive so quickly.

"You have nothing to apologise for, good brother. An awful lot has happened since we set sail from Halia, sadly, very little of it good. Commander Vorgo has shown himself to be a traitor. He…"

My words were halted as Abel raised a hand to quiet me before speaking.

"Believe me, I have seen Vorgo's treachery. He has been weakening Halia, ready for Va'heashes' next attack. He allowed the outbreak of disease I told you about to get worse, deliberately ignoring all my suggestions and hampering my efforts to quell the virus. Plus, I have been seeing odd fellows hanging around the castle, whom I do not recognise and who do not look like they belong. Any effort to ask about their identity is met with feeble excuses or silence. Unfortunately, I do not believe Vorgo is the only traitor. I am all but certain that other Halian Officers have been seduced by Va'heash's promises of power and decided to become another of his pets."

"I am sorry to interrupt, but we cannot dally. This battle may have been won, but more Purgorites are not far off. We need to get on board our ships and set sail without delay so that we can get a good head start." Advised a newcomer, a Halian naval officer I did not recognise.

"Commander Kane, we have not met. I am Sea Captain Cheval. I work with Captain Barlow, who brought you over here. I am to escort you and your soldiers back home." Came Cheval's more formal introduction.

Only a matter of minutes later, I was sitting with Brother Abel on some wooden crates at the port of Tul'voor, as we waited for our ship's preparations for sailing to be finalised. We would be sailing back home on a much faster and more modern ship than Oceanwolf, which was called *Caethlion*. As well as our surviving group of nine, there were a few dozen Halian troops who had come as part of the relief force, who would be sailing back on a separate vessel. I was gladdened to see 2Lt. Palos had been stabilised and the arrow safely removed from his chest. Morse was sitting faithfully by his master's side, pleased to see me again. Brother Abel stroked Morse's head fondly and gave the hound a smile.

"Morse was not himself after you left. He would whimper whenever I went to visit him at the kennels. When the rest of us were getting prepared to sail over here, it was almost as if Morse could tell what was happening. He would look at me with desperate eyes and wag his tail until I thought it would fall off. I am sorry, but I could not leave him at home." Abel told me.

"Young Morse here saved my life, I reckon. Bringing him was a wise choice, I would say." I responded.

It was then that I told Abel, with a heavy heart, of all the Halian lives that our mission had claimed. The most painful to recount were those of Major De'Beresford and 1Lt. Simon Fester. I was still devastated that we had to leave their bodies behind in enemy territory and could not bury them properly. Abel was sympathetic, as was only to be expected.

"I'm sure that you did all you could here, Marcus. It's time to get back to Halia, where I'm afraid more problems await."

I stood up as Sea Captain Cheval told us to climb aboard and make ourselves comfortable. I knew that Va'heash would only triple his efforts in assembling a monstrous navy before continuing the chase across the seas. The demon was in full hunter mode and knew that Halia had been weakened and was ready for plunder. Our time in that land was over. Halia was waiting for us. It was time to get home and get ready!

Notes

★Veronot = summer

★ Aogasti = summer month comparable to August

★Lenfer = Hell